A TASTE OF SHOTGUN

OTHER TITLES BY Chris Orlet

In the Pines: A Small Town Noir

CHRIS ORLET

A TASTE OF SHOTGUN

Copyright © 2018 by Chris Orlet

All rights reserved. No part of the book may be reproduced in any form or by any electronic or mechanical means, including information storage and retrieval systems, without permission in writing from the publisher, except by a reviewer who may quote brief passages in a review.

All Due Respect
An imprint of Down & Out Books
3959 Van Dyke Rd, Ste. 265
Lutz, FL 33558
www.DownAndOutBooks.com

The characters and events in this book are fictitious. Any similarity to real persons, living or dead, is coincidental and not intended by the author.

Edited by Chris Black and Chris Rhatigan
Cover design by JT Lindroos

ISBN: 1-946502-92-8
ISBN-13: 978-1-946502-92-6

For Trina

*Now you've reached the part
where all the mess begins.*
—Martin Goldsmith

ONE

I was late getting to the prison.

I stopped to piss at a Shell station outside Green Mount and my mind took to wandering and when I pulled back onto the highway I must have turned north instead of south. Fifteen minutes went by before I realized I was driving in the wrong direction. Oh well. Vince had waited four years for this day, another hour wouldn't kill him.

Still, it was just like me to screw up his release day.

The Shawnee State Work Camp lay at the butt-end of the state, not far from where the Ohio and Mississippi rivers collide. Shawnee was a nothing town in one of the poorest counties in the state, maybe in the country. You want to see perfect, abject poverty in all its wondrous manifestations—economic, spiritual, intellectual—where the whites are just as poor as the blacks but the dumb fucks still think God blessed them with a superior skin tone, go to Shawnee. If you ask me, the only reason anyone stays here is because he's too dumb to find the way out.

The work camp was a new facility, cost state taxpayers three hundred million, but you'd never know that from looking at it. It was shabby, like a massive shed or army

A TASTE OF SHOTGUN

barracks constructed of discounted sheet metal. Windowless with looming guard towers and razor wire fencing choked by wild oats and ragweed, like the contractors tried to blend the building into its bleak surroundings.

The landscape was flatter than a bookkeeper's ass and a feral February wind roared over the fields and snapped the ragged flags on the official flag pole.

Out front of the gate two dudes sat hunched on a bench smoking cigarettes. Each had a prison-issued backpack resting at his feet. I parked the van in the five-minute pick up area and kept the engine idling while a guard gave me the stink eye from his heated shack. I studied the two guys on the bench. The smaller, wiry guy was Vince Carroll. Other than the scraggly beard, he didn't appear to have changed much in the eight months since I'd seen him last. He wore a black wool cap and a brown Carhartt jacket over a black hooded sweatshirt and a pair of ratty Levis. Same as always. I had no idea who the other guy was, but he looked like a larger version of Vince, tangled beard, wool cap, and some kind of heavy pea coat. I eased out of the van and strode over to the bench. Neither one made to get up.

"Hey little brother," I said.

The big fella spat hard and said, "You're late."

I glanced at Vince.

"Probably got lost," Vince said and flicked away his cigarette. "Ain't that right, big brother?"

"Only twice."

Vince grinned back at the big fella. "Never had a sense of direction worth a dick."

Vince stood up and gave me a bear hug with enough pressure to crack a couple short ribs.

"Good to see you," I said.

"Good to be seen."

I stooped to pick up his backpack, but he got there first. "How you been?"

I immediately regretted such a stupid question.

"Living the dream." He swung the backpack over his shoulder.

The big fella said, "If you two are about done with your little gay reunion, I'm freezing my balls off here."

I gave Vince a look, but he was already moving across the icy lot toward the van.

"Damn, I thought I'd feel different being outside them gates," Vince said. He paused a moment and shrugged. "Nope. Feels the same. You feel any different, Pritch?"

"Feels a hell of a lot colder," Pritch said and tossed away his butt.

I sidled up alongside Vince and jerked my head toward the big guy. "What's his deal?"

"Oh," he said, "I told Pritchard we'd give him a ride."

My face fell. "Uh—"

Pritchard must've overheard us talking. He glared at me, daring me to contradict my brother. I leaned in toward Vince, voice lowered. "Where're we taking him?"

Vince shrugged. "How would I know? I just met the ugly sonofabitch twenty minutes ago." He turned to Pritchard. "Where to, Pritch?"

Pritchard seemed to think that over. "First strip club we come to."

Vince ran his hand over his scraggly beard and laughed like it was the funniest thing he'd ever heard. "Not a bad idea." He blew into his hands and gave the van a once over. "Hey, cool ride. Nice and roomy. New?"

"A year old. It's Reva's."

"Who's Reva?" Pritchard said.

"Denis' wife."

"Who's Denis?"

Vince halted and draped his arm around my shoulders. "This is Denis, dumb ass." He rolled his eyes and sighed loudly. "You see what I've had to put up with? I ain't talked to anyone with an IQ over eighty in four years."

"Don't expect too much out here, either," I said.

Pritchard went around to the back of the van and tossed his backpack into the cargo area. He snorted loudly.

"What?" Vince said.

Pritchard nodded toward me. "His wife ate cocks twenty-four-seven."

I turned to Vince, dumbstruck. Had he just insulted my wife? Vince went around to the back of the van. I thought he was going to knock Pritchard into next week, only he started chuckling. Christ. The last thing I needed was to get into a brawl in front of a state prison with some Neanderthal ex-con. I clenched my fists and took a step toward Pritchard. "What'd you say about my wife?"

Vince held up a hand and pointed toward the back bumper. "Your license plate, dumb ass."

I studied the plate. 8KX 247.

It took a moment to register. "Oh for god's sake!" I said. "I never even noticed that."

"Somebody down at the DMV sure hates you," Vince said. He laughed again and moved toward the driver's side. "I'd find out who's responsible for that if I was you."

I stared at the license plate, surprised I'd never noticed it before; amazed that it took a caveman to point it out.

I shook my head. No way could that have been an honest mistake.

"You coming?" Vince called.

"Uh huh." I thought about calling Reva at work. Wouldn't she be surprised? Driving around for a year with those plates. But I didn't want to talk to her about it in front of Beavis and Butthead.

"How about giving me the keys?" Vince said. "I haven't been behind a wheel since forever."

"Do you even have a license?" I said.

"What do I need a license for? It's not my van."

I shook my head. "I'm driving."

Pritchard climbed in the sliding door and Vince eased into the passenger seat and strapped on his belt without even being told. Then he glanced out the window. "Drive by the guard shack."

"I've got a better idea," I said. "Let's *not* drive by the guard shack."

As we rolled off the lot, Vince ran down the passenger side window and flipped off the guard with both middle fingers.

The guard didn't react. Good for him.

We pulled onto the highway and pushed north into a light snowfall, the heater cranked as high as it would go, a long three-and-half-hour drive ahead of us. In the back seat Pritchard hacked up a mound of phlegm. "How do you roll down this window?" he said.

I pressed a button to unlock the back window.

"Never mind," he said, swallowing.

I threw up a little in my mouth and washed the bile down with the last of the morning's cold coffee. So it was going to be that kind of day.

Vince sat quietly beside me; he alternately took in the

bleak landscape and stared hard at my profile. He said, "You look good. Family life agrees with you."

"No complaints," I said.

He nodded. "So. How're my niece and nephew?"

"Good. Growing like weeds."

Vince broke into a smile. "Got any pictures?"

I slipped my phone out of my back pocket. Steering with one hand, I pulled up some recent photos of the twins with the other and handed the phone to Vince.

He grinned. "Them are some good-looking kids," he said. "Must take after their uncle."

Pritchard leaned over the back seat. "Let me see."

Vince ignored him. "Jesus. Look how much taller Mandy is than her brother. Last time I saw them they were like the same size."

"That'll happen," I said.

"She playing YMCA ball?"

"They both are."

Vince smiled. "Just like we did."

"Well, like I did. You mostly rode the bench."

"You're nuts. I was a superstar," Vince said. His eyes went distant. "I sure would like to catch a game."

"There's three left."

"Yeah? I'm going to catch one of them."

I believed he meant it. He went through every picture on the phone before handing it back.

The highway cut through long stretches of dead browns and rusted grays, past the occasional slanting barn and distant cow cluster, amid dull landscapes of forgotten things. You could taste the emptiness like the last sip of beer.

Vince took out a pack of Camel filters from his jacket and cracked the window.

"What're you doing?" I said.

"What's it looking like?"

"Dude, you can't smoke in here."

Vince stared at me and tried to gauge my earnestness. "Seriously? Bro, I did not put my life on the line in Iraq so I couldn't smoke a fucking cigarette."

I sighed. "I know. It sucks, but Reva will have a shit fit." I tried not to sound like a whiny baby—with only moderate success. Vince fumed and tossed the pack of cigarettes and the chrome Zippo on the dashboard. Pritchard snorted from the back seat. I'd about had it with him. I was five seconds from stopping the van and dropping his dumb ass on the side of the highway.

"We'll stop at the next rest area," I said. My lame attempt at reconciliation.

"Forget it."

Vince switched on the radio. Sammy Hagar. For a while he and Pritchard argued over the music selection. Pritchard was partial to classic rock: Seger, Van Halen, Lynyrd Skynyrd, old man crap, while Vince preferred old country. Same as me. Pritchard called it "twangy hillbilly shit" and the two almost came to blows. I reached over and fiddled with the dial till I came across a Christian radio station. We quieted down to listen. I turned up the volume, hoping for a few laughs. Predictably, the husband-wife team spent ninety percent of the time soliciting money from their poor, stupid, gullible Christian radio listeners who probably didn't have a pot to pee in. Give us your cash or the commies and queers win. I didn't see anything funny about that, so I snapped off the radio and we drove awhile in blissful silence. I'd glance in the rearview mirror every once in a while hoping Pritchard had fallen asleep. Nope. Wide awake, arms crossed over his chest, staring angrily out the window. God knows what he had to be angry about. He was a free man, after all, with a free ride.

Vince's eyes drooped heavily. I thought he might've nodded off, but after a moment he turned to me and said, "Why didn't you bring Reva?"

"What?"

"Why didn't Reva come along?"

"She had to work."

"Who's Reva?" Pritchard said.

"Don't worry about it," I said.

"She the one from the license plate?" he said.

"Boy, you are treading on thin ice," I said.

Vince turned around in his seat. "Why don't you mind your own business?"

That shut up Pritchard for a while. Vince turned to me and said, "Where's she working these days?"

"She got on at the library, the children's section."

"Really?" He thought that over. "She'd be good at that."

"She likes it a lot."

"I bet the twins love it."

"Yeah. Next best thing to her being home all the time."

"They like to read?"

"They love to read," I said.

"Just like their dad."

"Nothing like their dad."

Vince laughed. "I read a lot at the work camp. Mysteries mostly. Mysteries and crime novels. That's about all they had in there."

"Crime novels? Really?"

"I know, you wouldn't think they'd allow that. But you want to get bad guys to read, you don't offer those romances or fat Russian novels."

I thought about that. "I guess that makes sense."

We made a pit stop at a Huck's convenience store outside of Pinckneyville. The genius of Mark Twain peddling Cheetos and Coca Cola and gas. I filled up the tank and went to the restroom to make room for more coffee. When I got back to the van, Vince was behind the wheel, cracking the neck of a pint of Jim Beam and hitting on a joint. He'd picked up a pair of mirrored aviator sunglasses, too, though there was no sunlight to speak of.

"I'll drive awhile," he said, and lapsed into a thirty-second coughing fit. "Damn, I ain't had anything that good in years."

I searched my jacket pocket. Sonofabitch. I'd left the keys in the ignition. "Didn't I tell you no smoking in the van?" I said.

"Cigarettes," Vince said between coughs. "You said cigarettes."

"And where the hell did you get a joint? I was only gone like five minutes?"

"Ask and you shall receive," Vince said.

"The Lord provides," Pritchard said.

Vince coughed and held out the joint. "Want a hit?"

"No, I don't want a hit. I want you to—"

"Hey, don't Bogart that joint," Pritchard said.

Vince passed the joint to Pritchard and kicked the engine over.

"Vince, you're not driving," I said. "You're stoned

and you don't have a license."

Vince adjusted the rearview mirror. "Fuck that. I did not put my life on the line in Afghanistan so I couldn't smoke a doobie in my brother's van. Now get in or we're leaving your ass." He slammed the driver's side door and threw the van into reverse. The van backed up fifteen or twenty feet past the pumps.

"Goddamn it, Vince," I muttered under my breath.

A mad look came into his eye and he giggled maniacally, the joint bobbing between his lips. Drugs, alcohol, four years in stir and traumatic brain injury were a bad combination.

Vince jerked the van forward and almost clipped my right shoulder. Pritchard urged him on enthusiastically. He threw the van into reverse, backed up, shifted into drive, and aimed the nose right at me. I suppose he was getting a big kick out of this. A little payback for time served. I had no choice but to make a break for the convenience store. Luckily, the wheels spun on the ice and failed to get traction. Halfway to the entrance I caught sight of one of the clerks, a big-boned twenty-something gal with chopped up green hair standing by the front doors, obviously dismayed at the scene unfolding in the parking lot. I rushed inside the store and strained to catch my breath.

"You know that guy?" she said.

"You mean that maniac trying to kill me? Yeah, that's my little brother. He just got out of prison like two hours ago."

"Looks like he's in a hurry to go back."

The van pulled up to the entrance and Vince laid on the horn and took a pull from the whiskey bottle. "Time to hit the road, bro! Get your ass in gear!"

I gazed at the clerk and shrugged and walked out the doors to my certain doom. Pritchard was now riding shotgun. "You're in back," he yelled through the rolled-up window.

I cursed under my breath and climbed into the back seat.

"Hold on to your Bibles, folks!" Vince cried and the van peeled out, tires squealing.

TWO

The snow picked up as we pulled back onto the highway. At times it was hard to make out where the snow-covered road ended and the wintry fields began. That didn't seem to trouble Vince; in no time the van was pushing seventy on the curvy, slick, rural two-lane, weaving in and out of traffic, blowing past Sunday drivers and big green combine harvesters and John Deere tractors on their way for winter maintenance.

I got all fetal in the back seat and closed my eyes and asked baby Jesus to please send a state trooper angel to pull us over before we wrapped around a tree.

As usual, baby Jesus wanted no part of me.

Vince rolled down the window and spat and left the window halfway down. "So what'd I miss?" he yelled over the roar of the highway.

I lifted my head. "What?"

"The past four years. Anything exciting happen?"

I thought about that. It was strange: four years had passed and not a whole hell of a lot *had* happened. I mean, I'd opened tens of thousands of bottles of Budweiser, poured countless whiskey and Cokes, washed untold dishes, mowed and remowed the lawn, taken the kids to a hundred ball practices, wasted a few thousand hours staring at the television. Just the mundane, everyday stuff of life. Other than that, not much had happened, except we'd all gotten older and deeper in debt. He probably had a lot more interesting time on the inside.

Of course, I wasn't about to say that.

The only noteworthy thing I could think of was five months ago our evil bastard of a stepdad died. Finally. Roy Gladson was Pop's cousin, only a hundred times more of a bastard than Pop ever was. By the time he married our mother, Roy was down to half a lung, one kidney, and a liver that looked like a dried-up meatloaf, and yet somehow the sonofabitch managed to hang on another eight years—out of spite, no doubt.

Roy owned a landfill on the outskirts of town, land that had been strip mined by Massie Coal till it looked like Hiroshima the day after the Japanese surrender. Roy came home every evening reeking like the mouth of hell. If Sara, our mother, complained about the stench, he'd say, "That's the smell of money, doll. The money that's keeping you and your brats housed and fed."

I told Vince that Roy was dead.

"Yeah, Sara told me," he said. "One of the happiest days of her life. She should've poisoned the sonofabitch years ago." He paused. "What was it he died of? A stroke?"

"Think so. Took her five hours to call nine-one-one. Told Chad she was taking a nap. Chad was like, yeah right. She never takes naps in the afternoon."

Vince grinned from ear to ear. "Good for her. I hope the sonofabitch suffered." After a moment, he said, "Sara inherit his dump?"

"It's still in probate. His daughter—the one in Florida—is trying to get it."

"Figures. Who's running it now?"

"No one. It's been closed since Roy died."

Vince shook his head. "Did he leave Sara anything?"

"The house. You talk about a dump."

Vince nodded. "She still hoarding shit?"

"She's gotten worse. Boxes piled to the ceiling. And she's getting so fat she can't fit between the stacks anymore. It's like she's trapped in there. Every month or two I have to go over and widen the corridors so she can get to the bathroom or the refrigerator. But God forbid I should throw anything out. You never know when you might need a newspaper from August of 2003."

Pritchard snorted and Vince turned and shot him a dark look. Then he turned back to me. "What about the Cadillac?"

"They sold it to pay doctor bills. Years ago."

Vince and I shared a look at this, then he turned to Pritchard. "Roy had this sweet red Cadillac DeVille convertible. Mint condition. He only took it out of the garage once a year. Memorial Day weekend."

Pritchard stared out the window. "Who the fuck cares?"

I could totally understand that sentiment. Who the fuck did care? I slipped off my jacket and rolled it up and laid it under my head for a pillow. Out the window I watched a stand of roadside timber roll past and the snow flurries tumble by in a cold ivory blur.

"What do you hear from Pop?" Vince said.

"Last I heard was the cancer had..." I paused. "What's the word?"

"Spread?"

"I was thinking of the technical term. Starts with an M, I think."

"Spread works."

"Anyway, it's everywhere, lungs, pancreas, liver, you name it. He could go anytime."

"And then what?"

"What do you mean?"

"I mean, he's going to die in prison right?"

"I hope so," I said. "If not, he's going to crap out in your trailer. He ain't staying with us."

Vince thought about that. "But they're going to bury him, right? Or cremate him? They ain't going to ship us the corpse and make us pay for all that?"

I shrugged. "I don't know. They'll probably cremate him and send us a box of ashes along with a bill."

"Let them try to collect from me."

Pritchard shook his head. "I can't believe the way you two disrespect your own father."

Vince hit the brakes. The van spun out and jerked to a stop in the middle of the highway. "Listen, pal," Vince hissed, "you don't like our company I can drop your ass off right here and you can walk back to Galesville."

"Galesburg."

"Whatever."

I sat up and peered out the back window. A tractor trailer was barreling down on us. Fast.

"Vince," I said. "That semi behind us. It ain't stopping."

"I see him," Vince said. He righted the van and we were once again underway.

Another five seconds and we would've been road kill.

After a moment something funny occurred to Vince and he let out a short laugh. "Hey Pritchard, why don't you tell Denis what you were in for."

"Fuck off."

"The Galesburg Kid robbed a Pizza Hut."

"Yeah?" I said. "Make off with a lot of dough?"

"Ha, ha, never heard that one before," Pritchard muttered. He turned and stared moodily out the window. He removed a pack of Winstons and a lighter from his coat pocket and started to light a cigarette.

Vince slapped the cigarette out of his mouth. "Hey, my brother said no smoking in the van!"

Pritchard gave him a murderous look. I thought for sure that this was it, one of them was going to die. "You know, I killed a man once," Pritchard said menacingly, his eyes narrowed to slits.

For a moment no one said anything, then Vince laughed sharply and turned to me. "If I robbed a Pizza Hut I sure as hell wouldn't be bragging about it. But Pritchard couldn't keep his pie hole shut." He waited a beat. "Get it—pie hole?"

"I got it."

Pritchard glared out the window. "I know the son-ofabitch who ratted me out," he said. "First thing I do when I get home is put that fucker down."

"That where you're from?" I said.

"Why else would I be going there?"

"Sounds like a craphole," Vince said.

"Home of Chuck Walgreen," Pritchard said with pride.

"Who the hell's Chuck Walgreen?" Vince said.

Pritchard rolled his eyes. "Jeez, what a bunch of rubes."

"Well, who is he?"

"Founder of Walgreens?"

"You say that like it's a good thing," I said. "All he did was drive five or six thousand mom-and-pop drug stores out of business."

Vince sneered. "And I did not put my life on the line in Afghanistan so some Galesburg asshole could lay waste to America's downtowns."

"That's capitalism, motherfuckers," Pritchard said. "You don't like it, go back to Russia."

I sighed and stretched out in the back seat, trying to ignore their inane chatter as the van fishtailed down Route 13. Vince's manic episode seemed to have passed and he was keeping close to the speed limit now. A sense of hopefulness ignited inside me, the hope I wouldn't die in some horrible smash up on the highway after all. As we approached a curve, we passed a Prius that had slid off the road, its nose pointing upward from the ditch like a sinking ocean liner. "Take that, liberal scum," Vince said.

Later, Pritchard's head slumped on his chest and he emitted the occasional bear-like snore. Every so often he'd cry out in his sleep: "Get off me!" Vince chuckled and turned on the radio to a classic country station out of St. Louis, but he kept the volume low so as not to awaken Pritchard. We both preferred him in an unconscious state.

I started to say something to Vince, something important, but he cut me off.

"So how come you didn't come see me the past eight months? You too busy?"

My sphincter tightened, but I'd been prepared for this. "I'm sorry, man. Things have been crazy with the twins. Every weekend there's been some out-of-town basketball game or volleyball game or something. You know how it is with kids."

"Actually I don't."

"Well, you can imagine."

"Yeah," he said. His tone was empty, hollow. I couldn't tell if that placated him or not. "You got the birthday cards with the pictures the twins made, didn't you?"

Vince nodded. "I got them." He was silent a moment, then he muttered, "You might've at least kept up the newspaper subscription."

I'd forgotten about that. I'd let the subscription to the *Belleville Daily American* lapse. "Yeah, I'm sorry about that," I said.

"Forget it."

He was silent. He was pissed. Who could blame him?

I was a thoughtless prick. No one knew that better than me.

THREE

I needed to talk to Vince, alone. I'd been putting it off because of our unexpected guest. When Pritchard had been asleep awhile, I leaned over the front seat and lowered my voice, just above a whisper. "Dude, we need to talk."

"Yeah? What about?"

"Your pal, Clay Goodwin."

"Huh. What's that shitbird up to?"

I paused. "Well, some might call it a shakedown."

Vince glanced at Pritchard, made sure he was asleep. "Say what again?"

"You heard me. And it's been going on awhile. A couple years ago he came to me and said he needed to unload some weed. Actually a lot of weed. Like old times, he said. I told him he had to be out of his mind—after what happened."

"Damn straight."

"So he says, 'That's right, I'm out of my fucking mind. So what?' He says he's into these East St. Louis niggers for fifty grand and if he don't come up with it soon they're going to feed him piece by piece to their pit bulls."

"What's that dumbass doing dicking around in East

St. Louis?"

"Trying to be a player, I guess."

Vince shook his head. "So what's that got to do with us?"

"Nothing, except if I didn't sell his shit, he says he'll have a little talk with Belleville Five-O, tell them what really happened the night Johnny Sika died."

Vince's hands tightened on the wheel till the knuckles whitened. "He can't be that stupid."

"He's that stupid and more."

His face turned hard. "He's a dead man."

I didn't say anything. I just let it hang out there.

"Two years ago? And you're just now telling me?"

"Wouldn't have done any good telling you before now."

Vince was silent.

"Besides, I thought I could handle it."

"And how'd that work out for you?"

"Not great."

Vince shook his head. "That little bitch." He was silent a moment. We both were. He said, "So what happened? And please don't tell me you've been selling his weed?"

"What else was I going to do?"

"I know what I would've done," he said through his teeth.

"Yeah and what good is it if we're both in prison?"

Vince stared out at the highway as the silence ticked by. A long moment passed, then he said, "So what's our cut?"

I hesitated. "Twenty percent."

"Twenty percent!"

We both looked to see if we'd awakened Pritchard. He was still sleeping like a baby, drool and all.

"Twenty percent?"

"You think I like this?" I said. "I got two kids. Think I wouldn't have told him to fuck himself if there was any other way?"

Vince shook his head. "Someone needs to bust a cap in that shit weasel." He breathed in steadily and stared through the windshield. "I'll tell you one thing, we ain't selling any more of that shit, that's for damn sure." His voice rose steadily, furious and hard at the edges. "Not one fucking ounce."

Too loud. Pritchard jolted awake. "What about an ounce?"

"Go back to sleep," Vince snapped.

"I wasn't sleeping."

Pritchard turned on the radio and an old Jackson Browne song came on. Usually I like Jackson Browne. Not this time.

Vince's eyes studied me in the rearview mirror. "Don't think I don't know what this is," he said. "I know exactly what this is. You think I'm going to handle this. Dumb ass Vince to the rescue again."

"That's not what this is about," I said in my most aggrieved voice.

"Forget it, bro. I did four years. I did it for our family and I never complained. Did I ever complain?"

He complained some, but I said no, he never complained.

"Damn straight, I didn't."

"Complain about what?" Pritchard said.

Some time passed before Vince spoke again. "You're going to fix this," he said. "Meanwhile you can tell Goodwin we're closed for business."

I nodded silently.

"What business?" Pritchard said.

"None of your goddamn business, that's what," Vince snapped.

He gripped the wheel and his jaw crept forward. "Somebody needs to bust a cap in that shit weasel," he muttered.

FOUR

An hour before we hit town it occurred to me that I'd forgotten to check on Vince's trailer. The last time I'd seen the trailer—it must've been two years ago—it was looking pretty rough. The screen door hung off like a broken arm, the front porch had collapsed and at least one window was busted out. Nothing that couldn't be fixed, but I'd also forgotten to turn on the electricity. And the water.

Pritchard yawned and gazed around blankly. "Where the hell are we?"

"Go back to sleep," Vince said.

Pritchard gazed out the window at the same snow-covered fields and low leaden skies. He blinked and wiped his nose with his sleeve. "Got any more of that Beam left?"

"You drank it all," Vince said.

"What about the weed?"

"You smoked it all."

"Man this getting out of prison sucks."

"What'd you expect, hookers and blow? If it weren't for my brother your ass would be walking home."

Pritchard didn't have anything to say to that.

We drove north listening to the heater rattle over some

moldy oldie radio station. We passed lopsided farmhouses ready to fall over. We passed some cows, who stared dumbly at us. They were covered in snow and looked cold and miserable.

Vince turned down the radio and said, "Speaking of business, how's the bar doing?"

"About the same," I said. "Barely holding on. Seems like every day another Buffalo Wild Wings or Hooters opens up out on the highway."

"They got real good wings, Hooters does," Pritchard said. "Let's stop at a Hooters when we get to town."

We ignored him.

"Parole board said I've got to get a job, but it can't be around booze," Vince said. "Any ideas?"

I shook my head. "You ought to talk to Chad. He's got connections. He knows everything that's going on in town."

"Who's Chad?" Pritchard said.

Vince sighed.

"Who's Chad?"

"He's my brother!"

"Jesus, how many brothers you got?" Pritchard said.

The towns were getting larger and closer together, large enough for fast food chains and gas stations and school buildings. Maybe even a cop or two. We were nearing civilization. We passed a roadhouse called Mott's Lounge and Vince jerked a sharp U-turn and whipped into the parking lot. We bounced over ragged asphalt and jolted to a stop near the front door. The parking lot was mostly empty.

I sat up. "What the hell—?"

"Pit stop."

"About fucking time," Pritchard said and kicked

opened the passenger side door.

Vince climbed out of the van and stretched some kinks out. "I've been waiting four years for this."

"Place looks like a craphole," Pritchard said.

"That's perfect!" Vince said. "Come on, dudes. I got four years of catching up to do."

I started to say something about needing to get home to pick up the twins from school, but it was pointless. I'd been in Mott's once before, back when I was single and looking for something other than the same old barflies, same old talk. Best I could hope was they'd slam a couple pitchers, shoot a few games of pool and get bored with the dive.

The bar was long and narrow like a shotgun shack and smelled thickly of stale beer and damp mops. Besides the bartender, a dirty blonde who looked like she'd seen a rough forty or so years, there were only two other people in the tavern, blue collars hunched at a front table drinking their lunch and staring idly at one of the many televisions positioned throughout the bar. We stomped the snow off our shoes, while the blue collars gave us the once over. The bartender glanced up from her smartphone and drifted over to see what we wanted. Her look was one of extreme boredom. Speaking as a tavern owner, her manner wasn't likely to bring back repeat business.

Vince leaned his elbows on the bar and studied the merchandise like a kid in a candy store. "Let's see. What'll I have for my first drink in four years?"

"You already drank a quart of Jim Beam," I reminded him.

"That doesn't count," he said and turned to the bartender. "A shot of Turkey and a pitcher of Bud."

"Really?" I said. "That's what you pick? Budweiser?"

"Tequila and a lime and another pitcher of Bud," said Pritchard.

The bartender lifted her eyes to me.

"Yeah, I'm good."

Vince nailed me in the gut with the back of his hand. "What the fuck, bro, ain't you going to drink a toast to my freedom?"

A flush crept across my cheeks. "Oh yeah." I turned to the bartender. "Give me a shot of Turkey."

She poured the shots and we picked up our glasses and raised them nose high. "To freedom," I said.

"I'll drink to that shit," Vince said.

"Fucking A," said Pritchard.

The whiskey hit my empty stomach and wired a signal to my brain that said, *What the hell is this? It's not even noon?* Pritchard sucked his lime, downed the tequila and smacked his lips loudly. Vince picked up his pitcher of Bud and strode over to the pool table at the rear of the bar. Pritchard followed. I sat hunched on a stool at the bar and studied the beer selection: Bud. Bud Light. Bud Lime. Bud Dry. Bud Ice. Bud Select. Bud Select 55. Bud Light Platinum. Bud Light Apple. I hated drinking before noon, which is why I didn't open the Lantern till three o'clock. Hell, I hate drinking before five o'clock. But I especially hated drinking shitty beer before five o'clock.

I ordered a Bud Light Lime-A-Rita and stared furtively at the bartender for something to do. I could see how she might've been a looker ten years, three kids, and two divorces ago. At least her hair was still nice, long and black, and she hadn't gone to fat. Not yet. But everything else was showing its age despite half-hearted attempts to disguise it.

She glanced up in the back mirror and caught me staring at her. "Want to start a tab?"

I reddened and took out my wallet and removed my credit card and slid it across the bar. "Guess I'd better."

She went over to the cash register. I lifted my eyes to the television above the bar. Some kind of game show was on. People in the audience dressed like animals and sandwiches and various household appliances and jumped up and down like they were on fire. The sound was off and a Waylon Jennings tune played on the jukebox, so thank god for small favors. I pretended the show was a video for the Waylon song, but it didn't quite work out. The only way it would've worked was if they had Waylon kick the crap out of the guy dressed like a Polish sausage.

The waitress came back and handed me the card.

"Declined."

"Oh for crying out loud." I took out my wallet again and pulled out another credit card. "Give this one a try."

This time the card worked and the waitress went back to being mesmerized by the dumb apps on her smartphone. I turned and leaned my elbows on the bar and watched Vince and Pritchard shoot pool. It was painful to watch. The Lime-A-Rita wasn't doing it for me, so I turned back to the waitress and cleared my throat and tried to get her attention. "How about food?"

"How about it?"

"Do you serve any?"

"No, but we got that." She jerked her head toward a large jar that sat at the end of the bar. The jar was about the size of a gumball machine and contained a murky gray fluid. Inside you could just make out something that resembled golf balls.

"What is it?"

"I think they're pickled eggs."

I took a sip of the Lime-A-Rita. "How old are they?"

The bartender shrugged. "Been here as long as I've been here."

"How long is that?"

Her eyes dulled as she thought that over. "Too long."

"Yeah, I'll pass."

She yawned but didn't bother to cover her mouth. "We got some jerky behind the bar."

I didn't say anything and the bartender shrugged and went back to leaning her ass against the bar cooler and staring at her phone. I picked up my beer and slid off the stool and strode over to where Vince and Pritchard were making a hash of a game of eight ball. You could tell they were seriously out of practice. I guess they don't have pool tables in the Shawnee State Work Camp. I guess that makes sense. Pool balls and cues are pretty much lethal weapons. Pritchard took aim at the four ball and the cue ball caromed off the four and knocked the eight into the corner pocket.

Vince tilted his head back and roared with laughter.

"We about ready to hit it?" I said.

Vince leaned over the table and racked the balls for another game. He lifted his eyes toward me. "What's your hurry? We ain't hung out in four years. You got something better to do?"

Apparently, the whole drive home was going to be one long guilt trip. "Fine then," I said. "Give me the keys and I'll pick us up some burgers. I can't drink on any empty stomach."

Vince dug the keys out of his jacket pocket. Then he

paused and dangled the keys in front of me, his eyebrows arched suspiciously. "You ain't going to run off and leave us, are you, bro?"

I frowned. "I just drove three-and-a-half hours to pick up your ass. If I was going to ditch you I'd have done it hours ago."

Pritchard chalked his stick. "I don't trust him."

I held out my palm. "Keys."

Vince tossed me the keys.

I drove to the nearest town, Callaway, pop. 1,097. I searched up and down the main drag for a fast food joint, but apparently the town was too small for even a Dairy Queen. I passed the remnants of a Hardee's. It looked like there'd been a fire; the walls were smudged black and the windows and doors boarded up. I turned and drove south and zipped past a patrol car hidden on a side street. I hit the brakes and held my breath, eyes fixed in the rearview mirror.

On went the lights. The cruiser pulled onto Main and zoomed up on my back bumper like a goddamn rocket and the cop whooped his siren at me. Well that little pointless side trip just cost me a hundred bucks. I cursed under my breath and pulled over in front of a boarded-up bank. I thought I sensed a panic attack coming on, so I fumbled through the glove box for a bottle of pills and popped a couple Ativan and immediately felt better. Everything slowed down just a little. Time. My pulse. The red and blue flashing lights. I gazed around at my surroundings. It seemed like every goddamn business in town was either closed or burned up; the town probably got all its revenue pulling over out-of-town idiots like me.

A TASTE OF SHOTGUN

Johnny Law took his old sweet time getting out of the cruiser. Nine or ten minutes dragged by before his door opened and he trudged through the gray slush up to my window. He was younger than I was by a good five years, which annoyed me. I'd noticed that most of the cops, bartenders, doctors, lawyers, I met were now younger than me. It's a hell of a thing to realize.

I rolled down the window and handed over my license and insurance card before he could ask, thinking just write me the goddamn ticket and let's not take all day.

"Clocked you doing forty-one in a thirty," the cop said and blew into his hands.

"Yeah. Sorry about that. I didn't realize I was going that fast."

He paused to study my license and then he fixed his eyes on me. "Have you had anything to drink?"

My blood turned to ice water. I wondered if he smelled the liquor on me, or maybe a town like this, you just expect everyone to be drinking or shooting up first thing in the morning. Surely that shot of Wild Turkey and a Bud Lime-a-Rita wouldn't put me over the limit...

"Just a lime soda. And a coffee this morning."

"Uh huh." He examined my insurance card. "Going anywhere in particular?"

I wanted to say, yeah, I'm going to the Nobel Prize Award Ceremony. The King of Sweden awaits. Fucking idjit. "I was just looking for some fast food, place to get a couple of burgers."

A car hissed by and some rube driver rubbernecked us. The cop gazed off down the street. "We had us a Hardee's once, but it burned down about three years ago."

"Yeah, I saw the ruins."

"Shame, too. That Hardee's drove my uncle's diner out of business, then it goes and burns down. Now we got shit-all, excuse my French."

Apparently we were good buds, now. Either that or he was just looking for some victim to jaw at.

"You could try the gas station," he said. "They sell hot dogs and nachos. The hot dogs are pretty good if you load them up with onions and relish. I wouldn't recommend the nachos. The cheese tastes like plastic. Looks like plastic too. Hell, for all I know it *is* plastic."

I didn't say anything to that.

He nodded thoughtfully. "I'll be right back." He turned and trudged back to the cruiser. Sometime later a second patrol car pulled up behind him and a female cop got out. She looked older than the male cop. Anyway, those two talked a while, flirted, I guess, then I started to worry about it taking so long, imagining all kinds of worst-case scenarios. Was there a warrant out for my arrest? Had I forgotten to pay a parking ticket somewhere? I vaguely recalled getting a speeding ticket about two years ago, but I paid a traffic lawyer to fix it for me.

Unless he'd forgotten.

That was entirely possible. I had a friend who'd gotten a speeding ticket in St. Louis, back before everyone carried a cell phone all the time. He asked a lawyer friend to take care of the ticket, but the lawyer forgot. Guess it wasn't a priority. Two months later my friend got pulled over in St. Charles County for a missing headlight and the cops found the warrant and cuffed him and dragged him off to the county jail. It took the city cops two days to come and pick him up, then he spent another day in the city jail before they finally let him call someone to bail him out. For four days, nobody knew where the hell he was. He lost his job because of it.

I'll bet that goddamn traffic lawyer forgot to fix my ticket.

At length, the cop walked back and handed me my license and insurance card. "Sign here."

I signed.

"I'll be back in a few minutes with a printed copy of your ticket and some instructions."

He turned and trudged back to his car. Evidently this traffic stop *was* going to take an entire day.

At least I wasn't going to jail.

Five minutes later, the cop tramped back, handed me the ticket and told me the court date. The fine for driving more than ten miles over the speed limit (but less than twenty), was ninety bucks. I shoved the ticket and my license into my shirt pocket.

The cop breathed into his hands again. "The Conoco is two blocks ahead. Go left at the light and take the first right you can't miss it. Just keep her under thirty." He pocketed his ticket book. "By the way, you got an interesting license plate."

"I'm aware."

"Yeah. Well, you have a good day."

I did just like the cop said, but damned if I could find the Conoco. I drove around another five minutes before I stumbled on it. Or maybe it was a different Conoco. Anyway, I went inside and bought their last eight dried up dogs and three small bags of chips. I ate my share in the van, then drove back to the bar, getting lost only once along the way.

Vince and Pritchard were waiting outside the bar when I pulled up. They hurried over to the van and jumped in. Vince had an inch-and-a-half gash above his right eye. Blood spilled down his cheek and jaw, but he didn't seem to notice or care.

"Shit man, you get lost again?" Vince said, strapping on his seatbelt. "It's fucking freezing out there." He turned up the heater to its highest setting. "Let's boogie."

I pulled out onto Main Street and pointed the van north.

"Can't this heap go any faster?" Pritchard said.

"I just got a speeding ticket," I said.

"So that's where you've been?" Vince said.

I ignored that. After a moment, I said, "Somebody going to tell me what happened back there?"

Vince twisted the rearview mirror and studied his wound. "Huh. Not as bad as I thought."

Pritchard leaned forward over the seat. "What'd you bring us?"

"Is somebody going to tell me what just happened?" I repeated.

"Probably leave a cool scar," Vince said. He pushed the mirror back into place. I readjusted the mirror.

"What's in the bag?" Pritchard said.

"Hot dogs. Chips."

Vince nodded toward Pritchard. "You missed it. Dumb ass here broke a beer bottle over some dude's head," Vince said. "Then all hell broke loose."

Pritchard reached over the seat and snagged the sack of hot dogs. Vince yanked it out of his hand.

"Don't be greedy, asshole!"

I looked at my brother. "Why'd he do that?"

Vince handed Pritchard a hot dog. Pritchard took a big bite out of the hotdog and spoke with his mouth full. "Fucking gay bar."

"Didn't seem like a gay bar to me," I said.

"You must be gay then," Pritchard said.

"What the hell does that even mean?"

Vince turned to me. "Where's the beer?"

A local patrol car screamed past. I recognized the same young cop behind the wheel.

"Jesus McChrist," I said, "you haven't even been out of prison two hours and you two have already committed assault and battery."

Pritchard mimicked what I said, but with a whiny girl voice.

I let it go. Another forty-five minutes and I'd be rid of them. Both of them. I kept the van under twenty-five, one eye glued to the rearview mirror till we were well outside the city limits. The cops never did come after us.

We passed a green birdshot-pocked road sign that said Belleville forty miles away.

I can do this, I told myself.

Vince let out a long belch. "Damn, I ain't had anything that tasty since I can't remember when."

"Probably four years," I said.

"Yeah." He looked through the bag for napkins, which I'd forgotten to pick up, then wiped his mouth on his sleeve. "Dude, why didn't you get any beer with the dogs? I told you to get some beer."

"Actually you didn't," I said. "Besides you just had how many pitchers?"

"Pull in at the next gas station."

I shook my head. "We're almost home, then you can drink yourself into a coma if you want."

"Why the hell'd you let him drive?" Pritchard muttered.

When they'd finished their lunch Vince tossed the empty bags out the window. He turned to Pritchard.

"Bus your table."

Pritchard ran down the window and tossed out his empty bags. "How much longer?" he said. "This is like being locked up all over again."

"We'll be there in a half hour," I said. "Just chill." I craned my neck to look at Pritchard. "By the way, where am I dropping you off?"

Pritchard shrugged and gazed out the window as we passed the familiar sight of the sewer treatment facility. "You got a couch?"

"You talking to me or Vince?"

"Either one."

I ignored him. Vince did too. Vince popped open the glove box and dug around among the CDs, reading the labels and commenting on my bad taste in music. "Hey, I remember this." He unsheathed my old hunting knife, a Fallkniven NL4.

"Huh. I wondered where that went to," I said.

Vince studied the blade, running his thumb along the edge. "This thing is fucking awesome."

"Let me see it," Pritchard said.

Vince ignored him. "Mind if I take this?"

"What?"

"It's just sitting in your glove box."

"That was a birthday gift...from grandad."

"I know it was a birthday gift." He turned and put his eye on me. "Dude, do I have to remind you what I did for you?"

I sighed.

"What'd you do for him?" Pritchard said.

"Mind your own fucking business!" Vince snapped.

Pritchard slumped back in his seat.

"Fine," I said. "Take it."

"Sweet."

"Anything else you want? My first born?"

"Which one's your first born?"

"Hunter. By six minutes."

"Naw. I'm good."

Pritchard leaned forward and rested his arms on the back of Vince's seat. "I don't think it's a good idea to give that psycho a knife."

Vince turned in a flash and planted the blade under Pritchard's chin. "One more word out of you and I'll gut you like a mud carp. Try me."

"Christ," Pritchard said. He fell back into his seat. "What a psycho."

Vince wiped the blade on his jeans and slipped it back into its sheath.

In a half hour I'll be home, I thought. So what if I get another ticket.

I pressed down on the accelerator.

FIVE

From the south you enter Belleville via Route 13. The monotony of fallow crop fields quickly gives way to the tedium of fast food joints, strip malls, auto repair shops, and decrepit 1940s cottages. Streets choked with pickups and the occasional muscle car. It's a town of thirty thousand. Thirty thousand slugs with no imagination, no interests beyond televised sports and crappy beer.

That's where I come in, with the sports and crappy beer. I've always had a love-hate relationship with Belleville. Mostly hate, but the fact is I fit right in here. I wouldn't feel right being someplace else. Some place better.

When I was a teenager all we talked about was getting out. Moving to Florida or Texas. A few of us did. A few of us joined the military, saw some of the world's real hellholes. Iraq. Libya. Pakistan. Afghanistan. Suddenly Belleville didn't seem so bad. Don't get me wrong, it was still bad, but now we knew it could be a lot worse. After our tours of duty most of us drifted back. Turns out you can drink bad beer and watch sports just as easy in Belleville as you can in Jasper, Florida or Denton, Texas. And the rent is cheaper.

To me, the best thing about Belleville has always

been that it's close to places that aren't Belleville. Places you could drive to or take a bus to. Like St. Louis. St. Louis was the best thing about Belleville. And that ain't saying much.

We grew up in the shadow of the Stag brewery, once the largest employer in town. When I was fifteen, the brewery was sold to some big, out-of-state operation. The new owners promised to keep the brewery open, but before the ink had dried on the contract the bastards had shut her down and tossed thousands of my neighbors out of work. And not just any work, but good-paying union jobs. As the seventies and eighties wore on the town's other major businesses followed suit. The stove factory. The shoe factory. Closed or moved overseas. Eventually, even the coal mines outside of town shut down.

The knockout blow came when a massive shopping mall opened in a nearby town. Ripped the barely beating heart right out of our one-hundred-and-twenty-five-year-old downtown while the city fathers stood around with their dicks in their hands and their thumbs up their asses.

The few shops that survived went under when the Super Walmart came to town.

Today, Belleville is a town in name only. It's more a collection of dilapidated houses ringed by fast food joints. The largest employer in town is the county jail.

We lose population every year. The middle class moves farther and farther out from town, sets up its own gated enclaves in pasture land and the poor drift in to take their place. Slumlords buy the homes for pennies on the dollar, rent them out to poor folks on housing assistance and illegal immigrants. Meanwhile, the houses, the neighborhoods, the schools deteriorate. It's the same old song all over the Rust Belt. There you have it. That's my town in a nutshell.

Vince's trailer was parked out back of our grandparents' house a half mile south of town. The little white farmhouse seemed to shrink in size every time I saw it. Soon it wouldn't look any bigger than a cheap doll house. Both grandparents were long dead and a single mom rented the place. Amber McFall worked as a waitress at Denny's and raised a two-year-old girl and tried her best to keep up a cheerful front, even though her world was pretty much shit. Amber was the kind of girl who never had a chance. She must have known that since she was twelve or thirteen. That's the age when teachers and school counselors begin telling a few select students that they have promise, that they can go far—as in far away from this dust bowl of dreams. But to the Amber McFalls of the world, they don't say a goddamn thing. Nor to the Denis Carrolls, the Vince Carrolls. They don't even see you.

Before he was sent to the work camp, Vince used to mow the grass and mend things on the property in exchange for parking his trailer rent-free. I don't think anybody mowed the grass or fixed anything since Vince went away. That was probably my job, considering it was my fault that Vince went away. At least partially.

Amber and some gal I didn't recognize sat on the front porch steps smoking cigarettes as we pulled up to my grandparents' house. Amber wore a long black coat with a gray fluffy hood over her beige Denny's uniform and she hugged her knees to her chest. Her friend had on a man's dark brown Carhartt jacket and a green stocking cap. Amber's little girl was bundled up in a gray bubble coat and green scarf and swung upside down from an old snow tire hung from a sycamore branch. The ugliest dog I'd ever seen—looked part rat terrier and part opossum—ran circles around the little girl, yapping stupidly. The little girl stopped swinging when we pulled up and hurried over and stood between her mother's knees and eyed us suspiciously.

But what really drew my attention was the trailer.

It was in far worse shape than I'd imagined. Besides the busted window, part of the roof had collapsed. So had the rest of the porch. Like I said, Chad and I had talked about fixing the place up before Vince came home—turning on the water and electricity and airing the rooms out a bit, but I guess we both expected the other one to handle it.

Vince eased out of the van and glanced at the trailer. "Man, the trailer has sure gone to hell the past four years." He glanced at me. "Thanks for keeping the place up, bro."

I didn't say anything. He was right. It looked like a meth lab had blown up.

"Probably skunks and shit living in there," he said. "Hell of a homecoming for a war hero."

That war hero thing was wearing thin. He'd been out of the service six years.

"That's your place?" Pritchard said, making a sour face.

Vince nodded halfheartedly.

"I don't know, dude. I think skunks got too much class to live there." Pritchard nodded toward the little white farmhouse. "What about that place? Can't we bunk there?"

"Who said anything about you bunking anywhere?" Vince said. Then he turned to me. "Who are the old ladies?"

"The one of the left is Amber. She's renting the house. And she ain't old. I don't know who the other one is."

Vince studied her. "She looks familiar."

She did, but damn if I could place her.

The rat-possum wandered over and sniffed Vince's hand. "You're an ugly little guy, aren't you?" he said. "Yes you are! Yes you are!" He squatted down and let the dog slobber all over his face. "What happened to Leah?" he said.

"She moved out two years ago."

"Really? Where'd she go?"

"No idea. Just moved out one night. Owed us four months' back rent." I paused. "Well, owed Sara."

We walked past Amber's Ford Escort and a dusty silver Camry and wandered over to the house. It occurred to me I should have warned Amber about Vince coming home.

Too late now.

"Hey Amber," I said.

Amber's face darkened and she pressed her little girl close. "Denis," she said coolly.

"This here's my brother Vince."

Vince grinned. "How do?"

I nodded toward the trailer. "Um, that's his place over there."

The three females continued to stare blankly at us. I nodded toward Pritchard. "And this here is…uh…" I shrugged. "Never mind about him."

A blackbird hopped on a satellite dish on the roof of

the trailer and Pritchard picked up a stone and flung it at the bird. He missed by a mile, but the stone shattered some more of the broken window glass.

"Fuck you, man."

Amber flared. "My little girl don't need to be hearing that kind of talk!"

Pritchard rolled his eyes and chuckled softly to himself.

After a moment, Amber lifted her eyes toward me. "This is my friend Erica." Erica looked away and blew cigarette smoke out her nose like she was bored beyond words. Amber whispered something to Erica, and her friend took the little girl's hand and led her inside. The mutt trailed behind them.

Amber stood up and cut her eyes toward me. "Denis, can I talk to you a minute?"

"Sure, hold on a second," I said. I went for my wallet and pulled out a cashier's check, which contained Vince's cut of the bar profits for the past four years. I turned to Vince and stuffed the check in his jacket pocket. "Your cut," I said.

He took the check out of his pocket and stared at it for a moment. "Really? That's it? That's four years' profit?"

"Uh huh."

He shoved the check back into his pocket. "I don't know how that place stays open."

"Tell me about it. Anyway, that ought to help you get on your feet."

"One foot, anyway."

"I'm going to take off in a minute. I got to pick up the twins. Let me know if you need anything, okay?"

"You're leaving?" he said, a look of concern etched across his face.

Pritchard had wandered over to Vince's pickup. He kicked one of the truck's four flat tires. "This is the truck you were talking about?" he said to Vince.

"Denis?" Amber called.

"Yeah," I said. "Coming."

I gave Vince a hug. "Good to have you home."

We moved around the side of the house. An empty concrete slab sat where my grandparents' air conditioning unit should have been. The slab was covered in colored chalk drawings. A house, a mommy, a little girl, a dog, and a cat. I looked around for a cat, but didn't see one. Amber drew on her cigarette and leaned in, her voice tight. "He isn't living here, is he?"

I shrugged. "That's his home."

"I know, but he isn't living here?"

"Well—"

"Denis, in case you forgot, I've got a little girl. You expect us to live out here alone with a pedophile?"

The wind picked up a little and made a raspy breath through the bare branches. Amber folded her arms against the cold and dipped her head. I studied the frozen crop fields beyond the treeline and thought how I just wanted to go home and sleep till this day was over. "He's not a pedophile," I said.

"No? What is he then? What was he in prison for?"

"He's harmless," I said.

She glared at me, waiting.

"He's a nonviolent offender, okay? It was a victimless crime."

"I read the papers, Denis. He killed someone."

"If you read the paper you'd know it was self-defense."

"Bullshit. He did five years."

"Four years. And that was for drugs," I said, before I realized how that sounded.

She shook her head disgustedly. "What about that other one?"

"Pritchard?"

She waited, tapped her foot.

"Armed robbery, I think."

"Goddammit, Denis!" she cried. "What are you thinking?"

I looked away. I'll tell you what I was thinking. I was thinking about that nap and maybe a hot shower. I wasn't asking for much. I studied the ground where dozens, maybe hundreds of cigarette butts littered the dirt. Among the weeds lay an empty pint of cut-rate vodka.

"You know that trailer isn't fit for fleas to live in," she said. "The roof's falling in. There's no water or electricity."

I shrugged. "I'm working on that. Meantime, you think you could run an extension cord out to the trailer? We'll deduct it from your rent."

Her eyes flashed angrily and she stamped her foot.

"Come on, Amber, where else is he going to go?"

"He could stay with you."

I shook my head. "You don't know my wife."

She lowered her eyes. Actually she did know my wife. My wife had babysat Amber when they were younger.

"Then he could stay with your brother," she said. "Or he could get an apartment. I don't care what he does as long as he doesn't stay here."

I looked over at Vince's old pickup parked behind the house, the tires cracked and deflated. I wondered if it would start. Probably not. Probably the battery was shot. That wasn't on me, though. Chad was in charge of Vince's truck.

I made a show of looking at my watch. "I need to pick up my kids," I said and turned to leave.

"Denis, where are you going?" she cried. "Denis!"

I turned the corner, leaving her on the side of the house with the butts and vodka bottles, and hurried back to the van. None of this was my problem. Sara owned the house. Let her deal with Amber. I had my own problems to worry about.

Vince and Pritchard stood on the porch of the trailer, gazing through the front door.

"It ain't so bad," I heard Vince say.

"Oh man, somebody took a shit on the floor," Pritchard said. "Is that human?"

I eased into the van and cranked the engine.

"Denis!" Amber said. She came around the corner of the house, looking pitiful and angry in the frozen mud of the front yard.

Vince turned and called after me, too. "Hey, bro! Wait up a second!"

I waved to them and slammed the door. I shifted the van into drive and made one-hundred-eighty-degree turn bouncing over the hard, rutted terrain. I turned up the radio so I didn't have to hear them shouting after me as I rolled down the gravel road toward home.

SIX

I never bothered to learn to cook, though when necessary I could rustle up a mean plate of scrambled eggs and bacon. My other specialties included chop suey from a can and cheeseburger macaroni from a box.

Tonight's special was spaghetti from a jar. Ground beef. Noodles. Sauce. Hard to mess that up. It was the twins' favorite. Mine too. Except for everything their mother cooked.

Once I fed the kids, they parked themselves in front of the television and turned to the kids' network. They were still too young for smartphones, so their transformation into zombies was still a year or two away.

I poked my head into the living room. "Don't you have homework?"

"Uh uh," Hunter said.

"I already did mine," Mandy said.

They were cute that way. They'd never tell on each other, but Mandy at least refused to lie.

I looked at Hunter. "So you *do* have homework?"

"I done it already," he said.

Eh. Good enough.

They were good kids, for the most part. Reva was dead set on them going to a good college. Not just go, but graduate. I went along for the sake of family harmony, but I always thought college is overrated. Way I see it, a man ought to learn a trade. I wished to god I'd learned to be an electrician. Something to fall back on when the bar finally goes bust, which could be any day. Besides, you go to college, likely as not you'll end up chained to a desk all day, staring at spreadsheets on a goddamn computer. I know a guy can make decent money chained to a desk, but still...shoot me now.

Of course standing on your feet eight hours a day opening bottles of beer for drunks ain't no picnic either.

Reva got home at half past five. The twins ran to greet her at the door—which they never did for me—and she asked them about their homework and got different answers than I got. She made herself a plate of spaghetti and a small salad. I cracked open a Stag and sat down at the table and watched her eat.

It had been gnawing at me all afternoon, the way I left my brother stranded out there in the boonies with a broke-down truck and a falling down trailer. Not even a cell phone for emergencies.

She forked some salad into her mouth. "How'd it go today?" she said.

"I wanted to talk to you about that."

Her fork paused in mid-air.

"Babe, that trailer isn't fit for a dog to live in."

"You were supposed to fix it up. Didn't you?"

I shook my head slightly.

Reva lowered her fork and fixed me with her eyes. "Denis, we already discussed this. I'm not having an ex-convict living in my house. Not with the twins."

"Reev, he's a war hero. You keep forgetting that. It'd do them good to be around a genuine war hero."

Reva poured herself a glass of wine. "I appreciate his service to his country, but he's not living here. End of discussion."

"Not even in the basement? He'd have his own entrance? We'd never even see him."

She gave me an exasperated look. "What part of 'end of discussion' don't you understand?"

I could feel anger swelling in my throat.

"Denis, I won't allow you to make me into the bad guy here just because I care about our children."

"And I don't?"

She shot me a dark look and set down her fork.

It was time to shut up. "Fine," I said. "I'll drop it."

"Thank you."

I got up from the table and took a long pull on my beer and went over and gazed blankly out the kitchen window. Four mounds of wet leaves I'd been meaning to bag and drag to the dumpster moldered in the back yard.

"By the way," I said. "Have you ever noticed the license plate on the van?"

Reva took a sip of wine. "What about it?"

"Go take a look at it."

"I'm eating dinner."

"Well you should take a look at it."

She scowled at me.

"It says 8KX 247."

"So?"

Then I saw it register in her eyes. She sighed heavily. "Grow up, Denis," she said and poured herself another glass of wine.

SEVEN

"I thought you were going to fix it up?" Chad snapped. "I thought I was going to take care of the truck and you were going to get the trailer ready."

He sounded pissed. He looked pissed. If Chad died tomorrow, that's what I'd remember most about him: being pissed. Mostly at me.

I stared down at my black tennis shoes. "I know," I said. "No excuses."

Chad shook his head at me and picked at the label of his bottle of beer.

I didn't say anything about him not fixing the truck. After all, none of this was his fault. It wasn't his fault he had two shitbums for brothers.

It was still early, so the bar was mostly empty save for a middle-aged dude and a much younger woman who carried on furtively in the booth under the old burned-out Falstaff sign. They both wore gray suits, which made me think they were attorneys. They were drinking dirty martinis and the chick giggled like a schoolgirl. The smell of cheating was on them thick as butter. From the goofy grin on the dude's face, I could tell the woman had her hand inside his pants. I had the TVs turned to some sports talk show and the sound off. Every once in a while the young woman got up and played something on the jukebox. New stuff I'd never heard before and hoped to god I'd never hear again. I was in a sour mood and was one more shitty song away from unplugging the jukebox.

I picked up a cocktail glass and inspected it for chips and lipstick traces for something to do. I'm bad about leaving lipstick on glasses. In the movies you always see bartenders polishing cocktail glasses, which only proves that movie directors don't know squat about bartending. Bartenders never polish glasses. Hell, we barely wash the glasses.

"I didn't think he'd get out so soon," I said in my defense. "It's not like we got a lot of warning."

"He said you just dumped him out there, with no phone, no electricity or water and a big old hole in the roof." He downed the last of his beer and pushed the empty toward me. I popped another Stag and set the bottle in front of him.

"I gave him a check for four thousand bucks," I said, exaggerating the amount some. "Besides, the trailer wasn't so bad. You run an extension cord out there—"

He glanced up at me with acidic eyes and I quickly looked away and leaned back on the beer cooler and folded my arms over my chest. "So what'd you want to tell me you couldn't say over the phone?"

Chad absently pushed the bottle back and forth between his hands. "Vince's parole officer called this morning. He missed his meeting."

I wasn't surprised. "Did you ask him why?"

"I don't know where he is. I drove by the trailer and he wasn't there. That chick who lives out there—"

"Amber—"

"—said she hasn't seen him in a couple days. Sara hasn't seen him either. You don't have a phone number for him do you?"

I shook my head.

Chad frowned and peeled at the label on the bottle. "By the way, she's looking for a new place."

"Amber is? Why?"

"Why do you think?"

"I guess that was a dumb question."

He scrubbed his hand over his face. "Look, we need to get Vince an apartment. And a job. And a phone. And when I say we, I mean you."

I nodded.

"You owe it to him. Big time."

"I'm aware," I said, somewhat testily. "What about the parole officer?"

"What about her?"

"She say anything else?"

"Yeah. If he misses one more meeting his ass will be on the first bus back to the work camp."

I took a bottle of Early Times off the back of the bar and poured myself a shot. Normally I don't drink at work. In a business like this, it would be easy to become a drunkard. Especially with my genes. But with Chad crawling up my ass I needed something to take the edge off and I'd already popped a couple Ativan since he came in.

"We need to have a sit down with him, before he gets into real trouble," Chad said. "I don't know, maybe we ought to go look for him."

I tossed back the whiskey and nodded. "He's probably crashing at some friend's house," I said, though I had no idea if this were true. But I sure as hell didn't feel like driving around looking for him. "I'll find him." I said, then tried to change the subject. "He told me he built furniture in prison, so I talked to this cabinet maker who comes in here. Runs a custom kitchen place. He wasn't too excited to hire an ex-con. Even one that's a war hero."

Chad sighed. "Too bad he couldn't work here." He pushed the half-full beer toward me and slid off the bar stool. "I got to pick up Darla from practice. Let me know if you hear from him."

The cheating couple were back at the jukebox. Billy Joel's "Uptown Girl" came on.

I cringed and picked up two cocktail napkins and jammed them into my ears.

Good thing we didn't have an icepick.

EIGHT

A red Honda Accord with a crumpled back fender sat in the driveway. No sign of Vince's beater, so he must've got it running. That was a relief. I parked my pickup and walked back to the trailer, stepping cautiously up the crumbling porch. A few of the boards had been nailed in place and the banged up screen door was back on its hinges. I knocked several times, hard enough to take the screen door off the hinges again.

No answer. I tried the doorknob and it opened right up. Inside was dark and the smell of urine knocked me back on my heels.

"Vince?"

Nobody home.

I took a step inside and flipped on the light switch. I guess they hadn't taken my advice and run an extension cord from the house. There was, however, a tarp over the gap in the roof that sagged with melted snow and ice and dripped into an overflowing plastic washtub. The place looked abandoned. Garbage, dirty clothing, empty beer cans, vodka bottles, roach clips. The smell of rot and despair. A new seventy-inch Sony television sat in the main room, still in the box. I half expected to be stampeded by rats any moment. Unless the trailer was too disgusting for them.

A voice rose up behind me. "Hey."

My heart leapt up in my throat and I turned and instinctively crouched in a defensive posture. Amber peered in through the door, an amused look on her face.

"Christ. You scared the crap of me."

"I thought that was your pickup," she said. She wrinkled up her cute little nose. "Jesus, smells like there was a sewage backup in here."

I closed the door behind me and joined her outside in the brisk, fresh air. Amber looked good, rested, her cheeks bore a healthy pink glow. "You haven't seen Vince have you?" I said.

"No, thank god." She gazed off toward the house. "His truck hasn't been here in a couple days. And trust me, I keep a sharp look out. I keep my windows locked up tighter than a frog's ass."

I bit back a laugh.

"Chad tell you I'm looking for a new place?"

"Yeah. I'm sorry to hear that."

She looked up at me briefly, then back at the house. "It isn't safe out here anymore."

I started to say that Vince was harmless, but decided not to waste my breath.

She hugged herself in the night air, shivering beneath her coat. "Last time I saw him was Monday. Him and that other one."

"Pritchard."

"Assholes woke me up at one in the morning. I was afraid to tell them to shut up. I didn't want to call attention to myself, and then the pooch starts barking and they came over and banged on my door for five minutes. Sounded like they were drunk. Or high. That was it for me."

I nodded sympathetically. "Have you found a place yet?"

"I'm going to stay with my parents till I find one," she said. "Why are you looking for him?"

"No reason," I said. Something in her tone made me uneasy. I took a step back.

She was silent a moment. "Cold, isn't it?"

"Cold as the hair on a polar bear's ass."

She laughed. "Want to come inside for a cup of coffee?"

It wasn't my imagination but I wasn't about to start that up again.

Still, it was nice to know she was still interested. Good for the old male ego.

"Thanks, but I need to find Vince." I smiled weakly and gave her arm a squeeze. "Take care now."

As I turned, I heard her laugh a low, scornful snicker. "The faithful husband," she said.

I didn't say anything to that. I hurriedly climbed into the truck and drove off in search of my brother.

NINE

I spent the rest of that afternoon driving past cheap motels and dive bars and twenty-four-hour diners hoping to spot Vince's Ford pickup. I cruised the trailer parks and slummy Section 8 apartment complexes, but found no sign of him. I drove by the topless clubs in the poor ghetto towns along the river. A shit ton of pickups, but none were his. When it came time to open The Brass Lantern, I gave up and drove back to Belleville.

As I turned onto Main Street, I spied his pickup outside the public library. The same place Reva worked and almost certainly the last place I would've thought to look. I parked the pickup on the street and went inside.

Maybe I shouldn't have been too surprised; the library is a popular hangout for the homeless and poor folks who can't afford the price of the internet. I found him upstairs slouched at a desk in the computer room. The room housed ten machines, old ones, and they were all in use. I came up behind him and coughed in my hand so as not to startle him. Sometimes ex-cons can be a little jumpy. Surprise them and you may find the business end of a Fallkniven NL4 in your spleen.

Vince was surfing some government website.

He turned and grinned at me. "Hey big brother."

"We've been looking all over for you."

"We?" He glanced around the room. "Got a turd in your pocket?"

"Me and Chad."

"Yeah, well one of you found me."

I pulled up a chair and sat down beside him. There were guys seated on both sides of him. One was obviously a bum, wispy gray hair, scraggly beard, age undeterminable. The other was a young Middle Eastern kid. He wore earphones and watched YouTube videos of some old bearded guy in white and black robes ranting about something. I rested my elbows on my knees and lowered my voice to a whisper. "I drove out to your trailer. Amber said you haven't been out there since Monday."

He continued tapping away on the keyboard. "Yeah, I can't live out there anymore. Bitch won't let me run an extension cord to the trailer and the power company says I owe them six hundred bucks from four years ago."

"I just gave you four thousand bucks."

"It's gone."

"How can it be gone?"

"Well it's going to be gone in a day or two. Found a sweet 2005 F-150. Thirty-five hundred plus trade-in."

I didn't say anything.

"Oh, and I bought a TV."

"I noticed." I glanced down at my shoes, then looked up. "So where are you staying?"

"Here and there. Few nights ago it got so cold we drove over to your place, see if we could sleep in the basement, or the garage, but somebody else was living there." He laughed. "It was like midnight and we were pretty fucked up. The old fart who lives there called the cops, so we had to boogie out of there."

"Mr. Halberstam."

"Who?"

"The guy who bought our house."

"Oh."

"When you say we—"

"Me and Pritchard."

"He's still hanging around?"

His eyebrows furrowed, then released. "Dude, why didn't you tell me you moved?"

"I thought you knew."

"How would I know if you don't tell me?" He paused again. I could feel the homeless guy's eyes on me, burning a hole in the back of my head.

"We went back to the trailer that night and nearly froze to death," Vince said. "Dude, I did not put my life on the line in Iraq and Afghanistan so I could freeze to death in a goddamn broke-down trailer."

I had nothing to say to that either.

Suddenly his eyes brightened. "Anyway, I was thinking I could sleep at the bar for a while. All I need's a little cot in the back room. Hell, I'll even sleep on that ratty ass sofa. That sofa's still there, right?"

"Uh…"

"I mean, I own a quarter of it."

"The sofa?"

"Funny."

"What about your friend?"

"Fuck him. I'm tired of him leeching off me."

The homeless guy wretched and spat on the carpet. Then he leaned in toward me and shouted, "You ever seen them pornos?"

Vince thought that was hilarious.

I leaned away. His breath smelled like Lucifer's ass.

I turned to the homeless guy and held up a finger. "Just a minute, okay?" I slid my chair over toward Vince. "Dude, if the cops see you anywhere near the bar they'll ship your ass back to the work camp."

"How're they going to know? I'll sneak in after closing time. I'll leave before noon. No one will ever know."

It sounded like a terrible idea. Not just because he'd get caught and shipped back to Shawnee and we risked losing our liquor license, but the last thing Vince needed was to be locked up with a bar full of liquor. Rent free. He needed to get back on his feet and get a place of his own. A job. A life. Only how was I supposed to tell him that? The guy largely responsible for his lousy situation.

The homeless guy leaned in again, his eyes all buggy. "They got giant rats in here. You feed them and they talk."

"Uh huh," I said. I moved my chair to the other side of Vince, next to the Middle Eastern kid. I sure as hell hoped he wasn't watching Jihadi recruitment videos. Was that racist of me? Whatever, it was better than that old dude's breath. "Look," I said to Vince. "I'll get the electricity and water turned on. I'll put it in my name. I should've done that before you got home. I'm sorry about that."

I'd have to figure a way to hide it from Reva, of course. She still regarded Vince as beyond redemption. Fortunately, I was home most mornings when the bills came in the mail. There was a good chance she'd never find out. Besides, how much could it cost to heat a trailer? And if she did find out? I'd cross that bridge when I came to it.

Vince logged off the computer and shifted in his chair.

"There's still the small problem of the roof."

"So let's patch the roof. How hard can it be?"

"It's going to take more than a patch. And the carpet's ruined, a window's busted out, the couch is shot…"

I sighed. "Okay. One thing at a time. Saturday morning it's supposed to get into the forties. I'll see if I can get Chad to help. He worked as a roofer one summer."

"On houses, not trailers."

I took a deep breath and let it out slowly. "You got to work with me here, bro."

He folded his arms across his chest. "In the meantime, where am I supposed to sleep?"

I muttered under my breath and got up and pulled my wallet out of my back pocket. Luckily, I'd been to the bank recently. I removed four twenties and four tens from the wallet and folded the bills and slipped them into Vince's jacket pocket. "Stay at the EconoLodge a few days, okay? Till we get the place squared away."

Vince studied me with a blank expression. "Big Money Grip," he said. "Is that why you were looking for me?"

"Actually, no. Your P.O. called. She said you missed your meeting."

"No way."

I shrugged. "That's what she said."

"No way. Bitch's crazy." He thought it over a moment, then logged back onto the computer. "Our meeting is tomorrow."

I sat down again and leaned back in the chair while he pulled up his email and scrolled through his messages. There was a new email from his P.O. with the subject line "Contact me immediately." He opened the email.

"Oh shit. I did miss my meeting."

"She told Chad she'd let it slide once. But just this once."

"That's real sweet of her."

After a moment I said, "Have you got a phone yet?"

"I'm looking at a few different plans."

I nodded. "What about job leads?"

Vince scowled. I could tell he was beginning to get aggravated with me.

"You know anybody who wants to hire an ex-con?" he said.

I didn't say anything.

"An ex-con with no fixed residence?"

He closed the email program. "Thanks for the cash. I'll get it back to you on payday."

"What do you mean payday?"

He nodded toward the blank screen. "I just applied for disability."

"That's what you were doing?"

"Uh huh. I got PTSD, remember?"

How could I forget? That had been Vince's one and only defense at trial, that he suffered post-traumatic stress disorder from the two years he spent in an explosive ordnance disposal unit in Iraq. A mitigating factor, the judge called it. It was something, the way his lawyer kept hammering home that Vince was a war hero, that he'd been wounded countless times, that he suffered traumatic brain injury. In the end, he got four years, instead of what could've been a lot more.

Still. I couldn't see how Vince was going to get back on his feet if he just laid around a motel room and smoked weed and played video games and lived off disability. It wasn't like he wasn't healthy. Physically, anyway.

"Can't you do landscaping or something like that?"

Vince turned on me, the angry blood pumping in his throat. "Fuck you, D! You do fucking landscaping."

"I—"

"Christ, man, you sit there in my bar sucking down beers all night long and bullshitting with friends and pulling down a nice salary and you expect me to cut grass with a bunch of wetbacks. Well fuck that."

Nobody shushed us or glared at us. Maybe they were afraid to.

This time I gave it back to him. I'd bitten my tongue long enough. "Look, man," I said and thumped my index finger on the computer desk, "you forget that I never asked you to take the rap. That was your idea. You insisted, remember? You ain't going to hold that over my head the rest of my life."

"Really?" Vince said. "You think—"

I'd had enough. I stood up, knocking over my chair, and stormed out of the room. I didn't look back.

Downstairs I ran into Reva as she came out of the break room holding a mug of hot chocolate. She lifted her eyebrows as I walked up to her. "Please tell me that wasn't you yelling upstairs?" she said.

I didn't say anything. She must have seen a vein pulsing on my forehead or the stormy look in my eyes, because she didn't pursue it. "Babe, is something wrong?" she said.

What wasn't wrong? I thought. Some douchebag is blackmailing me, my brother is giving me a mile-long guilt trip, and the bar is losing money hand over fist.

"Everything's fine," I said. I gave her a peck on the cheek and told her I'd see her later.

I had a bar to open.

TEN

I was in the walk-in cooler checking inventory when I heard the front door open.

"We're closed!" I called.

"Denis? You back there?" A vaguely familiar female voice.

I set my clipboard on a case of Busch bottles and strode out to the bar. Amber McFall stood in the doorway, dressed in her Denny's uniform, and damn if it didn't look good on her. Like a sulky Chrissie Hynde in that "Brass in Pocket" video. Over the uniform she wore a white jacket with a furry hood. The jacket stopped at her nice, big, round hips.

I slipped behind the bar, instinctively putting a barrier between us. "Hey, there, Amber. What brings you by?"

She sauntered across the room and laid an envelope on the counter. Her perfume smelled like something a stripper would wear. Cotton candy-ish and intoxicating in a sleazy kind of way.

"I wanted to drop off the rent and give you my thirty days' notice."

My heart sank. She hadn't been kidding about finding a new place. Damn, I hated losing a good tenant, especially someone who paid the rent. And on time for the most part. Not that *I* got anything out of it. The five hundred bucks went right into Sara's checking account, but for some reason it was my job to find the tenants, put the ad in the paper, interview prospective tenants, do the background checks (which I seldom did). Sara sure as hell couldn't be counted on to do that. Or much of anything. It was all a huge pain in my ass.

I opened the envelope and thumbed through the bills. "Find a place, yet?"

Amber chewed her bottom lip. "We'll be moving in with my mom and dad for a while. I just don't feel safe living out there in the boonies all by myself. Me and the baby."

I nodded. "Since Vince moved in."

"Well him and that creepy friend of his. And then there's Tusk..."

I slipped the envelope into my back pocket and lifted my eyes. "Tusk?"

"My boy...*ex*-boyfriend."

I nodded again. Tusk. I pictured a bald, burly redneck with a bushy goatee and wrap-around sunglasses behind the wheel of a mud-covered heavy-duty pickup with the Stars N Bars adhered to the back window. The kind of asshole who went around calling himself a "patriot."

"This Tusk been a problem for you?"

"I never knew a man that wasn't a problem for me."

I could see that. Women like Amber were lowlife magnets. Not that it was her fault. Not completely, anyway. No doubt she encouraged their advances, at least at the start. And once a guy like that gets any kind of encouragement, there's no discouraging him. They're like a feral dog. You feed him once and you're stuck with him—till one of you dies.

Fact is, I'd rolled in the hay with Amber a time or two myself. Years ago, before she moved into my grandparents' house, before she had a kid. She used to stop by the bar after work and hang around till we were the last men standing. I'd lock the door and turn off the sign, then I'd make her another drink and we'd play the jukebox and chat aimlessly a few minutes and when we couldn't stand it anymore we'd go to the back room with the ratty old couch. I'm still not sure how it happened, except that she wanted it too and I was too weak to resist. Yes, I was married at the time, and yes, I felt like a complete ass afterward, but it never stopped me. I got no excuses, except to say that I can be a real sonofabitch sometimes.

Anyway, after a few tumbles, after I got her out of my system and a kind of sickening dread set in, I put an end to it. A blind man could see that Amber was a living, breathing train wreck. Visions of boiling bunnies invaded my dreams. Luckily, she took my rejection in stride. "I always figured you'd dump me after you fucked me a few times," she said.

Whatever guilt I'd been feeling quickly gave way to annoyance. "I *am* married, you know."

"That didn't stop you before."

I shrugged. I mean, what can you say to that?

Now, Amber gazed off over the bar at the rows of empty booths and tables and blew a few stray strands of hair from her eyes.

"Well, I'm sorry to see you go," I said, hoping to wrap things up. "You were a good tenant."

"Uh huh," she said. "A good lay too."

"Yeah," I said. I flushed and swallowed hard. "Let

me know where to send the deposit."

"It's on the envelope."

I looked at the address. 10 Harrisonville Street, O'Fallon, Illinois.

"Oh, right."

There was a long, uncomfortable silence. A vehicle swooshed by on the street in front of the bar, playing loud, bassy rap music. I cleared my throat. "I was, um, just doing inventory."

"Uh huh."

"I should probably...you know..."

"Sure."

I extended my hand over the counter. "Well, good luck."

She looked at me quizzically. "Afraid to come out from behind your little fortress?"

I grinned stupidly and said, "Uh huh."

Amber laughed and shook her head. "Goodbye Denis."

I watched her go, her ass twitching under the tight beige uniform. I watched her till she went out the door and I let go a heavy sigh. Behind me someone snickered and I turned to find Clay Goodwin seated on a stool at the end of the bar. He wore an olive shooting jacket with the hood down and an orange and camouflage Stag cap even though deer season ended months ago. He must've slunked in the back way.

"I saw you staring at that ass," he said. "I may have to start eating at Denny's."

I was in no mood for that shit weasel. What's more, he was a day early for the pickup.

"Give me the usual," he said. The usual was gin and tonic; instead I went over and pulled a Budweiser out of the cooler and slammed it down in front of him. I left the cap on.

"You expect me to drink this? It's going to explode all over me."

He sounded like a whiny little bitch. "So don't drink it."

He scowled. "How about a glass?"

Clay Goodwin had all the personality of a doorstop and none of the charm. I don't suppose he had a friend in the world. Usually you'd feel sorry for a person like that. Not so with Goodwin. You'd rather feel sorry for an incontinent skunk. He pulled a pack of Marlboros out of his jacket pocket and set them on the counter where I could see them. You weren't allowed to smoke in bars. State law. I didn't say anything though. He tore off the cellophane wrapper. "I hear Vince got out," he said.

So much for inventory. I grunted and squatted behind the bar and pulled out the maraschino cherry bottle from the refrigerator and began filling the tray.

"That was quick," he continued. "What'd he do, three years?"

I set down the jar, picked up the remote, and turned on the televisions. All four of them. I didn't want to talk to the bastard, and he knew it.

"Four," I said. "With time served."

"Must've been a good boy inside."

I didn't say anything to that.

He lit a cigarette. I'd tossed all the ashtrays. They were just cheap, black plastic ones anyway. That's why he wanted the glass, for an ashtray. I set a rocks glass on the bar and made him get up after it.

He inhaled two of my beers and watched a game show. I noticed he got very few answers right. Or questions, as they're called on this particular show. I ignored him and went over to the door and pulled the chain on the neon sign.

He turned and watched me. "I get it. You think you're better than me. Because you run your daddy's bar. Because you got a nice respectable wife and two cute little kids. That's it, ain't it? 'Course I ain't ever been kicked out of the service. And I ain't never killed nobody."

He paused and watched me closely.

"No, you leave that to your brother," I said.

Goodwin twirled the beer bottle in his fingers and gave me a look that could've melted my spine. I regretted saying that. Why the hell had I brought his psychotic brother into this?

"What about Randy?" he said.

"Forget it."

"Sure, I'll forget it." He smiled and cleared his throat. "So, you got something for me?"

There it was. I went behind the bar and rested my hands on the counter and gave him a blank look. "You're a day early, aren't you?"

He shrugged. "So I'm a day early?"

"So nothing," I said. I turned and went to the back room and found a box of envelopes. From the safe I took four fifties, ten twenties, and a fifty and slipped them into an envelope. It wasn't much. It certainly wasn't going to make anyone rich. I suppose he and his crazy ass brother had other stooges like me who peddled their dope and were probably happy to do it. I went back to the bar and slid the envelope toward Goodwin.

He peeked inside, counted the bills. "Business a little slow this week?"

"What would you know about business?"

"Very comical," he said. Then his expression turned grave. "You wouldn't be trying to short us?"

"It's all there minus my twenty percent. You want, you can weigh the product."

"Damn right I can," he said. He sniffed and wiped his nose with the back of his hand. "Only I got more important things to do."

"Yeah? Got some kittens to drown?"

He grinned like it hurt and shoved the envelope into his coat pocket. "Very comical," he said.

I folded my arms across my chest. "Here's an idea. Why don't you get a job instead of blackmailing small business owners?" I knew I was pushing him hard, but I couldn't help myself.

"I got a job," he said. "My job is keeping secrets, and believe me it ain't easy, keeping secrets. Especially with a mouth like I got."

I kept telling myself that one of these days I was going to call his bluff. But two years had gone by and I hadn't done a damn thing. It was like I was waiting for something to change, only nothing ever did. I turned and went back to the walk-in cooler and got a couple of cases of Pabst, hoping he'd be gone when I got back.

Nope. Still there. He downed the last of his beer and stubbed out his cigarette.

I began stocking the coolers. "Speaking of Vince," I said, "he might not take too kindly to a shakedown."

"Shakedown!" Goodwin said, his tone one of mock umbrage. "Denis, if you want to dissolve our partnership, just say the word. I'll happily take my product elsewhere." He slid off the stool. "Who knows? Maybe I will get a job. One that doesn't require keeping so many damn secrets." He zipped up his jacket. "Give my best to the wife and kids," he said.

I didn't say anything.

After he left I picked up his rocks glass and pitched it across the room at the door. I just missed shattering the thousand-dollar storefront window.

Then I took a long, deep breath and glanced around the room.

What the hell was I doing, anyway?

Right. Inventory.

ELEVEN

Sometimes when I'd take the twins to a Cards game or sit in the stands watching them play basketball, I'd think about my kid brother and everything he'd sacrificed for me and my family. I owed Vince a lot—more than I could ever repay. I know it sounds nuts, but if I had it to do over again, I wouldn't let him take the rap for me. Not because I'm sick of the endless guilt trip I've been on these past four years, but because I don't think I would've screwed things up like Vince did.

I would've remembered to hide the goddamn dope.

My sense of direction may be for shit, but I have a memory like a steel trap. I don't forget things. Whether it's big things or little things.

This can be both a blessing and a curse because there are a lot of things I'd like to forget.

For starters, I wouldn't mind forgetting my whole rotten adolescence. They say what doesn't kill you makes you stronger. But I've always thought that's a lot of hooey. Lots of people get sick, break bones, and never fully recover.

Maybe they're talking about mental toughness.

I don't know. I'd trade all the mental toughness in the world for a normal childhood. Any day.

A TASTE OF SHOTGUN

I guess you could say we were a typical Midwestern blue collar family—hardworking, hard-drinking, education-scorning. No different than any of our neighbors. Whatever happened outside our screen door didn't concern us. For years, Pop labored at a stove factory earning barely enough to keep us in house and home. Pop was a drunk of heroic proportions, the very definition of the functional alcoholic. He somehow got up and went to work every morning and put in eight hours in front of a blazing furnace. A real role model, in a fucked up kind of way. Come quitting time he'd make a beeline for his twin brother's bar, where he'd spend the remainder of the evening getting tighter than a Texas tick. It wasn't just the work that made him drink. My mother is quite possibly the most unpleasant person I've ever known. She's got all the maternal instincts of a dingo, which is why we've always called her Sara and not mom. I guess I would've drank myself stupid too if I were married to her.

In those days, Pop's twin brother, Chuck, owned half of The Brass Lantern. When Chuck and his girlfriend Debra were killed in a motorcycle accident (Chuck's Triumph struck a center divider on Route 113, though there were no skid marks and no witnesses) Pop suddenly found himself in possession of half a dive bar. Chuck was not only Pop's twin, he was his best friend. Ironically, Chuck's death was probably the greatest piece of luck Pop ever had in his miserable life. Just a month before Chuck died, Pop had been laid off from the stove factory, so inheriting half the bar turned out to be a godsend. He hung a black and white portrait of Chuck behind the bar like a shrine. The faded, fly-specked photo shows Chuck sitting sidesaddle on his sleek red Triumph

TR9, his face half concealed behind aviator sunglasses and a cigarette, a pretty girl with long straight hair in a tank top and bellbottom jeans (Debra?) beside him. Forever forty-five. The shrine graces the bar to this day.

Pop spent the next decade happy as a pig in shit. Inheriting half a bar—a lawyer friend of Chuck's owned the other half—meant Pop had a lot more time to drink. Most nights he was too shitfaced to stagger home, so he'd pass out on the ratty little sofa in the back room. If he could make it as far as the sofa. Sara would give him hell the next morning—or afternoon—when he finally dragged his sorry ass home, which was the reason he stopped coming home.

Without Pop to bitch at, Sara, who was experiencing an astonishing, record-setting episode of weight gain, directed all her pent-up rage toward us kids. It wasn't long before Chad and me spent all our free time at the bar, where we earned a few bucks taking out the trash, tearing down boxes, stocking coolers, washing dishes, mopping floors, and drinking up Pop's liquor on the sly, before stumbling home drunk to face Sara's wrath. Sometimes Sara would send Vince to fetch us home. We used those occasions to initiate the lad into the pleasures of cigarettes and alcohol. It wasn't long before she forbid us to go to The Brass Lantern at all.

Then she filed for divorce.

At first we were thrilled. Thrilled at the prospect of Pop getting custody of us, of living with him at the dark and boozy Brass Lantern. We'd string up a couple of hammocks in the back room like on *Gilligan's Island*. It seemed plausible. We figured any judge with a lick of sense would have to realize what a monster Sara was and happily turn us over to our alcoholic saloonkeeper father.

A TASTE OF SHOTGUN

We underestimated Sara.

She wasn't just ornery, she was as manipulative as a pedophile priest. If forced to, she could act perfectly normal. She could play the part of the aggrieved wife better than Meryl Streep.

She got full custody.

The judge told Pop he'd have to attend Alcoholics Anonymous for six months before we'd be allowed to spend any meaningful time with him. I think he lasted about half a meeting. First smoke break he snuck out the back exit, never to return. We didn't blame him too much. Drinking was the only thing that gave Pop pleasure in this world.

Sara moved us into a little rental house in the suburbs. We paid three hundred bucks a month. Water and gas were extra but there was no charge for the mold and bedbugs. After we moved away we saw very little of Pop. Birthdays, holidays included.

Then, out of the blue, Sara remarried. No doubt to the only man who would have her—Pop's cousin Roy Gladson, owner of a small but surprisingly lucrative dump. Roy turned out to be ornerier than Sara. I remember my teen years as the equivalent of living in a pit full of rudely awakened rattlesnakes. By then, Chad was in the navy and living the good life on a nuclear submarine, while I drifted here and there, staying at friends' homes and sleeping on their bedroom floors when their parents allowed it, or trailer-sitting for this barmaid I knew when she went to the Outer Banks to work in the summer, sleeping outdoors in a hammock that smelled of mold and sex. I'd lie awake under the stars dreaming mad dreams of being rich and famous (I was, in turn, going to be a rock star, an actor, and a five-star general). Pathetic pipedreams, but they kept me going till I was old enough to enlist in the military.

When we were kids, Chad and I built a clubhouse under the roof of our outdoor patio, and one winter I stayed there. I would've died of hypothermia if it hadn't been for a pair of stray dogs I befriended. I'd haul those flea-ridden mutts up into the clubhouse every night and we'd crawl inside my gamey old sleeping bag. I owed those dogs my life. They stuck with me that whole winter, but when spring came they trotted off somewhere never to be seen again. (I told that story to Reva once, and she said those dogs were probably my guardian angels. I said I was no theologian but I was pretty sure guardian angels don't have fleas.)

I found all manner of creative ways to stay alive. Soon after our house went on the market, I jimmied open a basement window and, off and on for the next five months, slept in my old room in the basement. That ended when a realtor caught me sleeping off a hangover one morning and I had to knock her down and make a run for it.

Sometimes when I couldn't take the hunger and cold anymore, I'd show up at Roy's house with my tail between my legs. Vince and I would crowd into his narrow little bed. We had to earn our keep working at Roy's dump, keeping the rutted mud roads clear of junk and shooting rats with an old .22, till I would inevitably do something wrong and Roy would beat the tar out of me and off I'd go again, in search of some new place to lay my head. Somehow I managed to graduate high school with a D plus average. At least I think I graduated. I never did see a diploma.

The military was a godsend. Soon as we turned seventeen, the three of us enlisted. Chad joined the navy. Two years later, I joined the army. When it was his turn, Vince followed me into the infantry. I never left stateside, spending most of my time in Louisiana and California. Two years later I was back in Belleville.

I'd just gotten out of the service—discharged after me and a buddy were busted smoking weed—and tending bar part time at The Brass Lantern when Pop married this barfly named Georgia. She was a few years older than Pop. Fifty-eight, but decades of cigarettes and vodka made her look closer to seventy-eight. One night as he was driving home from the bar, his new, old wife by his side, Pop swerved to avoid a coyote and lost control on the slick highway and slammed into an overpass. His new, old wife sailed like a home run ball through the windshield. Cops said she split right down the middle.

They said Pop was three times the legal limit. His third DUI. He pleaded no contest to gross vehicular manslaughter and was given ten years in *the* Menard State Penitentiary. Overnight I went from part-time bartender to managing The Brass Lantern. Chad refused to have anything to do with the place. He said the bar was cursed and suggested we rename it The Devil's Lantern.

I was all for it. I thought the name sounded cool, but it turned out he was joking.

When the old woman's family talked of suing Pop, he quickly signed over the bar to Sara and her three sons.

That's how I came to own a quarter of The Brass Lantern.

And that's who the Carrolls are. We sure as hell ain't the Brady Bunch. But neither are we the Sopranos. Chad, at least, seems to have his head on straight. The guy's ambitious, clean-cut, smart—not book smart, but he's got common sense and common decency. Just don't get him started on politics. The wires in his brain begin to sparkle and fry when he starts talking about liberals and *mooslims* and wetbacks. Apparently all those hours sitting in his ambulance soaking in right-wing talk radio turned his brain to mush.

It was too bad, because as a kid Chad seemed mature beyond his years. He was always the sober, clear-eyed one. I guess he had to be with parents like ours. I used to envy him, look up to him. Then as now, when I had a problem, I went to Chad, not Pop or Sara. At report card time he'd forge Sara's signature and did it in such a professional manner that we never got caught. Where I got Ds and Fs, he got solid Cs without even trying. In the navy, he worked as a corpsman aboard a nuclear sub. After he was discharged, he joined the volunteer fire department and found work as an EMT. He got involved in politics and ran for coroner once, but lost by a handful of votes to a woman whose father had held the job for four decades. After that he went about things more methodically. He joined the Masons. He began attending the biggest Protestant church in town, even though our family was nominally Catholic and he'd seldom gone to mass. The guy was determined to be somebody and he knew how to go about it.

It paid off, too. If it hadn't been for Chad's political and social connections, the city would've shut down The Brass Lantern long ago.

Vince was a whole other story. He was the wild one in the family, in and out of trouble since seventh grade when he was expelled for bringing a handgun to school. A rusted old .38 he'd found at the dump. He wasn't going to do anything with it. He just wanted to show it around like any normal kid. It didn't even have a cylinder. Didn't matter. He wasn't allowed back. Every morning he had to take a special school bus across town to a special school for special students. He'd been a normal kid till they introduced him to the delinquents at the special school. That school was like an apprenticeship program on how to be a thug. Vince's teenage years were a blur of petty crimes and hijinks, always trying to show how crazier or wilder or braver he was than the next kid.

It was funny though. It didn't matter what he did. He could've blown up a federal courthouse and Sara would've still considered him her little angel.

As soon as he turned seventeen, Vince volunteered to disarm IEDs in Iraq. He survived two tours of this—despite suffering multiple head injuries—was decorated and became something of a local hero. For a month or two. Then he went back to being the crazy kid who brought the handgun to school.

Compared to my two brothers, I was just some lowlife who operated a dive bar hemorrhaging money like a Wall Street trader on a cocaine binge. Pretty much the only thing that gave my life an ounce of meaning was Reva and the twins, though you'd never know it from the way I behaved.

I was saying how much I owed my little brother. Reva had no idea the sacrifice Vince made for our family. That was my idea—to keep it from her. God knows why, but for some reason she had a high opinion of me and the truth would have devastated her. So we let her go on thinking that Vince was the black sheep, which she was disposed to think anyway.

We were, however, all in agreement on one thing.

The next generation of Carrolls was going to be different. There would be no more homeless Carrolls, no more underage Carrolls working in dumps and saloons. Reva made sure of that. Our children would go to college. They would read books. And they would definitely not inherit a bar. Ours would be the last generation of Carroll barkeepers.

And drug dealers...
And ex-cons...
And killers.

TWELVE

Clay Goodwin lived in a fortified compound off HH Road, half-hidden among a stand of cedars, tamaracks and jack pines.

It started out as a ranch but had been added onto willy-nilly, the whole thing enclosed by a tall hurricane fence topped with razor wire. Two ill-tempered pit bulls roamed inside the fence. Goodwin liked to say the area outside the fence was strewn with landmines, but Goodwin was full of shit.

The nearest habitation was a ruined farmhouse several hundred yards down the road that looked like it had been abandoned during the Great Depression. Behind the compound stood a small stand of ash trees bordering limestone bluffs. Somewhere in the vicinity, in small clearings deep in the county nature preserve, Clay and his brother Randy cultivated marijuana plants. Rumor had it that on occasion some of the county's more desperate meth heads would strike off in search of the Goodwins' pot fields never to be seen or heard from again, except for one poor bastard who was allegedly found strangled with his own intestines. Having met Randy a few times I had no trouble believing it. That sonofabitch was a special kind of crazy. Even the cops steered clear of him.

I left Kelsie in charge of the bar and drove over to Sara's house with the intention of borrowing Roy's old pickup. I didn't want anybody recognizing my truck. I turned off her house alarm and eased inside. I found Sara asleep in her bariatric lounger in front of the screaming television, a box of half-eaten pizza on her lap. I was careful not to awaken her, just eased into the kitchen and snatched Roy's keys off the key holder and slipped out the kitchen door.

The rotten tobacco smell of the cab brought back all kinds of unpleasant memories. The worst of which was Roy pouring a cup of warm tobacco spit over my head when I got caught sitting in his Cadillac DeVille. I was thirteen.

I sat in that stinking truck wondering why I hadn't killed him then and there. Just put the bastard out of his misery.

I knew why. I was still just a kid. And by the time I got back from being kicked out of the army, the bastard was dead.

The pickup's battery was dead, of course, so I had to jump it with my truck, then I drove out Route 3 to HH Road east of Goodwin's compound. I'd say it was a reconnaissance mission, only I had no real plan in mind, just a vague idea that involved payback. I slipped on a pair of aviator sunglasses and a ball cap and parked Roy's truck on a side road three hundred yards from his gravel driveway and trained my binoculars on the windows. The vantage point sucked. A line of red cedars hid the ranch house from view. I could just make out his Chevy Colorado parked in the driveway and the lights in the ranch house glowed dully behind battered blinds. No sign of the bulls. They were probably holed up somewhere warm.

The longer I sat there, the dumber I felt. What was I going to do, tunnel under the fence and knock on his door and run? Toilet paper his trees? Set a bag of dog poop afire? What I really wanted to do was rattle his brains, but all that would do is start a war. A modern-day hillbilly feud. I'd be leaving the bar at one o'clock in the morning to find Randy leaning against my truck thumping a crowbar against his palm...

I'd just about decided to go home when a crunching sound rose up ahead of me and I looked up to find a silver Sierra 1500 rolling toward me. The truck slowed as it approached. That was my sign to leave. I tugged at the bill of my cap, set down the binoculars, and slammed the pickup into reverse.

The truck jerked and the engine stalled.

The Sierra eased up alongside. A fogged-up window ran down and a fellow who looked to be in his early sixties, with a face like a badly peeled potato, gave me a wooden look and said something over the grumble of his V8.

I tried the key again. The engine made a lot of racket but refused to turn over.

I went to roll down my window, but the handle was missing. I opened the door halfway. "Excuse me?"

"Can I help you?" he said, his voice as gravelly as the road.

Which really meant: Who the hell are you and what are you doing out here where you don't belong?

"Car troubles," I said, and laughed stupidly.

"You can't park here."

Perhaps he hadn't heard me over the noise of his engine. I tried again. "I'm not parked here. I'm having car troubles."

"Well, you need to leave."

God, I hate people.

So he had heard me; he was just being a horse's ass. I tried the engine again. A rapid click from under the hood and the familiar sound of a drained battery.

I wasn't going anywhere. I cursed under my breath and turned angrily to the driver. "Look, old man, this is a public road, okay? You don't own it. So piss off."

"If you don't leave, I'm calling the sheriff."

It was like he hadn't heard a word I said. I sat there in a daze, wondering what the hell happened to neighborly country folks helping out their fellow man? Actually, I know what happened. They've gotten so paranoid about crime, so scared of tweakers and dope fiends breaking into their homes and stealing their guns and raping their womenfolk they've become mistrustful and hostile toward every stranger. They're more scared of crime than city dwellers.

The man nodded toward the seat and said, "What are them glasses for?"

It took me a moment. At first, I thought he was referring to my sunglasses, till I realized I'd forgotten to put away the binoculars.

"You're out here breaking into people's houses, ain't you?" the old man said. "Goddamn it, I knew it. You're out here casing Goodwin's house. I'm calling the sheriff right now."

The old fart was onto me. I sunk back into the seat. "You wouldn't mind giving me a jump first? I mean, before you call out the militia?"

The old man reached over and opened his glove box. When he turned back toward me he had a phone in one

A TASTE OF SHOTGUN

hand and a handgun in the other. The gun was old and looked like something he might've carried in Vietnam. "Don't even think of driving off now," he said.

The revolver didn't faze me as much as him thinking I could drive off with a dead battery. A pair of jumper cables lay coiled on the passenger side floor. I bent over to pick them up.

"Keep your hands where I can see them!" he cried.

"Look old man, I'm just pulling out my jumper cables, okay? Don't fucking shoot me."

"How do I know you ain't got a sawed-off shotgun under that seat?"

"Because that would be against the law," I said. I grabbed the jumper cables and I eased out of the truck, slow enough that I didn't startle him. I slammed the door. I expected to eat hot lead at any moment.

"Where you think you're going?" he said.

I ignored him and walked around to the front of Roy's pickup and felt around the grille till I found the latch and popped the hood. Meanwhile the old man was on his phone telling a dispatcher that he'd caught him a dope fiend on HH Road. "One of them damn tweakers," he said. "Probably the one who's been breaking into all them houses." Then I heard him read off Roy's license plate number.

This was not going to end well.

After I'd attached the cables to the battery I strode up to his window. "Say, while we're waiting for the seventh cavalry, how about popping your hood?"

The old man glared at me and went back to his phone call. "That's right," he said. "Looks like the same feller that broke into my tool shed and stole my riding lawnmower last month—"

I stood there and weighed the likelihood of getting my stupid head blown off. Then I decided I didn't care anymore and opened the old man's car door and reached in under the steering wheel and pulled the hood lever. The hood popped.

The old man kicked like a wasp bit him and fumbled for his revolver. "What the hell you think you're doing?" he yelped.

By then I had the hood up. I connected the cables to the posts and hurried over to Roy's pickup and eased into the front seat and turned the key. The old man bounded out of his truck and ripped off the cables, though not before the engine turned over. He flung the cables to the road and came over to the driver's side and waved the revolver under my nose. "You ain't going anywhere till the sheriff gets here."

I slid across the seat, got out on the other side, and walked to where the cables lay in the frozen dust. "That a fact?" I said. I picked up the cables and walked back to the pickup and tossed the cables behind the seat.

"I already gave the sheriff your license number," he said.

"Well then it's a good thing it ain't my truck."

I wasn't worried about the old man and his popgun anymore. I leaned on the door of the pickup listening to the engine. It sputtered but it didn't die. A beautiful sound, like a clear bubbling stream in springtime. I turned to the old man. "Before I go, you mind telling me what law I broke?" I said. "And I don't mean the imaginary ones in your head."

The old man thought about that a moment. "You broke into my truck and used my battery without my say-so."

A TASTE OF SHOTGUN

I reached into my back pocket and took out my wallet and fished out a five-dollar bill. "For your troubles," I said. I crumpled up the fiver and stuffed it into his jacket pocket. "You know back in my day folks didn't charge for a jump," I said. "Folks were more neighborly. Not frightened little chickenshits."

The man stared at me, his eyes bulging with anger. He sputtered and fumed, but I could see he wasn't going to do anything.

I climbed into Roy's pickup and gave the man a stare. "You have a good day now, hear?" I went to strap on my seatbelt and only then did I notice my trembling hands.

I didn't try to put the truck in reverse and back out of there. I didn't want to risk stalling again. Instead, I gunned it and drove straight down HH Road. I took the long way back to Sara's house, only getting lost twice on the way.

I wondered how many cops would be waiting for me when I got there.

THIRTEEN

A squad car idled in front of the house. From behind the living room curtains, Reva's face peered out, a look of concern in her eyes.

I turned into the driveway and parked the truck and walked over to the cruiser. Behind the wheel sat Sergeant Butch Stakoff. Kelsie probably told him I took the night off.

I'd gone to school with Butch, K through 12. He was a bully then and he was a bully now. Only difference was he'd turned professional. He'd married a cousin of mine, Lucinda. One of the few good things about living in a small city is there's a good chance you're related to at least one policeman, or judge, or alderman, so it's less likely some cop will lodge a broom handle up your rectum if there's a chance of running into you and the wife at next month's family reunion.

Stakoff eased out of the cruiser and zipped up his coat and shoved his hands in his coat pockets. "Evening, Denis," he said.

"Butch."

The guy on the radio had said it was twenty degrees, but the wind made it feel half that. Stakoff gazed off down the long, empty street where the plowed snow was

A TASTE OF SHOTGUN

stacked up on the curbs twelve inches high. One of the neighbors, an old Italian woman, rolled a trashcan out to the curb. Probably waited till I pulled up to do it.

"How's the family?" Stakoff said.

"Pretty good." I glanced toward the house. Reva had gone from the window. "Yours?"

"Not bad. Lucinda's about to finish her second round of chemo. She sure will be glad when that's over."

"Give her my best," I said.

"Sure."

I kicked at a piece of ice. "Now that we got that out of the way—"

He grinned. "Got a call from the sheriff about an hour ago."

"Did you now?" I said. "How's Sheriff Creech getting along these days? How's the gout? Any change?"

He ignored me. "He was talking with Art Oberneferman. Art says you two had an altercation this afternoon, out on HH Road. Said you were casing Clay Goodwin's house. He seems to think you were involved in some of the recent break-ins."

"What makes him think I was out there?"

"Well, the description for starters. And the truck was registered to your late stepfather. Sheriff called your mother and she told him you stole her truck."

"Borrowed her truck."

He paused. "Anyways, I told Art that that doesn't sound like you at all. Told him you're a business owner and your wife's the town librarian and you got a couple of sweet little kids."

I shook my head. "No sir. Don't sound like me at all."

"He said you entered his vehicle without permission and jumped your pickup with his battery."

"Art said that?" I said, clucking my tongue sympathetically. "Poor guy must be off his rocker. I'd heard Art was coming down with Old Timer's Disease. Getting senile. Damn shame, too."

Stakoff stuffed his hands into his jacket pockets and his eyes locked on mine, but not in a hard way. A half smile formed on his lips. "Damn lucky he didn't shoot you."

"That's me, Mister Lucky. I ought to spend more time at the casino."

The smile faded. "Want to tell me what you were doing out there?"

"Last time I checked HH Road was a public road. It ain't Art Oberwhoferman's nor anybody else's business what I was doing. You'd think an old fart like that would've learned to mind his business by now."

Stakoff took out a rag and loudly blew his nose. "Okay, Denis. Just do me a favor and stay away from Art's place, huh? I mean Goodwin's place. He'll forget about it in a day or two, and I can tell the sheriff I talked to you. Fair enough?"

"Anything for an old friend," I said.

He shoved the rag into his back pocket, nodded and turned and strode back to his cruiser. "Too goddamn cold for this shit," he muttered aloud.

I watched Stakoff leave, then I turned and waved at my neighbor, who was dragging a second trashcan out to the curb. I started up the driveway, thinking things over. I was hot. Not at Stakoff, who was just doing his lousy job, and not at the paranoid old man, but at Goodwin.

There had to be some way to put an end to this goddamn nightmare.

So why couldn't I think of it?

A TASTE OF SHOTGUN

Maybe Vince knew something I didn't. Goodwin was *his* friend, after all. Had been, anyway. Vince was the one who brought Goodwin to the card game that night when our usual fourth pulled out. I've thought about that a lot since, how if our cousin Trey had been there that night everything would've been different.

Trey was blood.

Goodwin was a piece of shit.

Fate, that's what it was. Lousy, rotten fate.

Reva waited at the door. I gave her a peck on the mouth and hung up my coat.

"Was that Butch Stakoff?"

"Uh huh."

"What'd he want?" she said. Her lips were pinched and dark circles rimmed her eyes.

"Not much. There was a fight at the bar Saturday night. One of the idiots is pressing charges. He wanted to know why I didn't call it in."

She wrinkled her brow. I couldn't tell if she believed me or not.

"I told him it slipped my mind."

"You didn't mention it before."

I shrugged. "We have a lot of fights. It's what guys do when they're bored. You know that. No big deal." I moved down the hall to the kitchen.

She followed me down the hallway. "If it's no big deal, why'd he drive all the way out here and wait out in his car for forty minutes?"

"Maybe he didn't have anything better to do."

The twins were in the living room playing some noisy video game. I stuck my head in and said hi. They said hi back without taking their eyes off the screen.

"Haven't they got homework to do?" I said, trying to

move off the subject.

"They did their homework."

I went over to the stove and lifted the lid off a pot. Empty. "Any supper left?"

"I'll warm up some stew."

That cheered me up some. Reva made awesome stew. She went to the refrigerator and took out a Tupperware container and warmed the stew in the microwave. She leaned against the counter and wringed her hands while we waited for the stew to warm up. "Aren't you working tonight?"

"Kelsie wanted more hours so I took the night off."

What was that now, four lies in a row?

I'd lost count.

I got a spoon from the utensil drawer. I figured I'd just eat out of the Tupperware container. "We should do something. As a family."

She raised her eyebrows. "Really?"

"Why not? We could watch a movie together or something."

Reva scowled. "They watch movies every night."

"I said 'or something,' didn't I?"

What the hell. I tried.

I took a bottle of beer from the fridge, twisted off the top, and sat down at the kitchen table. Tried to think of some way I could even the score with Goodwin but my mind was a blank. The microwave beeped and I ate the warmed up stew and drank the beer and listened to Reva talk about Hunter's problems at school, Mandy's friend who made her cry, and Reva's mother's skin cancer. Everyone had problems, but they weren't for me to fix.

Besides, I had my own problems.

And I couldn't think of a single thing to do about them.

FOURTEEN

St. Patrick's Day weekend. The punks and drunks were lined up three deep at the bar. Jägerbombs were half price in honor of the Apostle of Ireland. A local band, Elvis Schmelvis, played on the small makeshift stage I'd set up in the back corner. Every time the lead guitarist rocketed into the air *ala* Pete Townsend, I cringed, expecting my shoddy workmanship to come crashing down, killing and maiming the entire band of degenerates.

Live music was a new venture for The Brass Lantern. I wasn't totally on board with the idea. It sounded like a lot of messing around for very little return, but if that night's crowd was any indication, I couldn't have been more wrong.

It was Chad's idea to book bands. He said it was the one thing we could do that Buffalo Wild Wings and Hooters and all the other chains couldn't or wouldn't do. I'd managed to veto all his other dumb ideas: Tenacious Trivia. Rock Star Karaoke. They were fads, I said. They showed desperation.

"We are desperate!" he said.

He had a point.

After that the bar was known as The Brass Lantern: Home of Occasional Live Music.

I'd never heard of this band before, but they came highly recommended by one of our regulars. Apparently they had a big following in St. Louis and the crowd got so big I had to call in Chad to help out behind the bar. When he bitched about having to work the early shift, I reminded him whose brilliant idea the band was.

Most weekends the bar begins to clear out around midnight, but that night it was around one o'clock when the band played its final encore and the crowd began drifting away to the all-night diners. I sent Kelsie home at one o'clock. Chad took off a few minutes later. I happened to glance up and spied the Goodwins seated at the end of the bar. I wasn't surprised to see Clay, but I don't think Randy had ever been in before. I'd heard he didn't drink or smoke. I wondered if he did anything except creep the hell out of people. I figured Randy's presence was Clay's way of sending a message not to fuck with him.

I took out some bags of trash and ignored the Goodwins as long as I dared. I had an armful of mugs and was headed for the sink when Clay reached across the bar and grabbed my arm. I almost dropped the mugs.

"Gin and tonic," he said with his rigor mortis grin.

I turned to Randy, trying not to gawk at the grotesque scar on his nose and forehead, a memento from a long-ago meth lab explosion. "You?"

Randy turned his head away. I shrugged and set down the mugs in the sink and went to work on Clay's drink. A handful of kids hung around talking afterwards. It made me feel better to have someone else around, even punks, only I wished Chad was still there. That goddamn Randy gave me the willies.

I pushed the drink in front of Clay and I turned up the lights and made last call. More people drifted out. I washed some glasses in the sink and waited for Clay to say why he was there.

I didn't have to wait long. "I was talking to my neighbor Art Oberneferman this afternoon," he said.

"Oberwhoferman?"

"Don't play dumb."

I shook my head. "Don't think I know him."

"No? He lives down the road from me. Said he had a little run in with you the other day."

"He did, huh?"

"Said you were parked out on HH Road surveilling my compound."

I wrinkled my brow. "Surveilling, huh? Is that even a word?"

"With binoculars."

Clay removed a pack of cigarettes from his shirt pocket and shook one out of the pack and lighted it up. I pushed a dirty rocks glass toward him for an ashtray. He blew a long plume of smoke toward the ceiling. "Stakoff said he talked to you."

"You seem to know all about my business," I said. "It's kind of creeping me out."

Randy stared blankly at the television above the bar. Not drinking, not smoking. Not nothing. Just being a psycho.

I excused myself and strode back to the walk-in cooler. I hefted a couple cases of Budweiser out to the bar and began stocking the coolers. I said, "Anything else you want to tell me?"

He slugged the gin and tonic. "Yeah. I thought you should know that if anything happens to me, my brother is going to come looking for you."

I gave him a look. "You think something's going to

happen to you?"

Randy lowered his dead, hollow eyes at me, but he remained silent. I guess he figured that was more effective than opening his toothless mouth. He was right. With those nasty burn scars and that limp and his reputation for torturing his enemies, he didn't have to say a word.

"Another thing you should know. My attorney has a letter." Goodwin stubbed out his cigarette and slid off the stool. "Let's just say it contains some pretty compromising stuff regarding you and the late Johnny Sika," he said. "Just an FYI from one old business partner to another." He pocketed his cigarettes and his eyes scanned the bar. The band was clearing the last of their equipment from the stage. "Almost forgot. My niece is going to stop in and see you. Her name's Erica. She's looking for a bartending gig and I told her you were hiring."

"Well, you were wrong."

"Not to worry. She's a hard worker."

"Like you?" I said.

He laughed. "Pretty much the opposite of me."

"The opposite of you is good."

He stopped grinning.

"I don't need another bartender," I said, "and I sure as hell—"

"Waitress then."

"We don't have waitresses."

He looked around the bar, the tables crowded with empties and dirty glasses. "Could've used a few tonight." He turned to Randy and said, "Let's go." Clay started for the door.

Randy slid off his stool, malice in his crooked smile.

"You have a good night," he said and limped toward the door. The short hairs prickled at the back of my neck.

It looked like The Brass Lantern was getting a new waitress.

FIFTEEN

One of our longtime regulars was a retired lawyer named Clark Sheppard. Sheppard had been a fixture at The Brass Lantern long before he and Uncle Chuck bought the bar. They'd been drinking buddies since high school. Chuck was best man at both of Sheppard's weddings. Sheppard had made a small fortune operating a small law firm downtown. He'd also blown a small fortune drinking and gambling. The point is, he didn't care if The Brass Lantern made a dime—he just wanted his favorite watering hole to remain open.

The way I heard it, Sheppard took it real hard when Chuck was killed. He didn't care for Pop much or the way he ran things, so a few years after Chuck died, Pop mortgaged the house and bought him out. The bar remained a sore spot between them. Sheppard tried other taverns, but there were always too many bikers, too many yuppies, or too many people in general, and a month later his ass was back on his regular stool slugging his usual Manhattans.

It got worse after Pop went to prison. Sheppard was even more disgusted when I took over. The way he criticized me you'd think he still owned the bar, or that it was my fault Chuck and Pop weren't around anymore.

A TASTE OF SHOTGUN

Far as I was concerned he could go get shitfaced somewhere else if he didn't like the way I operated. What was one bar fly, more or less?

In recent years we'd reached a kind of truce. I didn't like him and he didn't like me, but as long as we kept the talk to sports and I didn't mess up his tab or short him on the booze, we tolerated each other.

Or so I thought.

It was early Sunday night. Sheppard and a realtor named Stan Henke were the only drinkers. Sheppard looked bored, staring blankly at a hockey game between Minnesota and Boston. I figured the time was right to subtly hit him up for some free legal advice. All he could do is tell me to go fuck myself.

"Been meaning to ask you something, counselor," I said.

He lowered his eyes, glanced at me briefly, then returned his eyes to the screen. He grunted something I took for a kind of half-hearted consent.

"So I've been reading this crime novel. It's a pretty good story, but something about it doesn't ring true, to my ears, anyway. Not that I know a whole hell of a lot about the law..."

"You got that right."

"Yeah. So this guy is murdered, you see, but before he's killed, he leaves a note with a friend. A letter. The letter says if he dies unexpectedly, the, you know, the guy who's telling the story, he killed him."

"The narrator?"

"Yeah. Him."

Sheppard took a swallow of his Manhattan. He wouldn't drink anything but Manhattans. And they had to be made with Canadian Club. Prissy old bastard disliked change of any kind. "You should probably stick with TV," he said.

I tossed a rag over my shoulder and hooked my thumbs in my belt. "I'm probably not doing it justice. It's better than it sounds. You see the dead guy thought the narrator might kill him. That's why he left the letter. Anyway, this letter is used to convict the narrator...of murder."

"You want to read a good crime novel?" Sheppard said. "Read James Ellroy. *American Tabloid.*"

"Yeah, thanks—"

"It's the great American novel, you ask me."

Nobody asked him.

"What was that other one of his I read?" He thought it over a moment, then he snapped his fingers. "*White Jazz.*"

"Yeah—"

"Now *there* was a book," he said, removing a pack of cigarettes and a lighter from his pocket. "Not like whatever that crap is you're reading."

He lit his cigarette. "Say what's the name of that book, anyway?" he said.

I tried to come up with a title, but I drew blanks. My brain froze up. After a moment, I said, "*The Crooked Letter.* I think."

Sheppard shook his head. "God, even the title sucks."

I continued. "So what I'm wondering is whether it's possible, you know, to convict somebody based on a letter like that?"

Sheppard gave me an odd look. "You do know that I was a tax attorney, right?"

Actually I didn't know. I just knew he was a scuzzball lawyer with a liver as big as a basketball. "What is it with you guys and all the specialization? Whatever happened to just plain old lawyers?"

"Whatever happened to smoking in bars?" he said with a shrug. He sipped his Manhattan and thought over my question. "I still think it's a terrible premise for a book," he said, "however, whether one could convict or not would depend on the circumstances. And the judge. A letter like that would likely be deemed inadmissible. Hearsay. You see, you're supposed to allow the accused the opportunity to cross examine the accuser. However, in this case the accuser is dead." He wrinkled his brow and thought it over some more. "Now if the prosecution makes the case that he's dead because of the accused's actions, a judge would likely allow that." He drained off the last of the Manhattan and pushed the empty glass toward me. "Guess what I'm saying is, it depends on the circumstances."

Just like a goddamn lawyer.

"The law's never black and white, is it?" I said.

He chuckled. "If it were, millions of lawyers would be out of a job."

I went to work on his Manhattan.

SIXTEEN

I must have talked to three dozen people who knew Clay Goodwin. I figured a dirtbag like Goodwin must've done lots of terrible things. Somebody had to know something. I button-holed every regular who walked into The Brass Lantern, including some real shitbirds. When that got me nowhere I visited most of the dive bars in the county and jawed with the bartenders and waitresses there. They all had Clay Goodwin stories, mostly about the deadbeat not paying his tab or getting drinks tossed in his face by women he'd insulted. I heard countless stories recounting the petty crimes he'd been busted for—drug possession, battery, DUI, unlawful possession of a handgun, public urination—but these were public knowledge. A month didn't go by that his name wasn't in the police blotter for pulling some stupid stunt. I spoke to a few of the women he'd gone out with; not one had a kind word to say about him, but none could give me a single thing I could use either. He'd used them as punching bags, sex toys, and ATMs. He was a Grade A asshole, but he hadn't done anything he hadn't already done time for—thirty days here for domestic violence, another thirty for DUI. His crimes were like him, small and petty. The whole effort was a bust.

It was the end of the line. Nothing left to do but call his bluff, tell him I was done peddling his skunkweed. Let him squeal to the cops if he dared and deal with the consequences. Maybe the cops would believe him, or maybe they'd be like, *eh, Vince Carroll already did the time. Close enough.* Might turn out Goodwin was bluffing the whole time. Maybe he'd figure he'd squeezed enough cash out of me, and a little more wouldn't be worth jumping at shadows the rest of his life. If he had any brains that's what he'd think.

Before I did anything, however, I wanted to talk to Chad. Like I said, he was the only one in the family with his head on straight. We'd drifted apart after Vince was sent away. He'd pretty much had it with me and Vince and the whole damn family. Who could blame him? Though now we risked losing the family business, so he had a right to know what was what.

Chad knew nothing about the shakedown. He knew we used to deal a little weed out of the bar, which he objected to. After Vince went away he threatened to sell his share of The Brass Lantern to a cop friend if I didn't cut it out. Not that he objected to weed in general. Chad and his now ex-wife Jana used to make Cheech and Chong look like teetotalers, but these days he had a reputation to maintain. These days Chad was the respectable, law-abiding Carroll. The one with ambition. He was going to be coroner or fire chief someday. Maybe county board chairman. That is if me and Vince didn't take a big dump on his political career.

Anyway, he had a right to know, just in case Goodwin wasn't bluffing and his other lowlife brother was suddenly tossed in the can. Vince sure as hell couldn't run the bar; the conditions of his parole didn't allow within a hundred feet of a tavern. Especially one where he was busted for drug possession.

It was a fine winter's day, blue sky, the air crisp and cool, temperature hovering around thirty-two degrees. I stopped by the firehouse on my way into work and found Chad in the parking lot sitting in his souped up ambulance listening to a right-wing radio station. He spent most of his time listening to conservative talk radio. Normally he sat in the lounge and watched FOX News, but not everyone liked to watch right-wing propaganda twenty-four hours a day, seven days a week, which is why he'd go sit in the ambulance.

I knocked on the window and went around and climbed into the passenger side.

"Where's Rocky?" I said.

"On the phone arguing with her daughter. Where else would she be?"

Chad's partner, Rocky—short for Raquel—was a single working mom with two teenage daughters who were always suffering some catastrophic social crisis and threatening to eat poison. Everyone thought Rocky and Chad were romantically involved because they were often seen sitting in the ambulance together, either in the parking lot or in a city park, but the truth was more mundane. Rocky was also a right winger and there was nothing she enjoyed so much as driving out to a pond to park and listen to FOX radio. It was better than sex.

A vacuum cleaner commercial came on. I'd noticed these talk shows were mostly commercials. Five minutes of ranting, twenty-five minutes of godawful commercials. I nodded toward the radio. "How goes the culture war, Captain?"

"Fucking liberals. Still trying to pass socialized medicine. I swear, if we don't take back the White House next year I'm moving to Canada."

"I'm pretty sure Canada has socialized medicine too."

Chad thought about that. "Then I'm moving to Ireland."

"I think every country has socialized medicine but us."

"Goddamn liberals won't be happy till we're just like all them other loser countries."

I wasn't sure what to say to that, so I went silent a moment, listening to more commercials. I let out a loud fart. I couldn't help it.

Chad scowled to me. "You need something or you just here to pollute my atmosphere?"

I cleared my throat. "Actually." I paused. "I thought you should know that, um, well…" I nodded at the radio. "Could you turn that off?"

Chad snapped off the radio. "Tell me what?"

"Promise not to go nuts?"

"Denis, quit fu—"

"Clay Goodwin's blackmailing us."

He paused. "It sounded like you just said Clay Goodwin is blackmailing us."

"Well, me really. But kind of us."

I could see the muscles in his forehead clench. A bad sign. Then he shook his head. "Denis, what the hell are you talking about?"

I took a sharp intake of breath and plowed ahead. "Okay. I've been selling a little of his ditch weed." I held up my hands. "But only because he threatened to go to the cops if I didn't."

He tensed. "Why would he go to the cops?"

"Tell them it was me who shot Johnny Sika. That I lied about that in court, which is, you know, perjury, I guess. He was going to tell the cops it wasn't self-defense after all. And that the weed they found was mine. Who knows what else? He could make up shit all day long."

Chad rubbed his hand over his stubble and stared hard out the smudgy windshield. He turned back to me. "How long's this been going on?"

"What, the dealing or the—"

He slammed his hand against the dashboard. "Yes! The drug dealing!"

I shrugged. "About two years."

"And you're just now telling me?"

"If I'd told you earlier you would've made me stop—"

"You're damn right I would've!"

"And Goodwin would've gone to the cops. And what good would that do? What good would that do Reva and the kids?"

Chad slowly shook his head. "Now's a fine time to start worrying about your wife and kids."

I dipped my head and stared at my shoes. "Anyway, that's what I came to tell you. I'm done selling his weed. I just wanted you to know in case he goes to the cops, and…you know."

Chad folded his arms over his chest. "And shits all over my good name, you mean. Everything I've worked for."

I looked out the window at nothing in particular. "I've been trying to dig up something on him—"

Chad stared at me, his jaw clenched like a fist. I knew what he'd say before he said it. "You just don't know when to quit."

I shut up. Thirty-five years old, and he still treated me like a kid brother.

A TASTE OF SHOTGUN

Anyway, the worst was over.

"There's a chance, a good chance even, that he won't do anything," I said. "Maybe he'll realize he had a good thing while it lasted, but now it's over."

There was a loud hiss of air brakes and one of the hook and ladders pulled into the parking lot and began the long, complicated process of backing into the bay.

"Get out," he said.

Chad turned the radio on. As the talk show host's voice filled the cab, the storm slowly receded from his eyes.

Rocky came out the back door of the firehouse and started across the lot toward the ambulance, no doubt looking for an ear to bend.

I'd said what I needed to say. I climbed out of the cab and got the hell out of there.

SEVENTEEN

It took most of a week to figure out where I'd seen her before. She was Amber's friend. We'd met the day I dropped off Vince and Pritchard at the trailer. Funny she hadn't mentioned that.

I was all set to tell her to hit the bricks that first night, tell her that her uncle was wrong, I didn't need another bartender, but it turned out we got slammed real hard that night. I figured I'd let her work and pay her a few bucks under the table and that would be the end of it. Then Kelsie called in and begged the weekend off. So I had her come in on Friday and Saturday nights. Next thing you knew, she was an official employee of The Brass Lantern.

Erica turned out to be a pretty good little worker. You'd never know she and Clay Goodwin were blood relations. She wasn't a bad looker either. Otherwise she was pretty much like all single moms with high school degrees, reeking of stale cigarette smoke and quiet desperation. Anyway, she was a welcome relief from Kelsie and her constant bitching about money and childcare.

Speaking of Clay Goodwin, he'd been conspicuously absent the past week, ever since he'd informed me about "the letter." Normally that would've suited me fine, only

A TASTE OF SHOTGUN

I was anxious to have it out with him. If he didn't drop by soon, I was going to go scare him up, if I had to look under every rock in the county.

It was Wednesday night, ladies' night, which meant the usual one or two leathery old women sitting at the bar drinking Budweisers and watching hockey next to their sullen husbands. It would take a lot more than half-price drinks to get young women into The Brass Lantern.

We closed a little before midnight, but Erica hung around awhile. She pulled up a stool and draped her coat over the back and nursed a rum and diet. I turned off the televisions and put on a David Allan Coe CD.

I could feel her eyes studying me as I counted the register. Something was on her mind. I half expected her to tell me that tonight was her last night, that she'd found something better.

She waited till I finished with the drawer then she cleared her throat. "Denis, can I ask you something?"

"Sure."

A pause. "How am I doing?"

"How—?"

"Am I doing all right?"

"You're doing fine. Why?"

She shrugged. "I get the impression you're not happy with my work."

"No, not at all," I said, waving my hand dismissively. "Why would you think that?"

"I don't know. I just..." She paused and stirred her drink. "Never mind. I guess I'm being silly."

"You're doing fine," I said. It was true. She was a fine worker. The regulars liked her. She had just the right combination of professionalism and flirtiness that kept the middle-aged guys coming back. Hell, most of the times I forgot who her uncle was.

That reminded me. I closed the register drawer and glanced up at her, trying to make my tone as casual as possible. "Say, you wouldn't happen to know where I might find Clay, would you? I've been trying to call him, but he must've changed his number."

"Tonight?"

"Uh huh."

She shook the hair out of her face. "Might try looking under a rock."

I laughed. "My thoughts exactly."

"Under a bus would be even better." She said it without any trace of humor or bitterness. Still, it took me aback. I poured myself a double of Early Times in a rocks glass and leaned on the dented beer cooler door and studied her.

"I figured you two were close," I said. "He got you this job, didn't he?"

She let out a small hard laugh, looked into her glass, and killed her drink in one swallow. "Trying to ease his guilty conscience," she said.

My ears pricked up. I went to work on another rum and diet and set the glass down in front of her. "Guilty conscience?"

The booze was kicking in. Her eyes took on a glassy appearance. Then she seemed to momentarily sober up. "Thanks," she said, "but can we not talk about him?"

"Whatever you say." To hell with that, I told myself. I wasn't about to let this opportunity pass. "I understand," I said. "I completely agree with you about the bus thing."

"Forget the bus. Somebody ought to put a bullet in his head."

Whoa. That got my attention.

I nodded and forced myself to keep my mouth shut. Just let her do the talking.

For a while she didn't say anything, just stared into her own personal abyss. After a moment she glanced up, her eyes wet and shiny. "You must think I'm awful."

"Not at all. Your uncle can be a difficult man."

"Difficult," she scoffed and her jaw crept forward. "You want to know what he really is?"

I nodded slightly.

"He's a goddamn rapist, is what he is."

My heart leapt into my throat. *Holy shit. Please God, please tell me she's not exaggerating.*

"Clay?"

"He should've been locked up years ago." She paused and her cheeks flushed violently. "Jesus, you must think I'm a nutcase."

I kept silent. I swallowed a large gulp of whiskey and watched a single tear drift down her left cheek. I came out from behind the bar and sat down on the stool beside her. I thought about putting my hand on her somewhere in a comforting way, but decided against it. The last thing I wanted to do was freak her out.

I went over my next line in my head. "Sounds like he caused you a lot of pain."

"I didn't even want to take this...this job," she said. "No offense, but..."

"None taken."

"I guess he thinks he's making up for what he did. What a joke." She opened her purse and pulled out a tissue and wiped her eyes and loudly blew her nose. "I'm sorry. I don't usually get like this."

"It's okay," I said. "Sometimes it helps to talk. I've

been a bartender all my life. I've heard it all. Us bartenders take a solemn oath, like a Catholic priest. What's said in the Lantern stays in the Lantern."

She laughed and looked up at me, her eyes glistening. "You're full of shit, you know that?"

"You got me pegged."

She blew her nose and went silent for a while. The hum of the coolers seemed incredibly loud and a snow plow scraped by on the street in front of the bar.

"I'm sorry. It's just that I'd forgotten all about it. Not forgotten, but, you know, buried it. Blocked it out, like it never happened." She paused. "That is till my mother called a few weeks ago and told me my aunt died. Like I gave a shit. Like I was supposed to grieve about that. I was glad she was dead. Only I wished she'd died twenty years ago. I know it sounds awful, but she let it happen."

I glanced into the mirror behind the bar, watching her. For a second our eyes met, then she lowered her gaze to her drink.

"God, I must sound like a raving lunatic," she said.

"Not at all."

Silence.

"You didn't know my sister Maggie, did you?"

"I don't think so."

"I thought you might've known her from school or something."

"No."

"Oh." She paused. "She saved my life, you know." She squeezed her eyes shut and fell silent.

I listened to the sound of the plow scraping on the pavement and studied her almost empty glass.

She went on. "We had different dads. They may as

well have been the same guys though. Neither one was worth a sow's turd." She shook her head. "In the summers we'd stay with our aunt and uncle. They lived way out in the country, by Coulterville. Middle of nowhere." She paused a long time. "Sometimes at night Uncle Clay would come into our room. The first time he came for me, I was only seven years old."

"My god," I said.

"Maggie dragged him off me. Said he should take her."

She breathed in steadily and looked down. "She was only twelve."

I didn't say a word, but I was thinking, *holy shit. This isn't real. This isn't happening.*

She continued, "I'd lay there in bed paralyzed with fear, listening to her muffled sobs, listening to him grunting like a wild hog. It went on for years. Till we got old enough to be on our own."

Nothing was said for a few moments.

"She knew about it. My aunt. She pretended not to, but she knew. She didn't do a goddamn thing."

"What about your mother? Didn't you tell her?"

"Maggie did. She didn't believe her. She called her a liar and a little slut. Beat her with a hairbrush. Even after Aunt Tilly left Clay, she wouldn't believe her."

I breathed in steadily and looked around the bar at nothing. "What happened to your sister?"

In the mirror I could see her face, swollen, her mouth bunched tight. She glared into her drink with scalding hot eyes. An inky trickle of mascara flowed halfway down her cheek. "She went away to college." Her body tensed and her eyes filled with rage. "Freshman year she hanged herself in her dorm room."

I squeezed her forearm. "Jesus. I'm sorry, honey."

"The college blamed it on stress."

She pressed her lips together and her chin trembled slightly. She dug another tissue from her purse and blew her nose. "I swore to god I'd kill him. When I got old enough. I promised Maggie." She dropped the tissue into her purse. "Instead, I pretended it never happened. Just pretended I never had a sister."

I nodded and squeezed her arm sympathetically.

Holy crap, here was the answer to all my prayers. And goddamn if Clay Goodwin hadn't dropped it right in my lap.

I slid off the stool and went back around the bar, feeling elated, better than I'd felt in months. I set the glasses in the sink.

My phone went off.

I didn't recognize the number. I glanced at my watch. It was half past midnight. I excused myself and answered the phone.

"Hey bro," Vince said.

"You got a phone."

"A burner."

I figured he wanted to stop by for a drink, or crash on the sofa. I didn't want him to do either.

"I was just closing up," I said.

"Cool, I'll be right there."

"Dude, I want to go home. I'm exhausted."

"Fine, then I'll just tell you."

"Tell me what?"

"It's about our friend," he said. "I don't think he'll be giving us any more trouble."

I walked down to the other end of the bar and cupped my hand over the phone. "Vince, it's late and

I'm tired. What are you trying to tell me?"

"Me and Pritchard followed Goodwin home tonight. Just now. You know that old baseball bat from when we were kids? The one you keep at the bar?"

My insides iced over. I glanced down the bar where Erica sat nursing her drink and pretending not to listen.

"You didn't..."

"Uh huh."

He sounded real proud of himself.

"Why the hell would you do that?" I hissed into the phone. "Jesus Christ, Vince."

He paused a moment. "I thought that's what you wanted? What the hell? You change your mind already?"

"Hold on," I said. I smiled at Erica and squeezed her arm as I walked past her. "Be right back." I strode back to the little office area by the walk-in cooler and sat down on the safe.

"Start over," I said. "Now what the hell happened?"

"I might've had too much to drink. You know how I get when I drink."

"Mean."

"Yeah," he said. "Anyway, Goodwin was at The Hideaway. The bar?"

"I know The Hideaway."

"Yeah. Little piece of shit. You know what he reminds me of?"

"Goddamn it, Vince. What the hell were you thinking?"

"What do you mean—"

"Christ man, you may have just fucked up our one chance."

He paused. "Wait, what?"

"I told you I was handling it," I said through my teeth.

Vince let go a mean little laugh. "Really? Since when? He's been shaking us down going on two years now. Sorry bro, but that ain't handling shit."

I could feel the sweat building on the back of my neck and my hands began to tremble. Talk about great timing. "How bad?" I said.

"How bad what?"

"Goddamnit, how bad did you hurt him?"

"I don't know. He ain't going to be running no marathons any time soon, I can tell you that."

"And why'd you get that moron Pritchard involved in this? Why is he still hanging around here anyway?"

"He wanted to." Vince paused a moment. "Jeez man, I thought you'd be happy."

"Yeah, I'm delirious."

I couldn't think straight. My chest started to tighten like a fist, like it does when I think I'm having a coronary. I opened the desk drawer where I keep the Ativan, but the orange container was empty. There should've been ten or twelve left.

"Dude, have you been stealing my Ativan?" I said.

"Those were yours?"

"Goddamn it, Vince. There were like twelve pills in there—"

"I needed them. I got issues."

"Issues. Can't you get a prescription from the V.A.?"

"I got an appointment with the V.A. in mid-July. If I'm still alive. That's as soon as they can fit me in. See how our government treats war heroes? It's a fucking outrage, you ask me."

"I still don't understand why you would do that—"

"What, take your pills?"

"Do that to Goodwin. You told me the other day you weren't going to do shit...Then you go and do this."

Vince chuckled. "I guess I couldn't help myself. Smug little bastard thought he could shake us down. And you weren't going to do a damn thing. You were just going to keep being his bitch. For a lousy twenty percent. And there he was, at the bar, looking all smug and weaselly. I don't know. Something just snapped." He paused. "I wish you could have heard him, bro. Crying like a little girl. Fucking pathetic."

After a moment he said, "Jesus, Denis, if you're going to change your mind you might let a brother know. Something like that could send me back to the goddamn work camp, know what I'm saying?"

"So did he recognize you? Did he know it was you?"

"No worries. I wore my bong gas mask. Scared the shit out of him."

"What about Pritchard?"

"No, but Goodwin doesn't know Pritchard from a bar of soap." He paused. "Dude, you need to chill. I told you he didn't recognize me."

He fell silent. I could hear Pritchard muttering something to Vince.

"What about your truck?" I said. "Your plates?"

"We parked down the highway and walked up. We jumped him while he was unlocking the gate."

I pictured the scene in my head, trying to peg where they might have screwed something up. "What about the bat?"

"The bat?"

"You were saying something about a bat."

"What about it?"

"You didn't forget it? You didn't leave it behind?"

"Man, you must really think I'm stup—" There was a brief pause. Some mumbled conversation.

"Oh shit," he said.

"What?"

"We've got to turn around," Vince said. "Don't worry, bro, I got this."

The line went dead.

I scrubbed my hands over my face and found his number under recent calls.

He didn't pick up.

I walked out to the bar. Erica was nowhere to be seen, but her coat was still draped over the back of the stool. The women's restroom door opened and she came out, the mascara scrubbed from her eyes. She looked at me and broke into a smile. "Your wife?"

"Actually, my..." I paused. "Yes, my wife. She misses me."

"That's sweet." She smiled. "I should get going. I just wanted to tell you I'm sorry for laying all that heavy shit on you. I mean, we barely know it each other."

"It's fine. It's what I'm here for. Well, that and watering down the booze."

She laughed politely and slipped on her coat and a pair of bright red mittens with sparkles. Kids' mittens.

"You all right to drive home?" I said.

Her eyes dulled a bit as she looked up at me. "Yeah. I'm fine. No worries."

"How about I walk you to your car?"

"Thanks, but I'm fine, really." She gave her handbag a light pat. "I've got all the protection I need right here."

"Condoms?"

She laughed and opened her purse and drew out a

small handgun. "Even better."

"Whoa," I said, taken aback. "Look at that."

"Meet Old Rusty."

It was an old Taurus 94 revolver. I didn't see any rust on it, though. Looked pretty well taken care of. "Where'd you get it?"

"An old boyfriend gave it to me. Wasn't that sweet of him?"

"No kidding? He still alive?"

She giggled. "Yeah. He's one of the lucky ones." She slipped the revolver back into her purse.

"Mind if I see it?"

"Sure."

She handed me the piece and I weighed it in my hand. Just like I thought. Cheap. Not much more than a popgun, but it ought to do the job if some creep surprised her in the parking lot.

I returned the pistol and she dropped it into her purse. Her eyes shone damply and she gave me a drunken half smile and said she'd see me Friday.

After she was gone, I turned out the rest of the lights and sat in the darkness, trying to decide what to do. I took out my cell and tried his number again.

The phone went to voicemail.

Goddamn it, Vince.

The cops were probably on their way to Goodwin's place now. They'd probably get there the same time as Vince.

I hope he'd enjoyed his couple weeks of freedom.

EIGHTEEN

I was up early the next morning. I was restless and couldn't sleep, so I figured I'd rustle up a hot breakfast for the whole family. Make myself useful while I waited to hear from Vince. He still wasn't answering his phone.

I made a hash of the bacon and eggs, but Reva appreciated it, even if the twins complained about the runny eggs and burned pancakes. Throughout breakfast Reva eyed me suspiciously.

I set down my fork and knife. "What?" I said. "Can't a guy make breakfast for his family?"

"So is this going to become a regular thing?"

I forked some eggs into my mouth. "We'll see."

Hunter said, "I like it when Mom cooks breakfast."

"Shut up and eat your eggs," I said.

"*I* like your cooking," said Mandy.

"Thanks, sweetie."

She stuck her tongue out at her brother.

Hunter cried, "Mom, she stuck out her tongue—"

"Knock it off, both of you," I said.

They'd be gone in a few minutes, off to school, and I could go back to sleep. Or back to lying in bed, thinking over all the stupid things I'd done. Not just recently, but throughout my whole fucked up life.

Except I couldn't do that either. I was too juiced up on caffeine and worried about Goodwin and what he might do or what he'd already done. There didn't seem to be anything to do but drive out to his place again. Let him know that I knew his little secret about his niece and what he'd done to her.

I made another pot of coffee and fired up my laptop. I thought about calling Chad to see if EMS had gotten a call about Goodwin last night, but decided that would be a bad idea. He'd just freak out on me again and it was too early for that kind of drama. I checked my phone and saw I had three voicemails from Vince. I trembled at the thought.

Someone knocked on the front door.

I got up and went over to the picture window and peeked through the blinds.

Several cops stood just outside the front door. My guts drew in a little, and I got that feeling I always get at the sight of cops, a racing heart and shriveling of the testicles. My first thought was that something had happened to Reva and the twins. A car accident.

My second thought was Clay Goodwin. He'd fingered me as the guy who waylaid him outside his house.

I steadied myself and opened the front door. A blast of arctic air stung my face. Butch Stakoff stood heavy on the porch. From the looks of it he'd been up awhile, outdoors in the sub-freezing night. Butch was accompanied by two young officers, who also looked hypothermic. They stood a little ways off on the ice-covered walkway. I felt self-conscious because I hadn't put out any rock salt. I couldn't help it.

I stepped out onto the porch, a mug of coffee in my hand. "Back again?" I said. "Everything all right?"

"Morning, Denis. Sorry to come by so early." He blew into his hands.

"My family okay?"

"Hmm? Oh, sure," he said. "Far as I know."

"Thank god," I said. "With these icy roads, you never know…"

Butch rubbed his hands together for warmth. "Denis, you wouldn't mind coming down to the station with us?"

My toes curled inside my slippers. So the bastard had gone to the cops after all. "Why?" I said. "Do you want to tell me what this is about?"

"What say we talk down at the station?"

"Jeez. You guys look all serious and shit. Have I done something wrong?"

Stakoff didn't say anything.

"Butch, am I under arrest?"

"We'd just like you to come in for a little chat, that's all."

"A little chat?"

"Uh huh."

"So I'm not under arrest?"

"Correct."

I nodded toward the other two cops. "Then why the militia?"

"Why don't you just pretend they ain't here?"

They looked like rookies. Young, doubtless former military, full of piss and vinegar, anxious to bust their first civilian heads. They returned my gaze with hard, empty stares. I turned back to Stakoff.

"Look, I'm kind of busy here."

He grinned. "Not too busy to assist your local law enforcement, I hope."

I shook my head. "Hell, when you put it that way." I

paused. "Mind if I call my wife and put on some decent clothes?"

"Sure, but keep the door open."

I sighed heavily and turned and mounted the stairs to the bedroom. I closed the bedroom door and sat down on the bed. I slipped my phone from my pocket and dialed Reva's number.

She picked up on the second ring. "Hey hon, can I call you back?"

"No," I said brusquely. "Reva, Butch Stakoff's here and he wants me to go down to the station with him."

A long pause. When she came back on I could hear traffic swooshing by on the street.

"Denis, what's going on?" Her voice was choked with anger and concern. Mostly anger. Not for the first time did I find myself wondering how much more of my shit she would take.

"I'm not exactly sure," I said. "All I know is he wants to talk to me. I have no idea what about."

"Denis, what have you done now?"

"Nothing," I snapped. "I haven't done anything. This may not even be about me."

"You must've done something or the police wouldn't be there!"

"I—"

"I *knew* this would happen when your brother got out of prison. I knew it!"

I stood up and walked over to the door. I opened the door and heard the squawk of Butch's radio transceiver. "I said I don't know what it's about. Look, do you think you can get off work and come down to the station? Maybe take an early lunch or something?"

"What am I supposed to tell my boss? I need to leave

work because my husband's been arrested?"

"I haven't been arrested." I paused and took a deep breath. All this quarrelling wasn't doing either of us any good.

Reva was silent, but I could hear her breathing heavily like she'd run a 5K.

"Babe, I swear to you I haven't done anything wrong," I said.

This seemed to break the tension somewhat.

"Why won't they tell you what they want?"

"I don't know."

"Did you ask them?"

"Of course I asked them."

The chill from the open front door blew into the house and the boiler kicked on.

"You don't have to come down now, but if I'm not home when you get off work, you might want to come down to the station and find out what's going on."

"Damn it, Denis."

"I know. I'm sorry."

"You're sorry? Denis—"

"Look, I got to go."

I hung up the phone and slipped out of my sweats and into some jeans and a sweater. Might as well look presentable. I grabbed my parka out of the hall closet and locked up the house. I followed Stakoff to the squad car and slid into the back seat. Various neighbors peered out from behind curtains, probably commenting smugly among themselves. *Always said them Carrolls were a bunch of no good white trash. Every single one of them.*

We drove off down the street, me sitting in the back like a wild animal behind some kind of cage overlaid with Plexiglass. I asked Stakoff if this was going to take long, and he said it was hard to say. The guy was a wealth of information. We were about halfway to the station when my chest began to tighten and I realized I'd forgotten to take an Ativan. Then my phone rang. I looked at the number. Vince. I let it go to voicemail.

NINETEEN

One of the young centurions escorted me to a small interview room, which turned out to be a claustrophobe's nightmare: gray walls, with a metal table and three mismatched metal chairs and a buzzing florescent light and one of those security cameras up by the corner ceiling. He said somebody would be right with me.

"Right with me" turned out to be an hour later. I used some of the time to listen to Vince's messages. The first one was a hang-up but the second somewhat cryptic message said he'd heard about Goodwin, and he needed to talk to me about that as soon as possible. I called him back and got his voicemail.

I rested my head on the table and shut my eyes and tried not to think about being locked in a tiny gray room for an indefinite period of time without my Ativan. It seemed to work. At least I managed not to freak out. At least my heart didn't start slamming against my rib cage like a jackhammer.

Around ten-thirty Stakoff came in. He carried a thick brown accordion folder under his arm and two coffees in Styrofoam cups. He pulled up one of the metal chairs and set a cup in front of me. A small plume of steam swirled above the rim. "Hope you like it black," he said.

I grunted.

"Sorry to keep you waiting."

"What else have I got to do?" I said. "You want to tell me what this is about?"

Stakoff slipped on a pair of glasses and removed a small tape recorder from his shirt pocket. He pressed the power button and set the machine on the table between us. "Voice activated," he said. "Pretty nifty. Only records what's said. No need to fast-forward."

"You must be very proud," I said.

He gave me a preoccupied look. "Huh?"

He removed a manila file from the folder and studied a sheet of paper. He belched softly. "So we're investigating a homicide that occurred around one o'clock last night."

"That's nice for you. What's it got to do with me?"

"The name Clay Goodwin mean anything to you?"

"Yeah, it means dirtbag."

"So you know him?"

"Who doesn't?" I felt my chest begin to tighten.

"Know him pretty well, don't you?"

"About as well as the next dirtbag," I said. I tried to keep my voice steady and I kept my hands under the table so he couldn't see them tremble. "Why?"

Stakoff gave me a curious look. "You okay?"

"Yeah," I snapped. "Can we get on with this?"

"Of course," he said, thumbing the stack of files. He appeared to find the one he was looking for and studied it a moment. He set down the file and looked at me over his glasses. "Didn't it come out at your brother's trial that Goodwin was supplying him with illegal narcotics?"

I tried to meet his eyes. "It was alleged. Never proven," I said. "And what's any of that got to do with me?"

"You're one of the bar owners, ain't you?"

"One of many. I still don't see your point."

He brushed that aside. "Vince. He killed one of the Sika boys during a drug deal, right?"

I nodded to the files on the table. "I sure hope that isn't what those files say. It was attempted robbery. Self-defense."

Stakoff leaned back and folded one leg over the other and studied me. "That's right. Attempted robbery. But we found drugs, if I recall."

The metal chair squeaked as I shifted. "Did something happen to Goodwin?"

"Funny you should ask."

"What's funny?"

"Goodwin's dead."

I stiffened, just for a moment. "Dead, as in—"

"As a doorknob."

I felt an icy wind blow up my spine. It wasn't possible. Vince would've told me. I tried to recall his last phone message. Something about him hearing about Goodwin and needing to talk to me.

I stared at the coffee cup, feeling too shaky to pick it up. "What happened?"

"That's what I aim to find out," he said. "And I will." He paused. "Look Denis, Clay Goodwin was never going to win man of the year. In fact, the world's probably a better place without him."

"I'm sure there's a point here somewhere."

"I'm going to ask you again what I asked you last week. What were you doing out by the Goodwins' place last week with a pair of field glasses?"

"Bird watching."

"Bird watching."

A TASTE OF SHOTGUN

I leaned forward on the table and folded my hands. "Yeah. You ever see a yellow-billed loon?"

Stakoff stared at me, his lips pressed tight in a rigid smile.

"How about a red-gartered coot?"

Silence.

I shrugged. "So what happened to Goodwin?"

Stakoff took a sip of coffee. "From the looks of it, somebody beat the tar out of him with a pipe and when they got tired of that they finished him off with a gunshot to the forehead."

"He was shot?"

"That's right. Now I'll ask you again. What were you doing out by Goodwin's house last week?"

There was no way Vince or the Galesburg Kid would have shot Goodwin. I knew my brother. Both my brothers were all about saving lives. Those of their fellow soldiers. Accident victims. Their ne'er-do-well brother.

I wracked my brain trying to figure out what was going on, but nothing made sense.

Then I remembered.

Erica Wainwright.

I slumped back in my chair. "Look Butch, I hate to toss a wrench into your investigation, but if I'm under suspicion for something, I should probably have a lawyer present. Someone to tell me to shut the hell up. Know what I mean?"

Stakoff held onto his coffee cup with both hands. "Well, sure, if you think that's—"

"So I'll just be on my way then." I rose out of my chair.

"Actually, we'd like you to stick around till we get the fingerprints back."

I froze halfway up. "What fingerprints?"

"The ones we found at the crime scene."

"On the bat?"

"What bat?"

"You said Goodwin was beaten with a bat."

"I said pipe."

I wanted to kick myself. Hadn't I just said I wanted a lawyer before I said something stupid? Something incriminating?

And he had it on tape too.

"I thought you said bat," I mumbled.

"Want me to play the tape for you?"

"I guess I misheard."

"Guess you did." Stakoff grinned. "We lifted us some nice fat prints off the murder weapon."

"So you've got the gun?"

He nodded.

"What kind of gun, if you don't mind my asking?"

"Why?"

"Just curious."

Stakoff took a sip of coffee and made a face. "Shit's awful." He set the cup down. "Care to guess?"

"A revolver?"

He brightened and sat up straight. "Hell if you ain't a good guesser."

"A Taurus 94?"

Stakoff grinned ear to ear. "You sure seem to know a lot about the murder weapon, Denis. Maybe you do need that lawyer after all."

"I don't know much, Butch, but I do know when I'm being set up."

Stakoff leaned back in his chair, his hands on his belt. "I'm all ears. So how are you being set up and by who?"

A TASTE OF SHOTGUN

"One of my bartenders showed me a Taurus 94 last night. Now that I think of it, she made sure I handled it too. Then she must've used it on Goodwin."

"Interesting theory. This bartender got a name?"

"Wainwright. Erica Wainwright."

Stakoff scratched the name down on the cover of a folder. "A gal, huh? I don't think I know her."

"She's Goodwin's niece."

He nodded. "So you're theory is...what? That Goodwin's niece beat him half to death with a pipe or, as you say, a bat, then shot him?"

"Old Rusty," I said under my breath.

"Say again?"

"That's what she called the gun. I just remembered."

I put my palms down flat on the table, the styrofoam cup between them. "Last night, we'd just closed the bar. It must've been eleven thirty, maybe closer to midnight. We were having an after-work drink—"

"You and Ms. Wainwright?"

I nodded. "She was telling me how when they were kids Goodwin raped her sister. She said she swore she'd kill him someday." I considered the wall for a moment. "I thought it was strange her telling me that."

"Why's that?"

"She'd only worked for me a short time. I barely knew her. You don't tell something that personal to someone you hardly know. Hell, you don't tell it to your best friend."

"Interesting. Anyone else hear this conversation?"

I shook my head.

He tapped a pen on the table. "I'm still not sure what you're getting at."

"I'm saying she shot Goodwin, just like she said she

would. And I'm her patsy."

His eyes dulled a bit as he thought over what I said. "Okay, but why would she set *you* up?"

"Hell, I don't know, Butch. Maybe I was convenient."

"Convenient?"

"Maybe. I don't know." I was silent a moment, considering things. "Where'd you find the gun?"

"The murder weapon? Why?"

"I mean, was it just lying there, waiting for you to trip over it?"

Stakoff seemed to think that over, but he didn't say anything.

"Doesn't that raise a red flag or anything?"

Stakoff choked down some more coffee and made a sour face. He leaned forward in his chair and tented his fingers under his chin. "Let's see if I got this straight. Out of the blue, one of your employees tells you that her uncle raped her sister, what, ten, twenty years ago? Then suckers you into putting your prints all over the murder weapon, then drives out to his house after work, beats the shit out of him with a baseball bat, shoots him in the head, and leaves the gun behind to frame you." He glanced at me. "Have I got that about right?"

I didn't say anything. When he put it that way, it did seem kind of far-fetched. Crazy, even.

"Well then," he said. "Open and shut. Case closed. Oh, except you still haven't told me what you were doing out there a week ago." He put his eyes on me flat and hard. "Well?"

I squirmed under his stare. "Like I told that old man—"

"Art Oberneferman."

"I was having engine trouble. So I pulled off the highway to check it out."

"You were a long way from the highway."

"I was looking for a good place to pull over. It ain't like them roads got shoulders."

"Uh huh," he said. "And the spyglasses?"

"You mean binoculars. They're for hunting."

He sighed heavily and reached into the folder and pulled out a sheet of paper.

"Got a hunting license?"

"Not on me."

He made a note. "We'll check anyway."

"Fine."

He held up three or four sheets of paper. "According to this report, Art said he saw you using them binoculars to case Goodwin's house."

"Can I see that?"

He shook his head. "Ongoing police investigation."

It seemed unlikely that the old man would've seen me using the binoculars, unless he had eyes like a hawk. "That's bullshit," I said. "He maybe saw the binoculars on my front seat, so he assumed that. They're for hunting. Besides, how good is his eyesight? Probably blind as a bat, a guy his age."

"Bats aren't blind," Stakoff said.

"What?"

"Bats. They aren't blind. They see better than people. Well, better than a lot of people."

"Whatever," I said.

Stakoff drummed his fingers on the table, thinking. "Back to that girl. Erica Wainwright. She a triathlete?"

"A what?"

"Maybe a bodybuilder?"

"Why are you asking me?"

"That beating Goodwin took, that wasn't done by no

normal gal. Unless she just got out of the Navy Seals."

I shrugged. "Maybe she had help," I said. "A boyfriend or something."

"Uh huh," he said, feigning boredom. "Last question. Where were you last night between say midnight and one?"

"I told you. I closed down the bar at midnight. Got home a little before one."

"You always close that early?"

"On weeknights, yes. If there aren't any customers."

"Then you drove right home?"

"I drove right home."

"Anybody see you?"

"See me driving home?"

"See you anywhere."

"My wife. When I got home."

Stakoff yawned and closed the folder. "I need some good coffee or I'm going to fall asleep right here," he said.

"Butch, listen to me. I know it sounds incredible, but it's the truth. Erica Wainwright shot her uncle because he'd molested her sister. For years, he sexually abused her. Then she left the gun behind to frame me. Left it just lying there for you to find. She'd probably been waiting months, maybe years for some sucker to come along and ask to see her gun. Didn't matter who. Just so she got his prints on it."

I studied his face. It was blank as an empty slate.

"Think about it," I said. "Why else would you leave the murder weapon at the scene?"

"It happens. You'd be surprised."

I hung my head and slowly shook it back and forth.

"Okay," he said. "Suppose you're right. Suppose it was a revenge killing. Why do it now? If, like you say, he raped her sister all those years ago, why now?"

"She told me she'd...what's the word. Repressed it. Buried it. Something about her aunt dying brought it back."

Stakoff sucked on a tooth. "Her aunt dying..."

I folded my arms over my chest. "I'm not going home, am I?"

"All depends on the print report," he said. "If your prints turn up on that weapon, I'd say we got too much *not* to hold you. Probably ought to check with the medical examiner too, see if she was beaten with a pipe or a bat."

"Butch, come on. Think about it. Why would I kill Clay Goodwin?"

"I can think of several reasons right off the top of my head. He was a small-time drug dealer. The Carrolls are small-time drug dealers. That's what small-time dealers do in order to become big-time dealers. They eliminate the competition."

"*Were* drug dealers," I corrected him. "And just one of us. Vince."

He paused. "Hell of a coincidence that Goodwin is murdered just a few days after Vince was released from prison."

He was silent a moment, then he stood up slowly with a middle-aged groan. "Anyway, you don't necessarily need a motive to charge someone with murder. Or to convict, for that matter. Not when you got fingerprint evidence and the murder weapon."

He watched me closely, waiting. "Anything else you want to add?"

"What the hell good would it do? I just solved the case for you and you don't believe a word of it."

"I'll admit it's a good story," he said, turning to go. "Now let's see what the evidence says."

TWENTY

Big surprise. The fingerprints recovered from the revolver matched my right index finger and thumb. Stakoff said they had no choice but to hold me.

One of the rookies put me in the "honeymoon suite," a plain, stark holding cell with a steel cot. The block was uninhabited except me and one other guy. I couldn't see him, but I could hear him alright. A young dude, maybe early twenties. He was dying to talk to somebody, anybody. I wasn't in the mood, but that didn't seem to matter to him. He wanted to know my name and where I was from and what I was in for and if I knew a guy named Kevin Carroll or Kevin Carroll's sister, Shelly, who he seems to have known intimately. After a few minutes I said I was going to take a nap. That only made him louder. Angrier. When I still didn't respond he started cursing and threatening to kill me.

Finally, at three o'clock, they let me use the phone in the day room. I called Reva collect. She sounded in a panic.

"Denis, where are you?"
"At the jail."
"I thought...why? What happened?"
"They're holding me."

"What do you mean holding you? Denis, did they arrest you?"

"Yeah. Kind of."

She took an audible breath. "For what?"

I told her. That is, I told her how Erica Wainwright was framing me. I told her what Erica had said about her sister. I told her about the fingerprints on the gun and how they'd gotten there. There were things I didn't tell her. I didn't tell her about Goodwin's letter. She'd likely find out in time, but there was a small chance it wouldn't come up.

I was counting big on that small chance.

She listened in silence. Let me tell you, it was awful, that silence. Worse than if she'd screamed at me, beat on me with her fists. I had no idea if she believed me or not. Then the sobbing started, like a calf in a hailstorm, and I wished to god she would curse me instead. Anything but tears.

She blew her nose and said, "What are they charging you with?"

"Homicide, maybe."

I heard a gasp followed by a long, unsettling silence.

I said, "It was the fingerprints. That's all they got."

"But you told them how they got there?"

"Of course I did. Only I don't think they believe me."

Reva was silent a long time. For a moment I thought she'd hung up. Then I heard a low moan.

"Reev, please don't..."

That only made things worse.

"Why didn't you tell me about this last night?"

"About what?"

"About this crazy woman?"

"I didn't know she was crazy. I thought she just needed to talk. That's what bartenders do."

"She was carrying a gun. Didn't you think that was strange?"

"Lots of women carry guns these days."

"I don't know any—" She paused. "Why are you defending her?"

"I'm not—"

"Denis, have you thought what will happen to us if you go to jail?"

If? I thought. *Where does she think I am?*

"I'm not going to prison," I said. "I promise."

For a while we were both silent.

"Babe, I think I'm going to need a lawyer," I said. I told her to call Chad. He was friends with a few lawyers. And I asked if she could drop off my Ativan.

She didn't answer. She seemed unable to stop crying.

I told her I had to go and that I loved her and the twins and I hung up before I had to listen to any more crying.

I went back to the honeymoon suite. Believe it or not, I'd only been locked up once before. For a DUI. But that was before the panic attacks began and besides I was drunk at the time so it didn't bother me too much and besides I'd passed out after half an hour. This time I was stone cold sober. I lay on the steel cot and all I could think was how I was never getting out, and how I'd I spend the rest of my days locked up in a little box, and everything started to go all swirly and my heart drummed in my chest and the back of my throat felt like it was on fire and I could feel the fear rising up like a geyser. There was a call button in the cell and I buzzed the desk and a woman with a voice like a glacier answered.

"I think I'm having a panic attack," I said.

"Can I help you?"

"I think I'm having a panic attack."

"The call button in the cell is to be used for emergencies only. Is this an emergency?"

"Yes! I'm having a panic attack."

"The call buttons are not to be used by inmates for routine communication."

"But...this ain't..."

"Is this an emergency?"

Hell with it. I lay down again. I took off my socks and tied them into a blindfold and tied them around my head and I tried to get my mind on something else, only the fear was too great and I couldn't think. I pressed the call button again.

"Violation of the call button rules is a level two offense," she snapped. "Horseplay with the system will not be tolerated."

"Fucking bitch," I muttered, but only after I'd taken my hand off the button.

Some time passed before I was taken back to the interview room. Stakoff came in a short time later, fresh as a prince after a long afternoon nap and change of uniform. He sat down across from me. "How's it going?" he said.

"That woman you got working the call station is a real piece of work."

Stakoff laughed. "Claudia. I don't think she likes men very much."

He took off his glasses and wiped them on a handkerchief and slipped them back on his nose. "Good news," he said. "We've located the niece. According to her statement, she left the bar at eleven o'clock and went directly home."

"How is *that* good news?"

"Well, it's good news for us." Stakoff glanced at me over his glasses. "Oh, another thing. She claims her uncle never raped any one. Especially not her."

"I never said he raped *her*. She told me he raped her *sister*."

He waited for me to finish, then he cleared his throat. "She seemed to take the news of her uncle's death pretty hard."

My hands carved through my hair, clutching a clump and releasing it.

Stakoff said, "You want to try again? You want to tell me how your fingerprints got on the murder weapon?"

"I told you," I said. "She showed me the goddamn gun."

"Yeah, you said that. But yours were the only prints."

That stopped me. I tried to think back to that night. How she was getting ready to go home. Putting on her coat...

"Red mittens!" I said. "She had on a coat and a pair of red mittens."

Goddamn, she was good.

Stakoff's face was grave, almost like he felt sorry for me.

"Mittens?"

"Yeah," I said. "With sparkles."

"Sparkly mittens."

I slumped in my chair, defeated.

Stakoff rubbed the stubble on his chin. "Look Denis, I got no choice here. I already spoke to the prosecutor. No way can we let you go—not unless you tell me something I don't already know."

I shook my head. I had nothing.

"In that case..." He stood up. "I'll make sure you get a chance to call a lawyer before I leave."

"So you're charging me?" I said. "With murder?"

"Well, that's up to the prosecutor."

I locked eyes with Stakoff. "So this is how it happens," I said. "All those wrongful convictions you hear about. Half-assed police work by shit-for-brains cops."

Stakoff gave me a solemn look. "This ain't the time to be making enemies, Denis," he said. Then he was gone.

TWENTY-ONE

My lawyer reminded me one of those guys who spent all his time on a sailboat. Or at fundraising dinners.

Or fundraising dinners on sailboats.

Russ Toohey was in his mid-thirties. He fancied gray suits with chocolate brown vests and pink pocket handkerchiefs, his long hair squeezed into a man bun. Somehow he was able to pull it off. Sure you wanted to punch him in his pretty boy face, but you also wanted to sail away with him to Party Cove. For years I'd seen him around the slow pitch softball diamonds and outdoor concerts, always with some hot little number on his arm, always driving a shiny black Porsche. The guy was a frog, a social climber on steroids. My first thought was I'd never be able to afford him. Not without selling a kidney or two.

I sure hoped Chad knew what he was doing.

I'd been locked up going on nine hours when I was marched back to the sweat room. Toohey stood up and squeezed my hand, bench-presser hard.

"Would you like a water?" he said. "Always bring my own supply. I'm having a San Pellegrino."

"I'm good."

"Cool," he said. "Have a seat." Toohey picked up a

leather backpack from the floor, removed a yellow legal pad and set the backpack down by his feet. He took a ballpoint pen from his coat pocket and scribbled the date on the pad. Then he took a long, awkward moment to study my face. "So, Denis, what's your story?" he said.

"My story?"

"Yeah. What's up?"

"What's up is I'm being framed."

"No, I mean, tell me about yourself. I want to know who Denis is."

Who Denis is? What the hell was this, a new age therapy session? I was definitely not in the mood for that kind of nonsense. I was being set up by a psychopath and this hipster lawyer wanted to get to know my inner child.

"I'm not sure what you want to know," I said, my jaw tightening. "I'm happily married. We have two kids, twins. I'm co-owner of a bar...Am I getting warm?"

"Cool," he said. He removed his iPhone from his jacket pocket and set it down on the table between us. I had the feeling he was trying to impress me with his phone, like it was the latest generation or something. Like I gave a rat's ass.

"What bar?" he said.

"The Brass Lantern."

He brightened. "I thought I recognized you from somewhere. You tend bar there."

"I'm the manager as well as one of the owners."

"Cool place."

"Thanks." I had no recollection of seeing him there, but I could just imagine him and his law school buddies slumming among our working-class clientele, getting a big kick out of fraternizing with the great unwashed masses.

"What else?" he said.

"What else," I muttered. "My record is clean except for one DUI, when I was twenty."

"Cool."

My shoulders sagged. If he said "cool" one more time I was going to reach across the table and throttle him. "Can we talk about why we're here?"

He nodded, blue-gray eyes twinkling. "Why *are* we here, Denis?"

"I told you. I'm being set up."

"For killing Clay Goodwin."

"Yes!"

He folded his hands and placed them before him on the table. "Do you know who's framing you?"

"This woman who used to work for me. Erica Wainwright. She's Goodwin's niece."

He jotted the name down on his legal pad. "And why do you think she's framing you?"

"I don't know. I mean, I know why she killed Goodwin. She told me. She told me he molested her sister when they were kids. And later her sister killed herself."

"Did she tell you this before or after she allegedly killed Goodwin?"

"Before."

"I guess I'm confused," he said. "Why would she confess something so intimate...right before she commits murder?"

I shook my head. "Because she's a psycho? Hell I don't know, Russ. All I know is we'd been talking about her uncle. We had a mutual dislike for him."

"But why would she frame *you*?"

I could feel my ears getting hot and the anger swelling in my throat. "I've been trying to figure that out. Maybe she knew Goodwin was blackmailing me."

Toohey slumped back in his chair and crossed one leg over the other. "Okay, Denis. Let's back up. You just said Clay Goodwin was blackmailing you. Why would he do that?"

I hesitated. I wasn't sure how much I should tell him. I wasn't sure how much I could trust this clown. "What I'm about to tell you...it doesn't leave this room, right?"

"Absolutely."

"It's like attorney-client privilege, right? It can't be used against me?"

"That's correct. I'm representing *your* interests, Denis. Not the state's. The only time I have to report anything to the authorities is when I have information that a crime's about to be committed."

I nodded, satisfied.

"You were saying something about Clay Goodwin blackmailing you."

"You remember how they arrested my brother after the cops found a stash of weed at our bar?"

"Refresh my memory."

"It was four years ago. During our usual Friday night poker game. Me and my brothers—"

"At *your* bar?"

"Uh huh. Goodwin was our fourth. Our usual fourth couldn't make it so Vince asked Goodwin if he wanted to sit in. We'd been selling a little of Goodwin's weed for him, a fifty-fifty split."

Toohey held up his hand, cutting me off. "Wait, you sold weed at The Brass Lantern?"

"A little...on the side. I mean, we didn't have a choice. The bar wasn't making anybody rich. Not with all the chains and microbreweries opening all the time.

And we were splitting the profits four ways. I had a family to support. And a mortgage. I needed a sideline. It was that or get a job delivering pizzas."

"Which is legal."

I glared at him. Like he'd ever deliver fucking pizzas.

"Go on," he said.

"Like I said, we were selling a little weed, to frat boys, mostly. They'd pay at the bar and go around back to collect. It was Vince's idea to sell Goodwin's pot. I didn't like dealing with him because, well, because he was a little weasel and he has this crazy ass brother."

Toohey nodded.

"So it's like one o'clock in the morning and the game breaks up and Chad takes off. A few minutes later one of the Sika boys comes around looking to score some weed. Only he's into us for two hundred bucks already. He's got a friend with him, but she's only got like twenty bucks on her. I told him to come back when he's got the two Cs he owes me. Same as paying a bar tab, you know? He's cut off. Anyway this ass clown, he must've been stoned out of his gourd, because he pulls out this combat knife and starts waving it around, and I'm thinking, man this dude's hopping down the bunny trail. So I'm like, 'Whoa, take it easy, chief, I'll get you a bag,' and he's like, 'Fuck that, man, I want all the bags and everything in the safe.' Well, screw that. No way am I doing that, you know what I mean? Not when I keep my uncle's Winchester right behind the door.

"I don't care how high or stupid he is, he's got to know he ain't getting away with robbing the Carrolls. So I pull out the Winchester to scare him. Only he don't scare. Like I said, he was all hopped up on goofballs and the crazy bastard grabs the barrel." I paused. "Next thing you know the gun goes off.

"Self-defense," I said.

Toohey gave me a long look and waited for me to continue.

"The blast just about cut him in half. There's fucking blood and guts everywhere. I'd never shot no one before. I mean, I was in the army, but I never left the States. So I'm freaking out. I start to call nine-one-one, when Vince snatches the phone out of my hand and tells me to think about Reva and the twins. He's like, with these rube cops there's no telling what could happen, they could fuck up a one-car funeral. He says he'll handle it. He'll call the cops and I should get the hell out of there, go home. Like I was never there. Then he grabs Goodwin by the neck and says, 'Denis was never here, right?' And Goodwin hesitates, because like I said, he's a fucking weasel. He says he doesn't want to get involved and he sure as hell doesn't want to lie to the cops—this from the guy who's never said a true word in his whole goddamn life."

Toohey held silent, listening.

"That's when Goodwin says there was a chick with Sika and she saw the whole thing. Vince says the bitch is a junkie and won't say shit, but Goodwin doesn't want to go along. He's got to be difficult. So Vince—I probably shouldn't be telling you this—but Vince picks up the Winchester and plants the barrel under Goodwin's chin and screams, 'You are involved, fucker!' So what's he going to do? He says, 'Okay, okay, whatever you say, Vince.' He's about to shit his drawers." I paused. "That was pretty much it."

Toohey pulled a lozenge of some sort from his pocket and slowly unwrapped it and popped it into his mouth.

"Hmmm," he said.

"I honestly didn't think anything was going to happen. I mean, it was self-defense. Anyway, Vince called the cops and me and Goodwin went home. Only in all the excitement we forgot about the five pounds of weed Goodwin had brought over, just sitting there stacked on top of the safe. I still can't believe it. We remembered everything else. We wiped my prints off the shotgun and everything, but in all the chaos I forgot about the weed and Vince thought I'd put it in the safe.

"I got about halfway home when I remembered. I tried to call Vince, but my calls kept going to voicemail. I must've called him a dozen times. I left messages."

I breathed in steadily and looked at Toohey. "Five pounds of homegrown staring the cops right in the face."

Toohey wrinkled his brow and leaned forward. "Now I remember. Travis Neighbors handled that one. Prosecutor didn't think it was a robbery, if I recall. Thought it was a drug deal gone bad, only he couldn't make a case. All they had on your brother was the dope. A lot of dope, though." He paused. "How'd they get Vince to admit the weed was his?"

"They said they were going to dust the packages. Vince's prints wouldn't have been on there, but mine sure as hell would've."

Toohey shook his head. "Not without a warrant, they wouldn't have."

I shrugged. "That's what Vince's lawyer said too. Only *after* he'd confessed."

He leaned back in his chair and nodded thoughtfully. "What else?"

I shrugged. "That's about it."

"Your brother served how many years?"

"Four."

Toohey glanced at me, a quizzical look on his face. "So where does the blackmail come in?"

"About two years ago, Goodwin pays me a visit. He wants me to start selling his weed again. Seems he's having a hard time moving product and him and his brother, stepbrother, whatever, got debts they can't pay. Only this time instead of a fifty-fifty split, it's more like eighty-twenty. He lets me know in no uncertain terms that if I refuse, he pays a visit to Belleville five-oh, tells them what really happened that night."

Toohey set down his pen and laced his hands behind his head. "You said it was a robbery. An act of self-defense. Why would it matter who shot Sika?"

"Right, but like you said, the cops and the prosecutor never really believed that story. Goodwin was going to tell them what they wanted to hear, that he witnessed the whole thing, that it was a drug deal gone bad or some shit like that."

Toohey looked grave. "Was it?"

"It was a robbery. Like I've been saying."

Toohey picked up his pen and tapped it absently on the legal pad. "So now the cops think you killed Goodwin because he was blackmailing you?"

"They don't know he was blackmailing me. At least I don't think they do."

He lifted an eyebrow. "Really? They don't know?"

"I don't think so. How would they?"

"That's motive, you understand. If they find out about that, they've got their case."

I was silent a long moment.

He continued. "So if they don't know about the blackmail, why do they think you killed him?"

"They have no idea. All they know is they got my prints on the murder weapon and that I was broke down by Goodwin's house about a week ago."

Toohey's brow furrowed. "What were you doing out there?"

"I was just out driving around. I do that sometimes when I want to think. You can't think at my house with the twins and the TV and all the noise. Then my piece of shit truck broke down. It just happened to be by Goodwin's house."

"And Goodwin saw you ought there?"

"No. A neighbor did. Some paranoid old geezer. He called the sheriff. And somebody told Goodwin."

"I'm confused. Why'd the neighbor call the sheriff? You said your truck broke down."

"Right. Broke down on a public road. The old fart thought I was a burglar or something. Like I said, he was like crazy paranoid."

Toohey shook his head. He scribbled a few notes on the legal pad. "Okay. Back to the niece. Ms. Wainwright. You told her you were being blackmailed?"

"I haven't even told my own wife about that."

Toohey stared.

"I've been thinking about this a lot," I said. "Maybe she knew, maybe she didn't."

"The niece?"

I nodded. "Maybe she suspected it. Or maybe Goodwin told her he was blackmailing me. For all I know, she could've been blackmailing *him* and threatening to go to the cops about the rape. Maybe he needed to shake me down to pay her off. Who the hell knows?"

"Whoa. This is starting to make my head swim," Toohey said.

"Tell me about it."

"Anyway, if she was blackmailing Goodwin, it wouldn't make sense for her to kill him. Why kill the golden goose?"

I shrugged. He had a point, damn it.

He took up one of the documents and studied it. "According to Stakoff, the niece denied the rape story. Said she never talked to you about her sister being raped. Stakoff said she was devastated by the news of her uncle's death."

I felt a lump in my stomach the size of a football. "She's lying."

Toohey set down the document and closed the file. "I got to tell you, Denis, this doesn't look great."

Suddenly things had stopped being "cool" I guess. I breathed in steadily and looked down at the table, my nails biting into my palms.

"However, we do have one thing going for us. Right now the prosecution doesn't know Goodwin was blackmailing you. That's huge. But those fingerprints on the murder weapon. That's going to be a tough one to explain away." Toohey shook his head. "First things first. We have a bail hearing in the morning with Judge Eckert. Just a warning: if he grants bail, it won't be cheap."

Of course not.

"Fortunately I know a guy," Toohey said. He stood up and pocketed his phone. "I'm going to do my best. Just try to take it easy." He hefted his leather backpack and opened the flap and dropped the notepad inside. Then he slipped the backpack over his shoulder.

He picked up his expensive bottle of water. "Kind of ironic, isn't it?"

"What is?"

"You get away with a killing you did commit and the county wants to charge you for one you didn't."

"Ironic don't begin to describe it."

TWENTY-TWO

Bail was set at two hundred large. Toohey seemed to think this was a great victory for us. He said downstate judges don't often grant bail in homicide cases, and when they do, it's usually a million bucks. Lucky for us, there'd been a last-second development.

The cops had traced the revolver. It seems the gun had been reported stolen four months ago from The Hideaway, a dive bar in west Belleville. Turned out Erica Wainwright had been a bartender there up until three months ago. She'd been fired, but the owner wouldn't say why.

Circumstantial, but enough to get a lower bail.

I had to come up with ten percent of that. Twenty thousand. Chump change for a tycoon like me.

Toohey went to speak to Dan the Bail Bondsman (*In the Can? Call Dan!*) and I was taken back to my home sweet cell.

I lay on my cot all afternoon with my socks tied around my head. It helped with the panic attacks if I couldn't see anything, and helped turn my thoughts from how I was going to spend the rest of my life locked away in a little cage till they found me dead some morning, hanged by my own trouser leg.

Toohey returned at seven o'clock, casually dressed in some kind of tight stretchy gray-striped capris, his long hair loose behind his ears. I asked him if he'd remembered my Ativan.

He nodded. "They would only let me to bring in one pill though. They're holding onto the bottle so you don't overdose."

He dropped the pill into my palm and I dry-swallowed it.

He seemed upbeat. "Good news. If all goes well, you should be free by morning."

I gagged on the Ativan.

Toohey stood up. "Sorry, I should've offered you some Fiji water."

I motioned for him to sit. On the second attempt the pill went down.

Toohey's grin was a mile wide. Those expensively whitened teeth of his lit up the inside of the room like a refrigerator light. "Cool, huh?"

I coughed and nodded.

"Just one thing. You'll have to put up your house for collateral. That'll mean filing a deed of trust making the bail company the beneficiary. I've already talked to your wife. She's agreed to sign."

"Really?" That surprised the hell out of me.

"And you'll still need about twenty-one K."

"Might as well be twenty-one million," I sighed. "Twenty-one thousand for a crime I didn't commit?"

Toohey shrugged. "I know. The point is to make sure you show up in court."

"The point is to make sure I remain behind bars." I shook my head. "I don't think I can swing that. We kind of live paycheck to paycheck."

"Hmm," Toohey said. He tapped the eraser of his pencil against his sparkling white teeth. "Do you have anything you can sell? Stocks? Bonds? Mutual funds?"

"You mean my investment portfolio?"

"Exactly."

"Ain't got one."

"Is there someone you can borrow from?"

I shook my head.

"How about a vehicle?"

"I got a 2009 Dodge Ram 1500. It ought to be worth about that."

"Truck's paid off?"

"Few months ago," I said.

"Cool," he said. "I know a guy who might be able to help us there."

Somehow that didn't surprise me.

So much for being free and clear.

"I'll just need the title." He stood up and slung his leather backpack over his shoulder. "Like I said, if everything goes smoothly you should be out early as tomorrow morning."

We shook hands and he rapped on the door.

"Just try to take it easy and remember I'm on the case."

"Cool," I said.

TWENTY-THREE

The next morning I was a free man. As free as an American male can be with a murder rap hanging over him and no wheels.

Not that the cops were done with me—not by a long shot.

I found Reva in the lobby of the jail. It was ten in the morning and she looked like she hadn't slept, but she seemed more relieved than angry. She let me hug her, but when I went in for a kiss I got her cheek. Still, it was more than I expected.

"How're the twins?" I said.

"I told them you went out of town on business. That was the first time I've had to lie to them."

I nodded. "Where are they?"

"With my parents."

I took her arm. "Let's get out of here." We walked in silence to the van, ice crunching under our boots. It had begun to flurry, small flakes drifting up and down on a biting wind. To be honest, Reva's behavior kind of pissed me off. This time I truly hadn't done anything wrong.

I went around and eased into the passenger seat. I waited till she started the engine. "You act like I'm guilty of something," I said. "Is that what you think?"

A TASTE OF SHOTGUN

She stared straight ahead, biting her bottom lip. "I don't know what to think, Denis. I had a feeling something like this would happen when Vince got out. I just knew it."

"Yeah, you keep saying that."

That pissed me off too, the way she kept blaming my brother for everything. I was more to blame than he was for the way things were. Of course I wasn't going to say that. Anyway, I was exhausted and it was all starting to get mixed up in my head. I couldn't wait to get home and take a scalding hot shower and maybe open a bottle of Jim Beam.

The last thing I felt like doing was fighting with my wife, but I had to defend my brother, at least a little.

"Babe, Vince had nothing to do with this," I said. I looked over at her and saw her tearing up. I kept my hands in my lap. I wasn't in the mood to get slapped in the face.

The van idled noisily and she bowed her head. "What's going to happen to us if you go to prison?"

"I'm not going to prison," I said. "I promise." I was just talking, trying to calm her down. I had no idea what was going to happen to me. Now that I was free—at least temporarily—all I could think about was that letter Goodwin had given to some lawyer. Whoever had it would be turning it over to the cops at any moment. If he hadn't already.

Reva turned to me. "Denis, I want you to tell me what's going on," she said. "The truth. No more of your lies."

"When did I lie to you?"

"You've started selling drugs again, haven't you?" she said.

My stomach had a heavy, sick feeling that made my face grow hot and my thoughts collide. "Of course not. Why would you even say that?"

I couldn't tell if she bought it or not. There was no reason for her not to believe me. So far, Vince had taken the blame for everything: Sika's shooting, the weed found at the bar. She probably blamed him for Goodwin's murder too. She had to have suspected something though, the way I always walked around with my pockets stuffed with twenty- and fifty-dollar bills, the text messages—which I know she sometimes read on the sly—the late-night calls to my cell phone from Goodwin.

Reva turned to me now. Her eyes flashed and sent a shockwave up my spinal column. "If you're lying to me, Denis, I swear to god I'll take the kids and leave you."

I swallowed hard. "Babe, I'm not lying."

She turned away. "God help us if you are."

TWENTY-FOUR

Four days after Clay Goodwin's murder a winter storm dumped three inches of ice on our town. There was the usual collateral damage: burst water pipes, fallen tree limbs that dragged down power lines, drainage ditches overflowing with wrecked vehicles. The town shut down. Out on the interstate, six tractor trailers piled up in a crunchy chain reaction you could hear two towns over. Motorists were stranded up to eight hours. Some ran out of gas or drained their batteries and deserted their vehicles like dead Palominos and wandered off in search of sanctuary, but found only abandoned houses. Lacking electricity, the homeowners had fled to motels or relatives' homes in other towns. Desperadoes broke into grocery stores and stole what little food remained on the shelves. Old folks froze to death in their beds.

I boot-skated down to The Brass Lantern to survey the damage. I expected to find the joint looted, the door kicked in, windows busted out, the booze hauled off in wheelbarrows. Surprisingly the bar was untouched. Later, after the roads were salted, I drove the van over to Sara's to check on her. Hers was one of the few blocks that hadn't lost power. She said that Chad had already dropped by to check on her and make sure her alarm system was still working. That was the main thing. The goddamn alarm. He'd brought over a bucket of Kentucky Fried Chicken and mashed potatoes and gravy. I felt stupid standing there empty-handed.

"I'll stop by again tomorrow," I said.

"Bring KFC next time," she said.

We lost power at our house, but we had an older home with a working fireplace. For warmth we fed the flames every scrap of wood we could scavenge, including fallen branches and the twins' high chairs. For light we burned kerosene lanterns and scented candles. We wrapped ourselves in ancient quilts, made hot tea and cocoa in the fireplace, and played stiff-fingered board games. We lugged the mattresses down from the bedrooms and slept in front of the fire. I stayed up most of the night sipping Southern Comfort and keeping the fire stoked and watching my family slumber in the mellow glow of the fireplace and tried not to think about what might've happened if I'd still been in the county jail instead of there tending to that fire. The idea of not being around for my family really freaked me out. Maybe for the first time.

By Monday the temperatures were in the low twenties and the neighbors began drifting home one by one. That afternoon Toohey called, asked if we could meet. I could just imagine what he wanted. I'd heard the county prosecutor was having his top investigators pull double shifts in hopes of finding something to tie me and Vince to Goodwin's murder. St. Clair County had more than its share of homicides, but most of the murders involved blacks so the cops weren't under a whole lot of pressure to solve or even investigate those cases. But the murder of a white man—even white trash like Clay Goodwin—

didn't happen every day. That moved things up to a whole other level. The cops got interested, the local news took notice, and the county prosecutor saw a chance to get his name in the paper, maybe win a few votes. They took it serious. Toohey said he'd drop by the bar around four.

The library remained closed so I borrowed Reva's van to drive to the bar and opened at three o'clock, as usual. There were a handful of customers, a couple of laid-off roofers, a lawyer, a young guy on disability who didn't look disabled in the least, and three frat boys who tried to score some weed and threw a hissy fit when I said I didn't know what they were talking about. They ordered a round of beers and stuck around awhile sulking, maybe hoping I'd change my mind. After they finished the round they left, I hoped for good.

At four on the dot, Toohey strode in wearing some kind of gay luxury parka. I nodded toward the back room and he followed me down the hall. He plopped down on the sofa while I perched on the corner of my desk.

"I see you survived the storm," he said. "The bar appears to have made it through unscathed."

"Uh huh."

"Cool," he said. "So how you doing? You holding up alright?"

"Like a champ," I said. "What'd you want to tell me?"

He popped a lozenge into his mouth and glanced around the room. "Little update. The prosecution is getting cold feet, their case is starting to unravel. First we traced the stolen gun back to a bar where Erica Wainwright was working, now she's MIA. They never had much of a case to begin with, if you ask me." He paused. "That was some fancy detective work on our part."

"Our part?"

"Well, my part. I was the one who found out she tended bar at The Hideaway at the time the gun was stolen. I mean, the cops may have known it, but they weren't commenting on it. I had to let *them* know that *we* knew, if you know what I mean."

"So, they arrest her yet?"

"They don't believe she killed anyone. They still think it's more likely you or Vince killed Goodwin and that it was drug-related. It's just too much of a coincidence that Goodwin turns up dead a few days after your brother is released. But right now, other than the prints, they got nothing. Don't get me wrong, the prints are huge. But as long as they don't find out about Goodwin blackmailing you, they'll have no choice but to drop the charges."

Toohey stood up, glanced around the room, at the walls covered with dusty framed photographs of my father and Uncle Chuck shaking hands with the semi-famous people who'd stumbled into the bar over the past forty years.

"Anyway that's the update." He studied the signature on a photo and whistled. "Wow, Buddy Hackett was here. Impressive." He stuck out his hand. "I'll let you get back to your customers."

After he left, I sat for a while staring blankly at Uncle Chuck next to Buddy Hackett's goofy mug. For a moment, I thought about running after Toohey and telling him about the letter. It would have been the smart thing to do.

That must be why I didn't do it.

TWENTY-FIVE

I needed a set of wheels, so I caught the cross-town bus to my mother's house. First time I'd been on a city bus since high school and it depressed the hell out of me, sitting among all those poor, mostly black people, folks who couldn't afford even the crappiest cars. Most of them seemed to be on their way to work too, which made the ride even more sad. I got off at 13th Street and hoofed it six blocks over melting sidewalks to Sara's house.

Sara was pretty much a shut-in. The only times she left home were for doctor's visits—a waste of time and money since she wouldn't do anything the doctor recommended anyway—and Christmas and Easter church services. She'd gotten so heavy she had a hard time prying her big butt out of her bariatric lounger, let alone walking. She was only sixty-two but her knees were shot and she required a heavy-duty walker to make her hourly trips from the refrigerator to the toilet. (While taking out her garbage, I discovered that she'd begun wearing adult diapers, no doubt to reduce the number of bathroom trips.) She'd stopped sleeping in her bed four years ago. The bedroom was too far away and besides the concept of day and night had lost meaning for her. She was somehow beyond time. She kept her heavy living room drapes closed all the time, so the only way she knew whether it was morning, noon, or night was by what show was on the TV. Not that it mattered what was on. She'd happily watch eight hours of some guy getting kicked repeatedly in the nuts. Her favorite show was the local news—horror stories of gangbangers shooting each other that made her even more afraid to go outside, never mind that those killings took place in the city, forty miles away.

The little bungalow was shut up tighter than Fort Knox, protected by two alarm systems (in case one failed) and a backup generator (in case the power went out or North Korean hackers sabotaged the power grid). She had bars on the windows and high-tech motion lights. The security companies made a fortune off her. If all else failed, she had her late husband's Remington pump-action shotgun, which remained permanently within arm's reach on the floor beside her chair. Even when the twins visited, she wouldn't part with the shotgun.

I can't imagine what she thought thieves would steal. Her old newspapers and empty pizza boxes? I couldn't see the point of living like that. I'd rather be dead. Not Sara though. Her only purpose in life seemed to be to stay alive. And eat. And watch TV.

A maze of boxes containing assorted junk snaked through her living room and dining room, with just enough space for a corridor to the front door and the handicapped accessible bathroom. With the exception of the fridge, she never used the kitchen, which was buried under boxes and broken appliances and trash that she was afraid to take outside. That was my job, to drive over to her house once a week (I usually made it every other week) and take out the trash.

A TASTE OF SHOTGUN

Her meals were delivered by Meals on Wheels, but they were seldom enough to satisfy her voracious appetite, so she'd usually pick up the phone and order a second course of Domino's Pizza. It was convenient because she didn't even have to heat the food up. They did everything but shovel the slop down her throat.

I pulled a flask from my coat pocket and slugged some gin and walked up the slush-covered sidewalk prepared for combat. Even if Roy's pickup was just sitting there, rusting on the concrete pad in the backyard, Sara wasn't going to give it up without a fight.

I knocked on the front door and let myself in. "It's me, Ma! Denis!" I called, hoping she'd hear me over the screaming TV and wouldn't blow my goddamn head off with the shotgun.

"Who's there?" she screamed. Sara had a voice like a sack of drowning cats.

"Denis!"

I had ten seconds to disarm the alarm. This was always a challenge because you never knew when she'd change the alarm code and not tell you. This time the code worked. I got it disarmed with two seconds to spare.

"Chad?"

"It's Denis!"

"Oh." She sounded disappointed.

I followed the corridor of pizza boxes and newspapers back to the living room. There she sat, squeezed into her lounger like an overcooked sausage, watching FOX News. Like her oldest son, Sara was a die-hard right-winger convinced the country was being hijacked by radical Muslim feminist communists and that the end days were coming soon.

"There's two bags of trash in the kitchen," she said,

by way of greeting.

"I'm not here about the trash," I yelled over the TV.

"Then what're you here for?"

There were few things I hated worse than asking my mother for a favor. I picked up a stack of newspapers and heaped them atop another pile of newspapers and sat down on the edge of the sofa.

"You're getting my papers all mixed up," she snapped.

"I'll put them back before I go. Just like they were."

"That's what you said last time and you got February's papers mixed up with January and December's." She turned back to the television. "If you didn't come to take out the garbage, what'd you come for? I know you didn't come to visit me."

You got that right, I thought. I cleared my throat. "I need to borrow Roy's pickup."

She turned and fixed me with a hard stare. "What happened to your vehicle?"

I'd decided to lie. It would be easier and I am all about easier. "It's in the shop."

"Didn't they give you a loaner?"

"No, Ma, that's why I need to borrow Roy's pickup."

"Roy would never have let you kids borrow his truck, you know that."

"Ma, we're not kids any more, and besides, Roy's dead."

"I know that. You think I don't know that?"

I could feel a headache coming on like a runaway engine. "What I'm saying is, it's your truck now. You can do whatever you want with it. You can sell it or you can lend it to one of your sons or you can drive it over Niagara Falls."

Sara frowned. "I'd never sell Roy's truck."

"Fine, Ma. Don't sell it—"

She held up her hand to cut me off and glanced toward the television set. "Quiet, I want to hear this."

The television set was enormous, about the size of a barn door. Roy hadn't been rich exactly, but he'd done all right for himself. One of those guys you hear about, a lot of money but never spends a dime, lives in a cluttered little house and eats fast food for every meal. His one extravagance was the enormous television. I waited till the talking head's rant was over, then I brought the conversation back to Roy's truck. "So? About the pickup?"

"What's wrong with your truck?"

"They're not sure."

"Why don't you drive the van?"

"Reva's driving the van, Ma. She's got to take the twins to school and then drive to work."

"What's wrong with the bus?"

"For me or Reva?"

"Either one of you. We pay good money in taxes to keep them buses running. People ought to use them or else we ought to get rid of them. Waste of taxpayer money, if you ask me."

I'd had enough. I stood up. "Ma, I ain't asking, okay? I need to borrow Roy's truck and that's that."

"What if I need it?"

"What are you talking about? You never leave the house." What's more, she'd need a forklift to get her big ass behind the wheel of that truck.

"What if I need to go to the store or to the emergency room?" she wailed.

"Ma, you get all of your meals and groceries delivered—"

"What if—"

"—and if you need to go to the hospital call Chad. He'll bring the ambulance personally."

"What if I want to go to church?"

"When was the last time you went to church?"

"Last month."

That was a lie. Probably. "Watch TV church," I said.

"It ain't the same."

"Goodbye, Ma."

"Denis James!" she bellowed.

I walked into the kitchen and found Roy's keys hanging on the key rack.

"Don't you take that truck!" she cried. "I swear to god I'll call the police!"

"Bye Ma."

As I closed the kitchen door, she yelled, "Don't forget to take out the trash!"

TWENTY-SIX

I got Erica Wainwright's address off her job application and drove Roy's foul, trash-reeking truck (windows down, heater on full blast) to her house. I wanted to look her in the eye when I asked why she'd ruined my life. The address turned out to be a snow-covered surface parking lot surrounded by ruined chain-link and choked with weeds and strewn with exploded garbage bags.

I sat in the truck, fuming, trying to decide my next move. I found Amber's number in my phone and called her. The call went to voicemail, so I put the truck in gear and drove out to Denny's, which sat just off the highway. Her Ford Ranger was parked on the back lot.

It was mid-afternoon and the place had mostly cleared out. Amber was chatting with an old couple in a back booth, a pot of coffee in one hand. I took a seat at the counter. She glanced at me and raised her eyebrows.

After a while, she drifted over behind the counter.

"Hey there. Surprised to see you here. Late lunch?"

"Yeah. I mean, no. Just coffee, please."

"Regular or decaf?"

"Whatever you got there's fine."

She turned over a mug and poured. "One decaf." She set the pot on a warmer and turned back to me. "How's

Reva and the twins?"

"Fine, thanks. How's uh…"

She waited, forehead wrinkled, watching me squirm. "uhhhh…"

"Shelby Lynn."

"Yeah."

"Shelby Lynn is real good. Thanks for asking."

I picked up a menu for something to do.

"You didn't come in for a cup of decaffeinated coffee," she said.

"Actually, no." I hunched forward, arms crossed on the countertop. "I'm a little worried about your friend."

"Which friend?"

"Erica."

"Erica Wainwright? Why? What happened to Erica?"

"She hasn't shown up to work for a couple of days. Been like three days."

"You called her?"

"Yeah, I called her. Her phone says it's out of service."

An old guy in dirty overalls and a Peterbilt cap at the far end of the counter signaled with his coffee mug. "Be right back," Amber said. She filled the old guy's mug and made some obligatory flirty small talk and drifted back.

"Let me try calling her," she said.

She slipped her phone from her apron pocket and walked back to the kitchen area. I sipped my coffee and swung my gaze around the restaurant. Old people, mostly, helping each other in and out of booths, hands cupped to their ears. Walkers parked like baby chairs at the end of tables.

"Got her voicemail," Amber said. "I asked her to give

me a call when she got a minute."

I set down the mug and screwed on a look of concern. "I think somebody ought to check on her."

"Since when do you take such interest in the welfare of your employees?"

I smiled, but I didn't say anything. "You wouldn't know her address, by chance?"

"So you haven't been to her place then?"

"No, I haven't been to her place," I said with a scowl. "Are you going to help me out here or not?"

"I don't know. She might not want me to give out her personal information."

I frowned at her.

"Couldn't you get it off her application?"

"I could, but I don't want to have to go all the way back to the bar."

"It'd be on the way."

I tapped my fingers on the counter.

"Oh, hold on." She grabbed her purse from under the counter and dug through it. A call bell rang and an order came up so she had to take care of that. Five minutes passed before she returned.

"Fifty-five Cheshire."

She was right, the bar was on the way to her house. I stood up and pulled out my wallet and put a ten down on the counter. "Thanks." I turned to go.

"If she asks, you got it off her application. Not from me."

"You're the best," I said and gave her a backhanded wave on my way out.

"The best what?" she said.

I let that hang out there.

TWENTY-SEVEN

I pulled up as Erica was walking to her car. Behind her, she pulled a small suitcase on wheels and she carried a bouquet of yellow roses. I inched down in the seat and drove on. Four houses down, I pulled over to the curb. Roy's truck was missing both rearview and driver's side mirrors, so I watched her out of the cracked passenger side. She eased into an older model Toyota Camry. The car was crammed with stuff, like she was leaving town in a hurry.

The Camry backed out of the driveway and headed south. I made a U-turn and followed, keeping a safe distance between vehicles, glad for once to be driving Roy's stinking but unrecognizable truck.

She turned onto Main and drove west, away from downtown. If she was leaving town, there wasn't a lot I could do about that. I sure wasn't going to follow her across the country in that old beater.

Main Street narrowed from three lanes to two. As the Toyota passed the Catholic church, her turn signal blinked on and she hung a right into one of the shabbier cemeteries in town. I pulled over to the curb and waited as the Camry disappeared from view. After a few minutes passed, I followed her inside the cemetery.

The cemetery reminded me of a creepy winter wonderland; beautiful in a ghoulish kind of way with the old growth oaks and hickories and weathered stones standing tall and capped with snow and ice. Just how the dead like it, I supposed.

The Camry was parked about a quarter mile in. Empty. I scanned the graveyard. The land rose on both sides of the road and was speckled with fresh graves. On one side lay thickets of pines where the land gave way. I spied her halfway up the hillside. She was placing the yellow flowers in a stone vase beside one of the newer headstones. I pulled up behind the Camry and parked but kept the motor running. Erica turned and glanced at the truck, then turned back. I bet that old truck creeped her out plenty.

I sat in the pickup a moment studying my next move. It wasn't too late to turn around, forget the whole thing, though if she *was* leaving town this would be my last chance to confront her.

What the hell. I reached into my jacket and pulled out the flask and took a good long pull, then I opened the door and climbed out. An icy wind sliced right through to my bones and stung my cheeks. I zipped up my jacket and started up the hill.

Erica turned again and studied me cautiously. I was too far away to make out her expression, but I assumed it was one of confusion and alarm. She must have recognized me by now and she glanced down the road like she expected someone to drive up suddenly. I gave her a quick disarming wave. "Hello!" I called.

She shielded her eyes and again glanced down the road. No one.

I went on, slipping in the snow every four or five

steps and cursing under my breath.

Erica watched me, unblinking. Her hand slipped into her handbag like she was searching for something. My thoughts went to the automatic she'd used to dispatch her uncle.

Old Rusty.

I paused a few yards away to catch my breath. "Quite a climb," I huffed.

She breathed steadily but didn't say a word.

"You're a hard one to track down," I said.

"Not hard enough, I guess."

I smiled at that. "I wanted to talk to you." I glanced at the yellow roses at the base of a headstone a few feet away.

Margaret Neel Wainwright
Dec. 4, 1989—Nov. 17, 2007
The Greatest Gift in Life is Love

"Your sister? The one you were telling me about?"

She nodded and her hand rifled through her handbag. She wasn't even trying to hide it. The short hairs on the back on my neck stood up. I swallowed hard. "That's what I wanted to ask you about," I said. "It seems you told the cops a different story than you told me. Made it sound like your uncle was some kind of saint."

Her eyes shifted toward the jagged rows of neglected graves. "I wouldn't trust anything the police say."

"So you didn't tell the cops that Clay never raped your sister?"

She bit her bottom lip. "Actually, I should be going. It's getting late." She took a tentative step.

I put out my hand. "Sure," I said. "But before you go

I got to ask you something..."

She halted. "I really should..." She tried to move around me, but I stepped in front of her.

"Won't take but a second," I said. "Really. I just want to know why you did it. Why you set me up?"

She cut her eyes up at me briefly then looked away. "You really don't know, do you?"

"Look, I can't blame you for wanting to kill your uncle. Who wouldn't? But why try to pin it on me?"

She squared herself but didn't answer.

"Did you know he was blackmailing me?"

She smiled at that. Even now I couldn't help but think what a pretty smile. But the way she kept her hand stuffed into her handbag gave me the willies.

"It wasn't that," she said.

"So what was it?"

I followed her gaze to a nearby headstone, not far from her sister's marker. I felt the backs of my legs go weak.

John Wayne Sika
Born 1990
Died 2010
Gone Too Soon

"We were going to be married that fall," she said. "If it wasn't for you."

I swallowed hard, my hands clenching and unclenching. "I don't know what you're talking about."

"Don't," she said, shaking her head. "I was there the night you killed Johnny. He was just a boy. A silly, impulsive boy. But you murdered him because you thought he was working with the cops."

"You're crazy," I hissed through my teeth.

That's where I'd seen her before. The chick in Sika's car. The one that got away. I pictured her face framed in the rear window.

"You'd have killed me too, if my uncle hadn't stopped you." She narrowed her eyes on me like blades. "Yeah. Uncle Clay saved my life. Ironic, isn't it?"

I didn't say anything. What was the point? The chick was crazy as a loon.

She went on. "And what happens to you? Not a goddamn thing."

I steadied myself and my sinews tightened like a spring. "Look, I don't know what you think you saw, or what that pedophile uncle of yours said, but I do know what happened that night. Your boyfriend tried to hold up the bar, or have you forgot about that? Have you forgot that he pulled a knife on me? Or the way he went for my shotgun? The cops investigated it. You know, real detectives."

Her eyes had gone distant and she shook from the cold. I was sure she had that handgun trained right on my guts, the trigger half squeezed. Something told me I was seconds away from finding out.

"Now you know," she said. Her hand slipped from the bag.

Fireworks exploded in my eyes, then searing heat, like a red hot poker rammed into my sockets. A loud high-pitched scream rent the air. It was a moment before I realized where it was coming from.

It was coming from me.

Goddamn pepper spray.

I flailed blindly. I lunged at her and my feet flew out from under me and I dropped like a bag of wet cement. I got to my knees just in time to receive a powerful kick in the groin. I sank back in the snow and howled in pain. I struck out again and caught hold of one of her boots and I felt her go down.

Then I lost her.

I scooped up handfuls of snow and scrubbed my eyes, rubbed them raw. My eyes burned so bad I hardly noticed the pain in the crotch.

I rolled on my back and listened to the sound of my blood pounding in my temples. I listened for the sound of footfalls in the snow, the crank of a car engine. But all I heard were some crows cawing from distant branches and vehicles hissing by on Main Street.

I wiped the snot and drool from my face and watched the world go from a blistering blindness to blurry. The first thing I could make out was Erica. She wasn't five feet away, lying at the base of her sister's tombstone. She didn't stir. My insides went all hollow. I crawled over to where she laid face down like a dark-haired snow angel. I squatted on my heels in the snow and gently turned her over.

Her eyes were half open and stared straight through me. A thin string of blood trickled out of her nose and a long purple bruise led to a deep ugly gash at the top of her skull.

She wasn't breathing.

She wasn't anything.

A coldness gathered in the pit of my stomach. This did not look good. It sure as hell didn't look like an accident. Not with all the footprints in the snow. Not with pepper spray residue all over the fucking place.

It had murder written all over it.

Try explaining this one away, Carroll.

I lost it for a minute. I grabbed her shoulders and

shook her till her brains rattled.

Nothing.

I braced my arm against the stone and hefted myself up and glanced around the cemetery, at the darkening woods and the last patch of light bounded by shadows. On the far side of the road, near the top of the rise, stood a stocky woman in a heavy gray coat holding a wreath of some sort. She looked right at me, her mouth agape.

Where the hell had she come from?

It wasn't hard to guess what was going through her mind. The old woman dropped the wreath, turned, and lumbered up the hill, fast as her stout little legs could carry her.

I started down the hill after her, waving my arms and trying not to startle her too much. "Wait!" I shouted. "Ma'am! Hold on! We need help!"

She disappeared over the rise.

"Hold on! We've had an accident!" I shouted. "We need help!"

I hoped to god she was alone so I could talk to her, reason with her, make her see it wasn't what she thought. I slipped and fell on my ass, twice, then raced across the road and up the other side, calling on her to wait. I stepped over the wreath she'd dropped when she crested the hill. "Beloved Husband," it read.

At top of the hill I paused to catch my breath. A gray Oldsmobile Cutlass was parked on the road. Other than that, the cemetery was deserted. I went on, following the footprints in the snow that led to a large tombstone not more than fifty feet away.

She was lying behind the stone, weeping silently. I scooped up another handful of snow and rubbed my eyes. Things were beginning to come into focus again.

I stood over the old woman and I untucked my shirt and wiped my eyes with my T-shirt. She lay there, flailing comically like an overturned tortoise. She was having a hard time catching her breath. "Don't..." she cried. "Please..."

I tucked my shirt back in and dug a couple of Ativan out of my pants' pocket and washed them down with a slug of gin. Best birthday gift Reva ever gave me, that flask.

Hell if I could figure what was wrong with her. Maybe she'd fallen and broken a hip. Maybe she was having a coronary. Anyway, there was nothing I could do about it.

The sun had dropped behind the trees and the hillside was sunk in gray shadows. Another half hour and it'd be dark. In the bare treetops, the biggest black birds I'd ever seen kicked up a terrific racket.

"Please..." she said. "I can't...breathe."

"Lady, I ain't going to hurt you. Just like I didn't hurt that other woman."

That other woman.

I walked back to the top of the hill and gazed across the road at my tracks in the snow and saw how they led to a small black mound halfway up the opposite hill. From the road you couldn't tell what was what. It could have been anything.

I turned back to the old woman. "What's your name?"

"I can't...breathe."

"Yeah. You said that. I asked you what your name is?"

The question pushed the color out of her face, and her lips trembled. "Hel-en."

I held out the flask. "Well, Helen, how'd you like a slug of Beefeater? Good for what ails you. No? A teetotaler, huh? Good for you." I took another slug and squatted on my heels beside her. "Okay, tell you what, Helen, I'm going to get you some help. You just hold tight, okay? Just take her easy, you hear?"

It seemed unlikely that anyone else was going to visit the cemetery that time of night. Unless it was some punk kids looking for a place to get high or a patrol car making sure there weren't any punk kids in here getting high.

But you never know.

I stood up and walked over to a large headstone. My shoes were packed with snow and my toes were frozen. I took off my shoes and knocked them against the headstone, then I slipped them back on over my wet socks feeling cold and miserable. I wasn't worried about the old woman. She wouldn't last long out here in the elements, and no one was going to stumble on her behind that big old stone, at least not for a day or two. And there was nothing to tie me to her. Nothing at all. But I *was* worried about Erica Wainwright. I couldn't just leave her lying about for the authorities to find. Too many people knew I was looking for her. And why I was looking for her. I'd have to move her. Somehow.

I couldn't think straight. I was too cold. Too tired. Too shook up.

Even if I got her into Roy's truck, there would still be the problem of her car. I'd have to get rid of her *and* her car. Permanently.

First things first. I had to move Roy's truck. I got to my feet and shuffled down the hill. Incredibly, the pickup hadn't stalled or anything. The engine continued to rattle and buck under the hood, like a miracle. The first break I'd caught in weeks. Months, maybe. I put her into drive and made a sharp U-turn and drove like hell out of the cemetery. I went a block east on Main and pulled into the parking lot of a Catholic church and parked the truck in the back lot by a dumpster like it belonged there. Like a regular maintenance vehicle. Then I climbed out of the pickup and hoofed it back to the cemetery. My heart rocked, hard, just once. Then it went back to beating normal.

No shortcut into the cemetery. A tall fence surrounded the graveyard, and the fence was too high to climb. I knew the cops would start patrolling the cemetery at dark, and it was basically dark now, so I picked up my pace, cutting through the church yard and following the fence to Main Street, before turning down the cemetery road. My shirt and underpants were soaked clean through. I pricked up my ears, but I didn't hear anything—no cries of help, nothing—except the light traffic on Main Street, birdsong, and the distant and mournful wail of a train whistle. Now officially my three favorite sounds.

I took out my cell phone and punched in Vince's number.

Come on, pick up, pick up...

"Yo!"

"Dude, I need a favor," I said. "Can you do me a favor?"

"Depends. Is it something I can do fucked up, because I'm totally fucked up."

"You mean like drunk or stoned?"

"All the above."

Great.

"I need you to go to Sara's and get the keys to Roy's dump and meet me out there in a half hour."

A brief pause on the other end. "Seriously?"

"Dead fucking serious."

He laughed. A stoned, nervous laugh. "Dude, what'd you do now?"

"We're wasting time, Vince. I'll explain when I see you. Can you do this for me or not?"

"What about Pritchard? Can he come along?"

"No! What is that dumb ass still doing here?"

"Want me to ask him?"

"No! I mean, I don't care—" I thought of something else. "You know anything about operating a backhoe?"

"Not a thing," he said. "Hang on." He was talking to Pritchard, but I couldn't hear what he was saying. "Pritchard knows how to operate one. I guess he's coming with us after all."

"Fine. Half hour," I said and hung up.

Down the road, Erica's Camry came into view. I punched Kelsie's number into the phone.

"I can't work tonight," she said by way of hello.

"I don't have time for this," I said. "How much?"

"There's no how much. I'm taking the kids to the movies. I promised. Get Erica to cover for you."

"Erica's M.I.A."

"Well, you should've been nicer to her."

"I was nice...I'll give you fifty bucks."

"What is it with you lately? Is there something going on I should know about?"

"What? No. Can't you take them to the movies tomorrow, to a matinee? I'll pay for it."

"Goodbye, Denis."

"All right. A hundred."

She told me to hang on. I heard her talking to one of her kids. "Not now. Mommy's on the phone..."

I walked on. I should've fired her ass years ago, the way she extorted money out of me left and right. It's the goddamn hospitality business. You work when you're needed. "Hundred and fifty," I said.

There was a pause. "Two hundred and you got a deal."

How much do you want to bet they were never going to a movie?

"Fine," I said. "Just get your ass over there."

I hurried past the Camry and mounted the hill. I shivered and squatted beside Erica's body, trying to figure out the best way to get her to the car. I'd figured I'd just toss her over my shoulder and carry her down that way.

That was a joke. She felt like she weighed a thousand pounds. I couldn't budge her, let alone lift her. That must be what they mean by dead weight.

I ended up dragging her down the hill by her boots, leaving a three-hundred-foot-long clue behind me. I hoped to god it would snow soon.

Halfway down the hill, I heard the old woman cry out. Probably mistaking me for some passerby. *Sorry Helen. No such luck.*

I paused to listen, to see if she'd cry out again. A pair of yellow headlights flared some two hundred yards down the road. I swear my scrotum shriveled to the size of a peanut. It had to be cops. Who else would it be, that time of day? And after dusk, a cop sees a car parked in the cemetery, he's going to stop. Investigate. No way around it.

I looked around for the biggest headstone and dragged Erica behind it. I leaned against the stone and tried to catch my breath. I dug out the flask. Empty.

I glanced off toward the timberline. If I made a break for it I just might make it without being seen. Might even make it back to the truck.

The headlights moved closer. One hundred yards.

What I wouldn't have given for a pint of Beefeater.

Eighty yards.

Or a couple of Ativan.

It was too big, the vehicle. Way too big for a cruiser. Too big even for a police SUV.

And it was orange.

I sagged against the tombstone and giggled like a lunatic. Relief washed over me like a wave of ice. A large dump truck rumbled by, spreading salt on the roads. The truck passed the Camry and continued on. It didn't even slow down.

I turned to the corpse. "Well, doll face, shall we go?"

Her keys were in the ignition. I opened the door, reached in and grabbed the keys, and went around back.

It took me five long minutes to get her ass into the trunk. I think I wrenched my back every way it was possible to wrench a back.

TWENTY-EIGHT

The headlights lit up the back of Vince's pickup. He'd parked at the front gate, next to the cheap wooden sign that read Roy's Dump. I pulled in behind the truck and Vince and Pritchard got out. An old Bad Company song wafted from his radio. I ran down the window and Vince rested his hands on the frame.

"Where'd you get this?" he said.

"Did you unlock the gate?"

"Uh huh," he said. "You want to tell me what's going on?"

"Less you know, the better."

He gave me a hard look. "Fuck that. You want our help or not?"

I turned off the headlights. "If we're going to have a long discussion, would you mind turning off your lights? And the radio?"

Vince frowned and went back to his truck and turned off the headlights, but he left the radio on at a lower volume.

I looked at Pritchard. "You really know how to operate a backhoe?"

"As good as the next guy."

Vince walked back pulling on a pair of leather work

gloves.

"So?" he said.

"We're going to bury this car."

Pritchard laughed. "I don't blame you. I wouldn't be caught dead driving a fucking rice burner."

"Seriously," Vince said. "What are we doing here?"

"I am serious. We need a hole big enough to push this car into. The way I figure it ought to take about an hour, the whole thing. If we can find the keys to the backhoe."

Vince wiped his nose on his sleeve. "Apparently, you've lost your mind. But that's okay. They have awesome drugs for that nowadays."

I glanced back down the road. Nothing but darkness.

Vince dug his hands into his jacket pockets. "I'm going to ask you once more, then I'm going home."

"Okay," I said. "It's an insurance scam. A friend reports her car stolen. I get half. If she gets caught, I still get half and she does all the time."

Vince shook his head. "Dude, are you that broke?"

"No, I'm doing this because I need a hobby."

Nobody laughed.

Pritchard said, "So what's our cut?"

"What do you mean?"

"If you get half, then I get half of that, so what's my cut?"

Vince said, "Why do you get half?"

"Because I know how to operate a backhoe. Kind of." He turned to me. "What's my cut?"

It didn't matter what I said, since he wasn't going to get a dime off me anyway. "Five hundred bucks."

"A thousand," he said.

"Fine, a thousand," I said. "Let's just do this."

Vince grabbed my arm. "Hang on, bro. What exactly

is my role in this?"

"I need you to give me a ride back to my truck. That's it. Nothing illegal."

"Except that makes me an accessory."

I shook my head. "I'm the accessory."

"I'm pretty sure what you're doing makes you an accomplice."

"What am I?" Pritchard said.

I started to say "a dumb ass," but I needed the dumb ass to operate the backhoe, so I ignored him and turned back to Vince. "All you're doing is giving me a ride. Think about it. If I called a cab instead, would the cabbie be an accessory? Or an accomplice?"

"If he was your brother and knew what was going on, yes."

Vince slipped his hand into an inside pocket and pulled out a pack of cigarettes and a lighter. He fired up the cigarette and blew a cloud of smoke over the roof of the Camry. "So I'm supposed to sit here while you two masterminds bury a car?"

"Basically."

"For an hour?"

"Hour and a half, tops." I turned to Pritchard. "How long to dig the hole?"

"As long as it takes."

I could've sworn I heard a sound come from the trunk. A soft moan. I glanced at Vince and Pritchard, but they didn't appear to have heard it.

Probably my guilty, overactive imagination.

I popped a few knuckles. "Move that piece of shit truck so we can get going," I said. "Time's a-wasting."

Vince shook his head and muttered "insurance scam" under his breath. He and Pritchard walked back to the truck.

There it was again. This time it sounded more like a knock. I reached into the Camry and turned on the radio to muffle the sound.

A Billy Joel song came on.

About the only thing worse than a Billy Joel song, I told myself, is a woman who's supposed to be dead knocking on the inside of your trunk.

TWENTY-NINE

Five o'clock rolled around. What used to be called happy hour, till the state legislature banned happiness. I stared at the local news on the screen above the bar (daily murder, sports, weather, cute puff piece involving animals, and ten minutes of asinine commercials) and chewed on a plastic stir straw. We had five customers, Clark Sheppard, and four Mexicans from the local Tex-Mex restaurant who drank Tecates, shot pool, and played annoying ranchero music on the jukebox. I say Mexicans but they could've been Bolivians for all I knew. I was telling Sheppard how I missed the old jukeboxes, the kind where you had to buy the records, so you'd buy records *you* wanted to hear. And when you got sick of those, you traded them in for different records. A perfect closed-loop system. Few pop songs can hold up to repeated play. Name me one record you don't want to stomp to bits with hobnail boots after you hear it ninety-five times. Even "Wichita Lineman" can't hold up to that many playings.

In Uncle Chuck's day, The Brass Lantern had an old Seeburg Select-o-Matic, probably worth a small fortune now. It was full of George Jones and Buck Owens and Chubby Checker records, but one of the last (and dumbest) things my father did, before they dragged his sorry ass off to prison, was trade it in for one of those digital jukeboxes that for a hefty fee can play any god-awful song ever recorded. You ask me, it was one of the worst business decisions he made. You never want to give up that much control over the music selection.

I told Sheppard, "Swear to god when that contract is up I'm sending that piece of shit machine back and getting an antique jukebox that plays nothing but old forty-fives. Nothing recorded after nineteen eighty."

I'd been saying that for years, but a vintage jukebox went for four thousand bucks on eBay. No way could I justify that expense, not when the bar was barely staying afloat.

Sheppard wasn't listening anyway, just staring blankly at the television screen and nursing his second Manhattan. Second one that hour. He seemed anxious about something. He kept glancing at the Mexicans then back at the TV.

Finally he said, "Denis, we need to talk."

"We do?"

"Yeah." He glanced over at the Mexicans again, then pulled an envelope from his pocket and set it on the counter and tapped it with his index finger. "You know what this is?"

I slung a dishtowel over my shoulder. "A yellow envelope?"

"Clay Goodwin gave this to me two weeks ago—for safe keeping." He fixed his eyes on me. "You remember Clay Goodwin, don't you?"

An anvil dropped in my stomach. Well, I'd been waiting for this. I just figured it'd be the cops waving the letter in my face, not one of my regulars. Not my uncle's business partner.

"So you know what's in here, I take it?"

"I got a pretty good idea."

He glanced around at the bar. The Mexes were gathered around the jukebox. He tapped his finger on the envelope again. "Some pretty damning stuff in there."

I folded my arms over my chest and glared at him. "Wasn't it you who told me a letter like that wouldn't hold up in court?"

"I said it depends. Now that I know the whole story, my professional opinion is that it will. Absolutely." His voice took on a patronizing, lawyerly tone. "You see a letter like this is considered deathbed testimony and deathbed testimony is an exception to the hearsay rule." His lips curved up slightly at the ends. "Sorry if I'm being too technical."

I didn't say anything, but I sure felt like punching him in his smug little face. I didn't care how old he was.

"Yes sir, I'd say this letter contains some pretty damning stuff."

"You said that."

"Bears repeating." He slid the envelope across the bar. "Go ahead. Take a look. I have the original."

I stared at the envelope a moment, like a detached finger. Christ, I thought, I'd just gotten rid of one blackmailer—well, Erica Wainwright had—and along comes another. Was this nightmare never going to end?

I picked up the envelope and studied the letter. It was about what I expected, but with more misspellings:

I Clayton Wayne Goodwin witnesed the murder of Johnnie Sika by Dennis Carroll the night of April 16, 2010 at The Brass Lantern tavern. Dennis Carroll threatened to kill me if I talked to the police which is why I didn't say nothing. Then two years ago Dennis stopped selling my weed out of his bar. I informed Dennis that if he continued to refused to sell my weed I would tell police how he mudered Johnnie Sika. Dennis said he or his brother would kill me if I did. I am writing this letter because I feel my life is in series danger. If anything happens to me it was Dennis Carroll who done it.

Well, here was the motive the cops were looking for.

I looked up at Sheppard. "I can't read this. I need my glasses." I went down to the end the bar and rooted through the lost and found till I found a pair of reading glasses. Goodwin kept a close eye on me, but his attention was diverted for a second when one of the Mexes came up next to him to order beers. At that moment I swapped the copy of the letter for an old electricity bill. If you didn't look close, you couldn't tell them apart. I went back down the bar and pretended to study the letter again.

"Okay, let's have it," I said. I slipped the bill into the envelope and shoved it into my shirt pocket. "How much?"

Sheppard grinned and held out his hand. "I believe you have something of mine."

"Oh," I said. I took the envelope out of my pocket and handed it over. He didn't look at it, just slipped it into his coat pocket.

"The way I hear it, the county prosecutor is building a pretty strong case against you," he said. "Fingerprints on the murder weapon. Witness saw you casing the victim's house. No alibi. Hear the prosecutor's got his whole team looking at you. I'd say it's definitely in your interest that this letter disappears."

"You're overlooking one small detail," I said. "I'm innocent. I didn't kill Clay Goodwin."

He stirred his Manhattan and smirked at the idea. "It doesn't matter to me one way or the other. Clay may have been a distant relative, but we certainly weren't close. And as for your guilt or innocence in his murder, that letter seems to indicate the former. Funny that."

My jaw tightened like a vise grip. "I'm going to ask you one more time. How much?"

Sheppard took on an offended tone. "Denis, please. I don't want your money. God knows you've got precious little of it."

I waited.

"However, there is one thing."

Of course there was. He wanted me to kill someone. Or steal something for him. A night with my wife, perhaps...

"You know I used to own this place."

"Yeah, you've only told me about a thousand times. And you only owned half of it. My uncle owned the other half—"

"Well, that's not quite accurate, but be that as it may, it's been a great sorrow to me watching the place go downhill."

I studied him, trying to anticipate where he was going with this. "You want your half of the bar back?"

A thin smile. "Not half, no."

I was incredulous. The sonofabitch actually expected me to turn over The Brass Lantern to him. Just like that.

What was it about me that people thought they could threaten and extort the living shit out of me and I'd just roll over and take it? Did I really come off as some candy-assed pushover?

God, it made my blood boil.

Sheppard glanced wistfully about the barroom. "When your uncle talked me into buying this place, I thought it would be a decent investment. Not a big money maker, of course, but something to do in my retirement. I was never one for golf or fishing."

"So buy another tavern." I said. "You own a law firm. You could buy a half dozen bars."

"Sure. But I'm rather sentimental about this place. Always have been. Spent some of my best times here."

Spent most of his times here, he meant. My knuckles throbbed and blood pounded against my eyes. "I knew you were a lowlife drunk with the morals of an alley cat, Sheppard, but this time—"

He held up a hand and dusted off his most obnoxious lawyer voice. "You know what, Denis? You're right. I have a sworn duty to my client—deceased though he may be. I owe it to him to turn over that letter to the proper authorities as per his wishes. It's the only ethical thing to do."

"Don't talk to me about ethics, you blackmailing piece of shit!" I lowered my voice and leaned in. "If you think me and my brothers are going to let you get away with this you're sadly mistaken."

"Denis, threatening people is what got you into this mess," he said, his voice grave. "Tell you what. I'll make this easy for you. We've got two plays here. I can turn over the letter to the prosecutor or you can return my bar to me and we call it square. What do you say?"

I gripped his forearm and dug my fingers into his arm, hard. There was no mistaking the fear and uncertainty that crept into his eyes. "Look, old man, you don't want this dive. You think you do, but you don't. First of all it's a money pit…"

He jerked his arm away from my grasp. He cleared his throat and smiled uneasily. "I will admit, your family has allowed the place to go downhill. But with a little money and the right people, I believe I can salvage it."

"I only own a quarter of this place, and I'm going to have to sell that to pay my lawyer. My family owns the rest. What am I supposed to tell them? Sorry guys, you've got to turn over your share of the bar because some goddamn vulture is blackmailing me?"

Sheppard flinched at the B-word. "I'm sure they'll do whatever's necessary to keep you and your family together, don't you?"

I thought about that. Chad, maybe. Vince, he'd want to lynch the sonofabitch. As for Sara, I had to laugh. You'd have to pry the title out of her cold, fat, dead hands.

A rage spread like a wildfire through me. A fellow can only take so much. My left hand crept along the speed rail and grasped the neck of a nice, full liquor bottle. My mind had pretty much shut down at that point and I was acting on impulse, pure animal instinct.

I glanced over at the Mexes. Good chance they were illegals anyway. They weren't going to say anything to anybody. Let him wake up five or six hours from now crammed into the trunk of a wreck at Roy's dump. He'd think twice before trying to shakedown the Carrolls again.

"Needless to say, if you mention this to anyone, I'll deny it," he said. "I mean, after I turn over the letter to the prosecutor."

My fingers clung to the sticky neck of a rum bottle. As I eased the bottle from the rail, the front door flung open and the bar flooded with light and noise as a group of realtors strode inside. Slowly, I lowered the bottle back to the rail and pulled back from the bar.

Sheppard turned. "You're in luck. I'm sure one of these fine people will be happy to help with the transaction." Sheppard slid off the stool and leaned in, his voice lowered. "One last thing. For obvious reasons I can't withhold this evidence from the authorities much longer. If you'd like the original, I'll need the deed signed over by Tuesday."

"This Tuesday?"

"Correct."

On his way out, Sheppard stopped and shook hands and slapped the backs of several of the realtors. He'd left a sawbuck on the bar. Two of the realtors, a guy and a girl, drifted up to the bar, smiling, laughing, asking me how I was doing and ordering several buckets of beers.

I dropped the ten in the tip jar and told the realtors I'd be right back. Then I wrapped a pair of bar rags around my knuckles and strode to the back where I spent the next five minutes punching the hell out of the inside of the walk-in cooler.

THIRTY

There was a time Reva would've waited up for me. Since the twins came along, those times were long gone. These days she had a schedule to stick to: put the twins to bed at eight, fix herself a drink or two, watch TV, and go to bed at ten. Most nights I'd get home around one o'clock, take a quick shower, and fall wearily into bed. Sometimes Reva would wake up and we'd talk about our days.

That night we talked.

I popped open a beer and sat in the rocking chair at the foot of the bed. I kicked off my shoes and propped my feet on the mattress and sipped my beer. Reva sat up and yawned and clutched a pillow to her chest for warmth.

"Aren't you coming to bed?" she said.

"After I finish this."

She studied me, trying to gauge my mood. "What's wrong, babe? Is something wrong?"

I turned the beer can in my hands and stared at the space between my feet. "Actually," I began. "There's been a..."

My voice trailed off.

A wave of concern passed over her face. "There's

been a what?"

"Development," I said. I'd thought hard about what I was going to say. I'd gone over it in my mind at least a dozen times and only drawn a blank. I had no idea how to explain this.

"Denis, what are you talking about? What development?" My wife had that look she sometimes gets: half alarm, half lit fuse waiting to blow.

"With the case."

"The Goodwin case?"

I shook my head. "Something else."

Reva stared at me, waiting for me to go on.

"I'm being blackmailed."

"What?"

"I—"

Suddenly she was on her feet. She had on her red winter flannels—white fir trees and gallivanting deer. She folded her arms across her chest and a look of bewilderment crept into her eyes. "I don't understand. Who's blackmailing you?"

"It's kind of a long story—"

"Denis!"

"Okay. Before he died, Clay Goodwin left a letter with an attorney. The letter says it was me, not Vince, who shot Johnny Sika."

She stared at me, confused. She shook her head. "Why would he lie about something like that?"

I looked away. "It's not a lie."

Reva sunk slowly to the bed and stared into space. For maybe the first time in her life my wife was speechless.

Not for long, though.

"You lied—"

"No. I mean, it was self-defense! He—"

"You *lied* to me." Her body tensed and her eyes filled with rage. "All this time—"

"It was Vince's idea—"

"Don't give me that shit, Denis! I know Vince. He does whatever you tell him to do."

She was shouting now, loud enough to wake the twins. The neighbors even. I leaned forward in the chair, elbows on my knees. "Look, babe, I know how this must sound to you, but, honestly, we were just doing what we thought best." I held up my hand, cutting her off. "Just hear me out. Please...We didn't think it would be a big deal. I mean, I had a family and Vince...well, he didn't. No matter who did it, it was still self-defense. Nothing was supposed to happen. We were just trying to protect you and the twins. Do you see?"

"That's how you protect us? Shooting people and lying to the police?" After a moment, she said, "My god, Denis, what else haven't you told me?"

I shook my head. "Nothing—"

"You said Goodwin was blackmailing you. Goodwin's dead!"

"Not Goodwin. Sheppard. Clark Sheppard."

"Denis, who the..." She lowered her voice a notch. "Who is Clark Sheppard?"

"He's the lawyer Goodwin gave the letter to. He used to own our bar—well, half of it—back when Uncle Chuck was alive."

Reva gave me a blank look. "A lawyer is blackmailing you?"

"I told you, it's crazy."

She looked at me briefly then back at the wall. "I don't understand. How can he blackmail you if it was self-defense?"

I swallowed hard. "Goodwin was afraid I might do something to him, so he wrote this letter and gave it to Sheppard. It says if anything happens to him I'm responsible. I wasn't going touch him, but he was a paranoid little freak, you know?"

She turned and looked at me. Her eyes glistened as tears formed. "But it's a lie. You didn't do anything. You didn't kill Goodwin."

"Of course not! I told you, his niece shot him then she tried to frame me."

A trace of doubt crossed her eyes. "Where's this letter? I want to see it."

I looked away. That wasn't going to happen. "Sheppard has it."

Reva shook her head. "What does he want? I mean, he's a lawyer. He's rich. What could he possibly want from us?"

I sighed and walked over to the far corner of the room and turned around. "He was supposed to give the letter to the cops, but he says he'll destroy it on one condition."

She waited.

"He wants the bar."

She let go a mirthless laugh. "He wants our bar?"

I nodded.

Her eyes widened in disbelief. "You're serious?"

"He used to own it. He wants it back. Otherwise, he turns over the letter." I paused. "It's fucked up, I know. But if the cops get that letter they'll arrest me for Goodwin's murder. They'll have to."

I went over and sat down on the edge of the bed. I tried to take her hands, but she pulled them away. "It's crazy. The whole thing. There's no other way to put it."

Reva stared into space. She said, "What kind of lawyer blackmails innocent people?"

I shrugged. I didn't have an answer for that.

I watched her closely. A single tear traveled over her cheek. Her eyes were unsteady on mine and kept sliding around the room like she was trying to find some kind of answer there.

She shook her head. "You killed that boy. That Sika boy."

I got up from the bed and stalked back and forth across the room. "It was self-defense. Goddamn it, Reva, you've got to believe me."

She almost laughed. "Believe you? I'm supposed to believe you?"

"I don't know what to say, except I'm sorry. I never wanted to keep the truth from you. I was only trying to protect you and the twins. I—"

At the word "twins" she turned and glared at me. Her look gave me a sudden chill. "Denis, what have you done?"

"Reva, come on—"

"I can't believe anything you say. Damn it, Denis, I— I don't even know who you are anymore."

Sour spirals came up from my stomach. It was like we'd crossed a line and on the other side everything would be different. And there was no way back.

"I can't," she said. "I've tried, but I can't anymore. I can't let the twins grow up like this. Blackmail. Murder. Drugs. Lies. I just can't."

She turned away.

I felt empty. I stood up and retreated to my corner of the room. I leaned against the wall and waited for the inevitable.

I didn't have to wait long.

"I'm leaving, Denis," she said in a flat, faraway voice. "Tomorrow I'm taking the kids and leaving."

"Honey," I said, choking on my own voice. "Come on…"

That was all I said. I was silent a long time, then I walked out of the bedroom.

I didn't even try to change her mind.

THIRTY-ONE

The next morning Reva called in sick. She dropped off the twins at school while I made a pot of coffee and moped around the house. Later we sat at the kitchen table and talked. Reva admitted she'd been a bit hasty when she said she and the kids would leave in the morning. There were phone calls to make, living arrangements to plan, clothes and other essentials to pack.

Then they would leave.

She did all the talking. I sat there like a dumb animal that had crapped on the carpet. That's what I felt like anyway.

"You don't have to go," I said. "I'll leave. I'll probably be staying at the graybar hotel by the end of the week, anyway."

She gave me a blank look.

"The county jail."

She frowned.

"I could stay at the Lantern for now. There's a sofa in the back."

"Don't try to be a martyr," she snapped. She dropped her eyes and took a sip of coffee. "I told the kids."

"You told them—"

"That we're moving out."

"Just now?"

"On the way to school."

I scowled at that. "That doesn't seem like the kind of thing you drop on a kid right before school." I tried not to sound too judgmental, but pretty much failed. "Weren't they devastated?"

"A bit late for you to take an interest, don't you think? Besides, they were going to hear it sooner or later. Might as well be sooner."

That burned me up. I got up from the table and put on my jacket and stormed out of the house. It was more than I could stand at the moment. She came to the door and called after me, but I ignored her.

I drove around for a while, feeling sorry for myself, wishing it wasn't so early so I could get drunk. Then I thought, who says it's too early? Plenty of bars open. I aimed Roy's truck in the direction of The Hideaway. When I drove past Russ Toohey's office I slammed the brakes and pulled up to the curb. I figured it was time to tell him about the letter.

Toohey was on his way out the door. Said he was expected in court in fifteen minutes, the usual traffic tickets and domestic violence crap. He slipped into a coal gray cashmere Chesterfield and flung his leather backpack over one shoulder and selected a cheese Danish from a silver tray on his secretary's desk.

"Let's walk and talk, shall we?"

"Sure."

"Care for a Danish?"

"I'm good."

"Cool."

His office was only a block from the courthouse, four buildings down from Sheppard's law office. The day was sunny and mild, the skies cloud free and robin's egg blue. Melting snow ran in rivulets along the curb.

"Don't let this weather fool you," he said. "It's supposed to snow tomorrow night."

I squared myself and said, "There's something I forgot to tell you."

"There always is."

"It complicates things."

"It always does." He swallowed the last of his Danish and licked his fingers. "Go on. You have my undivided attention."

I told him about Goodwin's letter. He didn't seem at all surprised.

"You saw the letter?" he said.

"I have a copy," I said. I reached in my back pocket and handed him the letter. He stopped on the sidewalk and unfolded the letter and slipped on a pair of glasses and quickly scanned the letter. His face betrayed nothing.

"Christ, another shakedown? What is it with you? It's not like you're rich."

"Tell me about it."

After a moment he handed the letter back to me and we continued on. "Who is it?"

"A lawyer. I'm not supposed to say who."

He frowned at me.

"Clark Sheppard. And if he finds out I told anyone, he's going straight to the cops with the original. Or so he says."

"Clark Sheppard? He's got some balls. And he gave you that copy?"

"I did the old switcheroo. He has a copy of my electric bill."

He grinned. "Won't he be surprised."

We continued on and Toohey shook his head. "Clark Sheppard. That surprises me. Although…years ago he was accused of filing false tax returns for a client. Must've been twelve, fifteen years ago. Never charged." He thought that over a moment. "I know he's been losing his war with the bottle for decades. But blackmail." He shook his head again. "What's he want?"

"My bar."

Toohey halted and studied me. "Seriously?"

I nodded.

"Well, I suppose if I were an alcoholic…" He chuckled. "Sorry. I don't mean to make light of your situation. Damn if he isn't ballsy and stupid."

"He's got the original. He's calling the shots."

We walked on again. "Too bad he's retired or I'd see him disbarred for this," he said. "How long have you had that letter?"

"Got it last night."

"Nice of you to share it with me."

I felt too stupid to say anything.

"Well, there's the motive the prosecution's been looking for," he said. "I'm not sure it's admissible, but if it is, needless to say, that would be bad for us." Toohey thought about that some more. "If I were a betting man, I'd bet he's bluffing. If he goes to the cops, he risks extortion charges and spending his last days in prison. And for what? A hole-in-the-wall saloon? No offense."

"I can tell you right now, Sara won't turn over her quarter stake."

"Who's Sara?"

"My mother."

We walked up the salt-covered courthouse steps and

Toohey, his brow furrowed, halted again. "I'm afraid I can't advise you what to do. It would be unethical. We're bordering on all kinds of ethical quandaries as it is." He paused. "How long did he give you?"

"Till Tuesday."

"Hmm."

My eyes flicked to the courthouse square. There wasn't much traffic for a weekday, but then besides hearings and trials there was never much reason to come downtown.

He wasn't going to tell me anything. I was wasting time when I needed to be talking to my family.

"I've got to get to court now," he said. "Sorry I can't be of more help to you."

We shook hands and he turned to go.

"Oh, by the way," I said, "do you handle divorces?"

He froze and turned around, his face grave. "I do," he said. "You?"

I nodded.

"We'll talk," he said.

THIRTY-TWO

I never did make it to The Hideaway. Instead I drove to Walmart and bought a new battery for the truck. I was done fucking around with that pickup. I installed the battery in the parking lot and I drove to Fire Station No. 2 to see Chad. I figured he'd be the most reasonable of the three.

The station was deserted, so I sat in the lounge and drank a Coke and waited. I must have killed an hour and a half watching idiotic game shows (I couldn't find the remote control) before Chad and Rocky showed up. Turned out a couple of horses had fallen through the thinning ice on a pond near New Baden and they'd been on hand in case any of the rescuers got hypothermia saving the horses. Luckily the firefighters had these brand new special ice water suits. Chad said they used a chainsaw to cut a path through the ice so the horses could get ashore. A happy ending. The newspaper was all over it. TV crews from St. Louis showed up, but too late to catch the action. Chad, however, had captured it all on his iPhone and sold the video to Channel 4 for two hundred bucks. Something told me he could've gotten more.

Chad made a new batch of coffee while he thawed out. He poured some coffee into a filthy World's Best

Dad mug. "I see Toohey got you out of the clink."

"Yeah. Thanks for finding him."

"He's a little precious, but he's smart." He held up the pot. "Java?"

I shook my head.

He turned to me. "Listen Denis, if this is what I think it is, I'm not interested. I don't want to hear about it and I goddamn sure don't want to discuss it. I got Toohey for you because Reva asked me to. But that's it. I'm done, you understand?"

He walked over to a bookshelf, picked up the remote, and turned on FOX News.

There was his iPhone footage. The horses, freed from their icy, watery grave, galloped across a field, joined by their relieved equine friends. Damn, it was a fine video.

"I should've held out for more money. Shit's going viral."

I sighed and stood up. Fuck it, I thought. I'm done. Let Sheppard turn over the letter to the cops. I didn't care anymore. With Reva and the twins leaving everything was shit anyway.

I turned to leave. I got as far as the door, when he called me back.

"Denis, why did you come here?"

"Forget it," I said, sulkily. I went out the door and walked across the lot to Roy's truck. As I eased into the driver's side, I felt Chad's hand on my shoulder.

"All right," he said. "You may be a fuck up, but you're still my little brother. So what's up?"

I didn't say anything for a moment, then I removed the letter from my pocket and handed it to him. "Goodwin wrote this about a week before he died. He gave it to a lawyer for safekeeping."

Chad read the letter slowly, his lips moving along with the words. After a moment, he lowered the letter and looked at me, his voice choked with fury. "Is this true?"

"I had nothing to do with Goodwin's death."

Chad stared at me.

"He wants The Brass Lantern," I said. "The original for the bar."

I followed his look to a crop field behind the station where a flock of wild turkey grazed. He said, "Who wants the bar?"

"A lawyer."

He looked confused. "A lawyer is blackmailing us?"

I nodded. "Clark Sheppard."

"The tax attorney? Uncle Chuck's friend?"

"Uh huh."

He studied the letter again. "He wants the bar? He wants our fucking bar? What kind of idiot would want that money pit?"

He handed the letter back to me. I leaned on the truck bed and stared at the ground, toeing a chunk of ice with my boot.

Chad shook his head and fell silent a long moment. When he spoke again, his voice had lost its heat. "You know I was counting on that bar for my retirement."

"I know."

"The guy's a lawyer. Doesn't he know blackmail is against the law?"

I shrugged. "I guess he figures I got more to lose. And he's right. We're talking life in prison if they pin Goodwin's murder on me."

His anger seemed to shift from me toward Sheppard. "He ain't getting away with this," he said.

A TASTE OF SHOTGUN

The back door of the station opened and Rocky came out and lit a cigarette. She waved to us.

Chad crossed his arms and leaned his back against Roy's truck and stared angrily into space. His furrowed brow suggested he was working something out in his head. "Fuck it," he said. "I'll probably die before I retire anyway." Then he wrinkled up his nose and took a step back from the truck. "What are you doing with Roy's truck?"

"Had to sell mine to pay my bond."

"That sucks," he said. He shook his head again and laughed shortly. "You know Sara will never agree to this."

"I don't know, maybe I can buy her share."

"With what? You just sold your goddamn truck."

I didn't have an answer to that. "Anyway, I appreciate it," I said. "I'd say I'd pay it back to you some day, but I don't know I can promise that. I'll try though. I'll pay back what I can."

"Forget it."

"No, I will."

"I said forget it," he said, his voice tense and hard.

I knew he'd come around. Chad was a good man. A good brother. No way was he going to let his niece and nephew go without their father.

Of course, if he found out Reva was leaving me and taking the kids, all bets would be off.

He slapped the roof of the cab. "Get this pile of shit out of here. It's stinking up the parking lot."

I smiled. "Thanks, man."

He nodded. "Good luck with Sara."

I climbed into the truck and let out a long breath. I turned the key and the engine clicked and hummed.

Dead.

Jesus Christ, a brand new battery.

Chad stopped halfway across the lot and turned slowly around. "Let me guess. You need a jump."

I stuck my head out of the open door. "Actually," I said, "How are you with replacing starters?"

THIRTY-THREE

Five minutes into the first quarter and already we were getting hammered by twelve points. It had been the same story all season. Our coach, a financial advisor named Dale Schuhardt, was one of these "equal time" guys who thought every player should get the same amount of court time, no matter his skill level. That's fine if the other side is playing that way too, if it's written in the league rules. Only it wasn't. The other team was playing all five of its best players and they were seriously kicking our eight-year-old butts. We had one of our good players out there, Billy Timmons, and the other four A-teamers, including Hunter, were getting splinters in their backsides riding the pine.

Another turnover. Criminently.

This is why we had a 4-9 record. Erickson had no business coaching a girl's field hockey team, let alone a boys' basketball team.

"Put in the A team!" I yelled.

Reva turned around and glared at me. I sat down.

Mandy, dressed in her cute little cheerleader costume, shook a pom pom in my face.

"Please don't do that, honey," I said.

She did it again.

Reva told her to cut it out.

Mandy looked at her mother. "When are we moving in with grandma and grandpa?"

"Soon," Reva said. "Now please sit down."

Someone slapped me on the back, hard enough that it smarted.

"Hey, bro!"

Vince plopped down beside me. He leaned over and smiled at Reva. "Hey Reev, long time, no see."

Reva returned an icy smile. "Hello Vince."

I turned to my brother. "What're you doing here?"

"Had to come see the next Lebron James, didn't I?" He leaned his elbows on his knees and glanced at the scoreboard. "I hope we're not visitors."

"We are."

"Ouch." He nodded toward the court. "Which one's Hunter?"

"He's on the bench. Third from the right."

"On the bench? What the hell?" He put his hands to his mouth and yelled, "Put in Hunter Carroll!"

Reva covered her face with her hands and Schuhardt glared up into the stands. Mandy dropped into her mother's lap and stared shyly at Vince.

"You must be Amanda," Vince said. "Why you're as cute as a bug's ear."

Mandy turned to her mother and pressed her mouth to Reva's ear. "Who is that?"

"That's your Uncle Vince," Reva said unenthusiastically.

There was a loud buzzer signaling the end of the first quarter. The lead had grown to fourteen points. I leaned toward Vince and said, "We need to talk."

"Christ. Now what?"

I jerked my head toward the exit. "My office."

We walked down the stands and out of the gym into a dark hallway that led to more hallways. Vince jammed his hands into his jacket pockets. "So?"

"I need you to sign over your share of the bar."

He laughed. "This just gets better and better."

"I'm serious."

Vince paused. "In that case, I'm going to need more information."

I gave him the letter, waited till he scanned it, then I laid it out for him, the long and short of it.

He handed back the letter. "I'll kill the rat bastard."

A handful of people drifted out of the gym toward the restrooms. I took Vince's arm and steered him through the front doors onto the icy front steps. I stood coatless in the bitter wind.

"You're not really thinking of giving that old fart our tavern? Christ man, are we going to let the whole town blackmail us?"

I watched a bus go by, exhaling plumes of exhaust that drifted in our direction. "I know how you feel—"

"Do you?"

"—but we've got to be smart about this."

Vince laughed. "Too late for that, bro. That ship done sailed."

"Chad's agreed to it. That leaves you and Sara."

He got an amused look in his eyes. "Sara? She wouldn't give away a fucking cold."

I shrugged. "She might."

After a moment he brightened. "Tell you what. I'll sign if you let me break a couple of his ribs."

I frowned. "He'll just file assault and battery charges and you'll be right back in the pokey."

"Not if I wear a clever disguise. I could wear my gas mask bong like last time."

"Forget it."

Vince's shoulders sagged. "Man, you're such a killjoy. You want me to sign over my share of the bar and you won't even let me crack a few ribs."

I shuffled my feet on the ice. "So what's it going to be?"

He glanced off down the street. "Hell, bro, you know I'll sign. Didn't I give you four years of my life? What's a quarter share of a bar?"

Of course he had to bring that up.

He paused. "While we're on the topic, anything else you want from me? A kidney maybe?"

"Maybe. I'll let you know when the time comes."

"I'm sure you will," he said. "It just pisses me off that that piece of shit lawyer is going to get away with this."

"Tell me about it."

The buzzer went off signaling the start of the second quarter. Vince removed a Kleenex from his pocket and blew his nose. "Dude, I don't mean to get all up in your business—"

"But?"

"—is everything alright?"

I tensed. "What do you mean?"

"You and the misses."

"Why?"

"I overheard what she told Mandy, you know, about moving out."

"Oh," I said. "Look, promise me you won't tell Chad about that, okay? He's only agreeing to give up his share because of Reva and the twins. If he finds out they're leaving he might change his mind."

"Shit man, that sucks," he said. "No worries though. If you need a place to stay, I got this trailer that's just sitting empty. There's no water or electricity and there's a giant hole in the roof, but it'll be spring soon."

"What would I do without you?"

He shrugged. "Let's go back inside. Fucking freezing out here."

I held the door for him. "You know they could've won this one, if just once they'd played their A team."

"You want me to break that coach's ribs? After the game?"

"Shut the hell up," I said.

THIRTY-FOUR

That left Sara.

I got Roy's truck started and drove over to her house on 13th Street and collected a week's newspapers off the lawn and carried them inside. I took four bags of garbage out to the garage and went back inside and cleared off an easy chair in the living room. The house still reeked of Roy and his dump, but Sara refused to open a window to air the place out, afraid some rapist might crawl in through the half-opened window.

I asked if I could turn off the television.

"Did you bring Roy's truck back?"

"I still need it."

"So do I."

No way was I going to have this conversation again. I stood up. "I'm going to turn off the TV for a minute."

"Why?"

"Because I want to talk to you."

"What about?"

"Can I turn off the TV first?"

"Why?"

"So I don't have to scream over it," I screamed.

She seemed to think that over a while. "You can turn it down, but not off."

"Fine." I looked around for the remote control. "Where's the remote?"

She shrugged. "How should I know?"

"Don't you use it to change the channels?"

"Not if I can't find it."

I shook my head and glanced around the room. "You've got like six of the damn things," I said, but she didn't hear me because I hadn't screamed it. I looked under some trash and newspapers and searched between the couch cushions. Nothing. I went over to the set and searched for a volume button. The TV didn't appear to have one, or if it did I couldn't find it.

"What do you want?" she yelled over the TV.

I let go a heavy sigh and plopped down on the couch. There was no good way to say what I had to say. It was like trying to tell someone they stink. You just had to spit it out. "I need you to sign over your share of the bar," I yelled. "Vince and Chad have agreed to sign over their shares."

She looked at me in disbelief, then she laughed. "Why on earth would I do that?"

"Because if you don't I could go to prison for the rest of my life," I yelled.

She looked at me blankly. "Lord, Denis James. What on earth have you done now?"

"I didn't do anything," I yelled.

"You must've done something—"

"I'm being framed!"

"Framed?"

"Blackmailed!"

"What?"

I got up and went over to the television and pulled the plug out of the outlet. The TV went black.

"What'd you do that for? I was watching that!" she cried.

I sat down again. "Look, Ma, it's a long story, but here's the gist. If we don't sign over the bar to this man, I could go to prison for the rest of my life."

"What man?"

"Clark Sheppard."

"Chuck's friend?"

"Yes."

"He doesn't own the bar anymore. I own the bar now."

"I know. I mean, we all do."

"Then why—"

"He's blackmailing me."

"Denis, I don't understand a word you're saying."

My shoulders sagged. Just like I figured. I'd have to explain everything, the whole rotten mess. Not that it would do any good.

I kept it brief. Just the facts. I told her it was me who shot Johnny Sika. Not Vince. I told her how Goodwin's niece was trying to frame me for her uncle's murder. I told her how Goodwin raped his other niece and how she killed herself. I told her about Goodwin's letter and how Sheppard wanted the bar in exchange for the letter. It was too much for her to handle, just like I knew it would be. Halfway through the story she grew agitated and stopped paying attention. She held her hands over her ears and screamed, "I don't want to hear any more of this!"

She was sobbing loudly now. It was a grotesque sight to see, my huge mother, quaking, struggling to catch her breath, choking on snot, hot tears gushing down her beefy cheeks. Then, suddenly, a realization set in and her face contorted violently. "Are you telling me my baby went to prison because of something you did?"

"No, Ma, the drugs were his too."

She tried to stand up, but gave up after two attempts. "He wouldn't do something like that unless you told him too. He listens to you. You led him astray. You're his older brother. You're supposed to watch out for him and set an example!"

My heart plopped into my stomach like a stone.

"How come you didn't go to jail too?" she cried. "If you were both selling dope. How come only Vincent went to jail?"

"What was I supposed to do? Go down to the police station and say that technically half the weed was mine? What about Reva and the twins? Vince wasn't blameless, Ma."

"He'd never have been arrested if you hadn't shot that man! To think I worry all day long about dope fiends breaking into my house and here I find my own sons are dope dealers." Her face went ghostly white and her eyes shut down. "My baby spent four years in prison for a killing he didn't do and now you have the nerve to come ask me for my life's savings?"

"Drugs, Ma. He got four years for dealing drugs. And I ain't asking for your life savings. Just your share of the bar. You've still got your savings and the dump and—"

"No I don't! The dump's in probate and Roy's daughter is trying to steal it from me, the goddamn bitch!"

Oh yeah.

"And now my own son wants to hand my bar over to a complete stranger." She locked eyes with me and pointed toward the front door. "Get out! Get out of here this instant and don't come back! You are an evil man, Denis James. You belong in prison with your father!"

Christ. I'd always known Vince was her favorite, but I honestly had no idea this would be her reaction. I got up and stood helplessly in the middle of the living room. "Look, Ma, I'm going to call Vince. He'll tell you how it was his idea. He'll tell you—"

A shoe knocked me on the side of the head. She took off her other shoe and prepared to launch it. "I hope you go to prison for the rest of your life," she screamed and flung the other one at me. It sailed wide. "Now plug that television set back in and get out!" She paused to check her breath. "And don't even think of taking Roy's truck!"

I plugged in the set and turned and walked out the side door through the garage. I rolled the garbage cans out to the curb and paused and looked back at the house. Then I eased into Roy's truck. I figured I'd call Vince anyway. Maybe he could talk some sense into her. Though, honestly, at this point I didn't much care.

THIRTY-FIVE

"No dice," Vince said over the phone. "Sara won't budge. I mean that both literally and figuratively."

So, not even her favorite son could convince her. Well, that was it then. I was out of options. If Sheppard wasn't bluffing...

At least Illinois no longer had the death penalty.

The next day, Reva and the twins moved in with her parents. She hadn't returned my last three calls, so I decided that if the truck started I'd stop by the library Saturday morning, prepared to make a scene if need be.

I *will* see my kids today, or else, I muttered to myself.

I walked through the big oak doors and marched up to the circulation desk. Reva was chatting with a harried looking woman and her two big-eyed, curly-headed rug rats. They had about three dozen books to check out. I figured a six-, seven-minute wait. Maybe longer.

"That's a lot of books," I said. "Can they read all those books?"

The woman turned and gave me an insincere smile and went back to chatting with my wife.

"I didn't know you could check out so many books at once," I said. "I thought there were limits. Used to be a limit of six books when I was a kid. I guess there ain't no limits anymore."

Reva gave the woman a pained smile and the rug rats regarded me curiously. The mother continued to ignore me.

"I think limits are a good thing for children. Vitally important, don't you think?"

The woman didn't respond. Reva scanned faster than I'd ever seen her scan books.

When it was my turn, Reva scowled and whispered, "Are you going to make me get a restraining order?"

"I wouldn't be here if you'd return my calls."

"Lower your voice." She scowled. "What do you want?"

"I want to take the kids to the zoo. Is that a crime or something?"

She shook her head.

"I just want to take them out one last time before they lock my ass up. Maybe forever."

A dour, middle-aged woman shot us a hard look from across the room.

"That your boss?" I said.

Reva half-nodded.

I turned and smiled at her. Then I turned back to Reva. "Seriously? You'd deny me one last afternoon with my kids?"

Another woman and her two little brats came up to the circulation desk with a stack of books. That's probably why she relented. She needed to keep her job now more than ever.

Roy's truck started so I drove over to Reva's parents' house and picked up the twins. Reva's mother didn't say a word to me and the old man was nowhere to be seen. Fine by me. If they'd noticed that the truck lacked seatbelts they would've raised a stink.

We got to the zoo at one o'clock and walked around in the twenty-five-degree weather and gaped at the polar bears and penguins and the seals all enjoying the hell out of the icy water. Three inches of snow had fallen overnight and on the way back to the truck we made a lopsided snowman and I lay down in the snow and showed the twins how to make snow angels. Basically, I crammed five years of fatherhood into one afternoon.

When we got back to the truck, the battery was dead and the twins got all whiny and pouty while I tried to flag down someone to give us a jump. It took thirty minutes before this good old boy in a pickup came to our rescue, and by then all the good feeling we'd built up from the afternoon was long gone.

That evening I went to Mandy's basketball game. I sat in the bleachers a row behind Reva and Hunter, sat there with a canyon in the pit of my stomach. I couldn't concentrate on the game. My thoughts were dark, all about how I was going to miss seeing my kids grow up, never see Hunter play high school football, never see Mandy go off to prom and college and, well, everything. Marriage. Grandkids.

At halftime I followed Reva out to the restrooms. She stood outside the men's room while Hunter went inside to pee.

"I'm not stalking you," I said, holding up my hands.

"Kids said they had fun at the zoo today."

Wow. That was decent of her to say. "Yeah. So did I."

She put her eyes on me flat and hard. "So, is your family going to sign over the bar to that lawyer?"

I shook my head. "Sara refused to go along with it."

She rolled her eyes. "Figures."

We were silent awhile.

"So, what are you going to do?" she said.

"Get my affairs in order," I said, with a shrug. "Hope the judge doesn't allow that letter into evidence."

She seemed lost in thought for a moment, then her eyes focused back on me flat and hard. "That's it?" she said. "You're going to hope?"

I rolled it over in my head. What the hell else did she expect me to do? Murder the old man?

"That's it," I said.

THIRTY-SIX

That evening Reva called. She'd phoned Sara and tried to reason with her. A complete waste of time, of course, but that she made the effort made me think there might still be a chance for us.

"She might be willing to sell her share for a hundred grand," Reva said. "I thought her share's only worth fifty thousand, if that?"

I stared out the back door at the empty driveway where the van usually sat. The house was freezing, but I wasn't sure how to work the digital thermostat. Reva always took care of that.

"It gets better. She said we didn't need such a big house and two cars. And she told me to tell you she wants you to bring back Roy's truck." She sighed heavily. "I'm sorry, Denis, but your mother is a real bitch."

"It ain't that," I said.

"No?"

"She blames me for Vince going to prison."

"I hate to agree with her, but she's got a point there."

I let that pass. "Say Reev, you think you could come over here and show me how to set the thermostat? I'm freezing my stones off here."

"You're a big boy," she said. "I'm sure you'll figure

it out."

"I've tried. I'm about ready to pull the damn thing off the wall."

"Goodbye, Denis."

It was too cold to sit in the house and I sure as hell didn't feel like building a fire, so around eight o'clock I got Roy's truck running and drove to The Brass Lantern where the thermostat was the old-fashioned kind. There was supposed to be a band playing, Arkey Neel and the Shitkickers. Kelsie was behind the bar chatting up the regulars.

I said hello to a few friends and sat at the end of the bar. Kelsie drifted down eventually, hands in the back pockets of her jeans, mouth bunched up. "The one night I'm actually scheduled to work and you show up."

I glanced around the bar. "Where's Arkey?"

"Cancelled. Something about his guitar player quitting."

"I thought they were a family band?"

"Families can quit each other. Happens all the time."

"Don't I know it."

"Hmmm?"

"Scotch and water, please."

She brought the Scotch and set it down on the bar and jerked her head toward the frat boys. "They were looking to score some weed earlier."

I glanced over at the college boys. Typical privileged assholes who'd grow up to vote Republican, move to the exurbs, and work twelve hours a day in a LEED-certified building where they drone on and on about core competencies, value-added synergies, and circling back for face time.

But now they just wanted to score a little ditch weed.

A TASTE OF SHOTGUN

"What'd you tell them?"

"I told them to fuck off."

I nodded. "Good girl."

Kelsie had made it clear when she went to work for me that she'd have nothing to do with drug sales. That was fine by me. The fewer fingers in the pie, the better.

Even without live music we had a decent crowd. A gang of Mexicans shot pool in the back, the college boys roared and guzzled pitchers of Bud Light, and a few regulars sat hunched at the bar idly watching the hockey game. Around ten o'clock Vince and Pritchard staggered in already five sheets to the wind. Vince no longer cared if he violated his parole, and I was done babysitting him.

They sat on either side of me and slammed beers. I could tell something was eating my brother and sure enough, after a few Stags, he started in on me.

"We ain't seriously going to let that guy get away with this?"

"I don't know what's going to happen," I said. "I guess we'll find out Tuesday."

"This is fucked up." He shook his head. "I did not put my life on the line in Iraq so some scumbag lawyer could blackmail my family."

Pritchard said, "Why *did* you fight in Iraq?"

Vince thought that over. "Uhhhhh...you know, to make America great again. I mean, safe for capitalism, or some shit." He shrugged. "Fuck? I don't know. All I know is I did not put my life on the line so we'd lose our bar."

"None of that makes any sense, what you just said," Pritchard said.

Vince ignored him and pulled on his beer. "You should've told him from the start: you turn over that letter, you die a long, excruciating death."

"I tried that," I said. "Though not those exact words."

"And?"

I shrugged. "He knew I was bluffing."

"Who said anything about bluffing?" He turned to Pritchard. "You in, Pritch?"

"Fuck yeah," he said. "In what?"

I shook my head. "Forget it, bro."

Vince twirled the beer bottle between his fingers and stared at the television. "All I'm saying is, he turns over that letter, he's a dead man."

"It ain't enough that one of us is going to go away for life?"

"Like I said, I did not fight the fucking Taliban to be fucked over by some scumbag attorney."

"I don't see how the two are related," Pritchard said.

Vince shot him a dirty look.

Pritchard raised his hands. "Hey, I'm in."

"No, you're not," I snapped. "Nobody's in. Now shut the hell up and drink your beer."

THIRTY-SEVEN

"My office," I said.

Sheppard followed me down the hallway to the small room in the rear of the bar where we held our Friday night card games. He took a seat at the poker table and studied the sofa against the back wall and his face folded into a possumy grin. "Your uncle and I lugged that sofa here from my law office thirty years ago. Probably hasn't been cleaned since."

I sat down on the safe. "You're probably right."

"Same poker table too. Except the felt's gone. Used to have some good times here. Playing five-card draw, Omaha Hi/Lo."

"We still do."

"Yeah?" He nodded and glanced around the room and studied some of the old flyspecked framed photographs. Then he paused and cleared his throat. "So? Do we have a deal or not?"

"One of the partners refused to sign off."

His lips pressed tight in a rigid smile. "Which one, if you don't mind my asking?"

"My mother."

"You're joking, right?"

"Nope."

"But the others—they agreed?"

I nodded. "Reluctantly."

"I'll bet I haven't seen your mother in fifteen years. She was a real sweetheart, as I recall."

"That don't begin to describe her."

Sheppard tilted his chair back and folded his arms over his chest. "So what do we do now?"

I shrugged. "This is your rodeo, not mine."

He chewed his upper lip and thought things over a minute. Then he leaned forward and laid his hands flat on the table. "Look, Denis, it won't do either of us any good if I turn over this evidence. Why don't I give you another day? Have another chat with Mother Carroll. I'm sure she'll come around when she realizes what's at stake."

"She knows what's at stake and she doesn't give a damn. Trust me, she won't change her mind."

Sheppard scowled. "Seriously? I'm giving you a free roll of the dice and you're just going to throw it away? I misjudged you, Denis. I thought you were smarter than that."

I shrugged. "You expected too much, counselor."

He drummed his fingers on the table a moment, then he shook his head and slowly stood up. "Well, no skin off my nose. I'll be able to buy this place for pennies on the dollar once the city shuts you down."

I didn't say anything to that. I watched him turn and stalk out of the room. So he wasn't bluffing after all. I pulled my copy of Goodwin's letter out of my shirt pocket and weighed it in my hand a moment, then I started down the hallway. It was my last play. He might think twice about going to the cops if he knew I had evidence of blackmail.

"Before you go," I called.

He paused halfway across the barroom floor and turned to look at me, his eyes flexed above a frown. Before he could respond, the front door flew open and a blast of arctic wind rushed into the room. Vince and Pritchard strolled into the bar. They stood there, silhouetted against the front door. I was as surprised as Sheppard to see them.

"What the hell is this?" Sheppard said.

"Hey Shep," Vince said. He shoved his hands into his jacket pockets. "Just the fellow we were hoping to see. Sit down. Let us buy you a Stag."

Sheppard paled and scanned the room for additional exits.

Vince turned, locked the front door, and pocketed his set of keys. He nodded toward me. "Give him one on the house, bro."

"Thanks but I have an appointment," Sheppard said. He turned and bumped into me as I came up behind him. He moved sideways along the bar like a panicky crab.

"What's the matter, Shep? Don't appreciate our hospitality?"

"Vince," I said, my shoulders sagging.

Vince held up a hand. "I got this, bro."

He moved toward Sheppard and pulled a pistol from his waistband, a .38 Special from the looks of it. He jabbed the barrel deep into Sheppard's gut. Sheppard let out a yelp like a puppy makes when you step on its tail.

Pritchard pulled a knife from his jacket. My eyes lit up. My Fallkniven NL4.

I turned to Vince. "What's he doing with my Fallkniven?"

"I gave it to him."

That set my teeth on edge. "You can't just give away my knife like that. It was a gift!"

"I know it was a gift," he said. "But it ain't your knife anymore. You gave it to me."

"Yeah, to you. Not to that dumb ass—"

The Fallkniven thudded into the hardwood floor not two inches from my big toe.

I glanced up to see Pritchard glaring at me, his eyes filled with darkness and murder. "I've had about enough out of you," he said. "Next time you call me a dumb ass will be the last time, you hear?"

He meant it. I stooped and pulled my knife out of the floor board and set it on the table.

Vince meanwhile shoved the .38 deeper into Sheppard's gut. "Fellas, fellas, let's try to remember why we're here." He turned to Sheppard. "Okay, Shep, fun's over. Let's have that letter."

Sheppard turned to face me, lips trembling. "What the hell is this? Have you all gone mad?"

"You heard him," Pritchard said. He gave Sheppard a hard shove. Sheppard stumbled and knocked over a chair, but he managed to remain upright.

"Christ, Vince," I said. "This is not helping."

Vince picked up the overturned chair and pushed Sheppard down into the seat. "I ain't asking again," he said. He gripped the butt of the revolver and clipped Sheppard sharply on the side of the head. Sheppard cried out and slumped to the floor. He folded up like a cheap lawn chair. He lay doubled over, cursing a blue streak.

Slowly he got to his hands and knees.

Before he could clip him again, I caught Vince's arm.

"That's enough."

"Hell if it is." He gave the old man a sharp kick in the ribs. "Think you could shakedown the Carrolls?"

Sheppard folded up again. "You're going back to prison for this," Sheppard said, coughing, choking on bile.

"Yeah? Then I'll make it worth my while," Vince said. His boot connected with Sheppard's ear. The crunch of steel-toed boot on bone sounded a lot louder than you'd think it would. Sheppard sank to the floor like a sack of wet corn.

I seized the front of Vince's jacket and dragged him away, just as Pritchard leapt onto my back. I flailed about, knocking over chairs and tables, as Pritchard wrangled me into a headlock. He had my windpipe choked off. I couldn't breathe and I couldn't shake him off. Finally I lost my balance and we crashed into a table. Chairs tumbled and scattered in every direction. Lucky for me, Pritchard took the brunt of the damage. I crawled to my feet and gave Pritchard a swift boot in the nuts, then I turned and tackled Vince just as he was about to kick out Sheppard's teeth.

I got one hand on the revolver. "Goddamn it, Vince. Let go!"

"Fuck you."

"Let go of the fucking gun!"

Something slammed into my back, something that felt like a Spanish fighting bull. Fucking Pritchard again. He buried his forearm into my windpipe.

"Let go of him!" Pritchard snarled between his teeth.

I'd just about pried the .38 from Vince's fingers when the gun exploded.

Pritchard let go of me and I worked my leg behind

Vince and body slammed him to the floor. The gun skidded across the floor, under the jukebox.

I lay on top of my brother a moment, both of us fighting to catch our breath, then I flopped onto my back. My ears rang like a fire alarm was going off next door.

I hadn't had the wind knocked out of me since high school football. While I lay there gasping for breath like a trout out of water, I heard a muffled: "Holy fuck!"

I slowly raised myself up on my elbows and followed Vince's gaze across the room.

Pritchard lay spread-eagled on the hardwood floor. The top of his head was gone. It looked like some klutz had kicked over a bucket of brains.

THIRTY-EIGHT

"Holy shit, bro! Ho-ly shit!"

My gaze shifted from Pritchard to the still smoking revolver under the jukebox.

"Whoa! It took the whole back of his head off," Vince said. From his tone you might think he was playing a video game.

I crawled over to where Pritchard lay. Yep. Deader than a slab of bacon.

"It just went off," I said. That was all I could think to say. It seemed to cover it.

"Yeah it did." My brother squatted beside me. "Bro, I am flashing back to OEF, big time." He got to his feet and strode over to the jukebox and picked up the .38. He set the revolver on a table beside the Fallkniven. The room reeked of gunpowder.

"What's OEF?" I said. I couldn't hear a damn thing out of my left ear, and the right one buzzed like a hornet's nest.

"What's OEF? Operation Enduring Fucking Freedom." He paused. "Well, I guess that would be OEFF."

He glanced around the room. "I don't know about you, but I could use a drink." He walked over to the bar and returned with a new bottle of Fireball whiskey and pulled up a chair. He cracked the cap and took a swig and passed the bottle to me. I sat on the floor and guzzled some and handed the bottle back. The whiskey sat in my stomach and smoldered like charcoal.

Vince stared at Pritchard's corpse. "You think anybody heard that?"

"I think everybody heard that."

Vince was silent a moment while we both pricked our ears for sirens.

"Do you hear hornets?" I said.

"I don't hear anything."

Vince, ex-bomb squad leader, ex-war hero, ex-con, was taking this a lot better than I was. I'm no health professional, but I'm pretty sure I was officially in a state of shock.

"Fuck man, what are we going to do with that?" he said.

I thought about that. I glanced over at Sheppard. He didn't look like he was doing much better than Pritchard. I picked myself up off the floor. I was sick and tired of making plans to dispose of corpses.

Though I wasn't about to put Vince in charge.

"Where'd you get that .38?" I said.

"Sara's house. It was Roy's. I think he found it at the dump years ago. Why?"

"So they can't trace it to us?"

He thought that over. "Seems unlikely."

I straightened in relief. I could faintly hear the hiss of air brakes on the street out front of the bar. The number seventy bus.

"Dude, we got to get rid of that," Vince said, cutting his eyes toward Pritchard. "We could take it out to the woods somewhere and bury it. Out behind Grandma and

Grandpa's place. There ain't no one there. The house is empty."

"Why do you keep saying that?"

He looked at me. "What?"

"You keep calling him *it* and *that*. He's only been dead like two minutes."

"What's it matter what I call it?"

"You did it again," I said. "How about some respect for the dead?" I couldn't believe I was saying that. About Pritchard. "Anyway, we ain't just going to dump him out back of the trailer. Use your head."

"Oh, that's right. I forgot you were the brains of this outfit. That's why there's a corpse and a comatose lawyer on the floor of your tavern."

"Our tavern."

"Suddenly it's *our* tavern." Vince lifted the bottle of Fireball and took a healthy slug and stared at the gory pattern on the floor. He chuckled lightly. "I didn't think Pritchard had so many brains."

"Glad you've retained your lame sense of humor."

He chuckled again, then he sobered and said, "You got any of that Ativan left?"

"No," I lied.

"What do you got?"

"I got a fucking mess on my hands, is what I got."

Vince sighed and stared at the floor. "Somebody's going to have to clean this up."

"Let's not get ahead of ourselves," I said. I jerked my head toward Sheppard. "We still got that ass clown to deal with." I walked over to where Sheppard lay. His skin was pale and the side of his head was a red pulpy mess. I nudged him with the toe of my shoe.

No response.

"Bastard better have that letter on him," I said. I squatted down next to him and turned him over. "Oh shit."

"What?"

Once again I felt the icy footsteps of death tramping up and down my spine. It was getting to be a familiar feeling. "Ohhhhh shit."

"What's wrong?"

"Dude, I don't think this fucker's breathing."

I squatted on my heels and plunged my fingers into his neck and tried to find a pulse. I couldn't tell. His neck was all cordy and thick. I was probably feeling around in the wrong place.

Vince took a slug of Fireball. "What're you saying?" he said.

"Hang on," I said. I got up and walked around to the back of the bar. I dug through the lost and found till I found what I was looking for—a little compact some gal left in the ladies' room ages ago. I went back and knelt beside Sheppard and placed the mirror up to his mouth. The mirror fogged slightly. But not so you'd notice. I shook my head and pocketed the compact.

"He ain't dead, is he?"

I sat on the floor and didn't say anything.

"Fuck, bro. I didn't mean to kill the old dude," Vince said, wringing his hands. It was the first time I'd ever seen my war hero brother act scared. Really scared. "Jesus McChrist, we got two fucking corpses here!"

I made no reply.

"Dude, we got to call Chad," he said.

I could feel anger swelling my throat. "Are you crazy? Hell no we ain't calling Chad!"

I hugged my knees to my chest, trying to think, but

my head still throbbed with blood and my ears still buzzed from the gunshot.

"You got a better idea?" he said.

"If you'd shut the hell up I might be able to think!"

That shut him up.

A moment passed before I came up with something. Something insanely stupid.

So insanely stupid it just might work.

"We're going to make it look like they were brawling," I said.

Vince gave me a dubious look. "Seriously? That's your plan?"

I nodded.

"These two? Brawling? Pritchard, yeah. I could see that. But the old dude? He's a tax attorney or something like that."

"You ain't helping," I said. I picked up the .38 and went around to the bar and found a bar rag and wiped the .38 clean, then I put the gun in Sheppard's grasp and aimed toward the wall. I pulled the trigger.

A dull click.

"What the hell?" I said. "You only put one bullet in this thing?"

"There were four, I think," Vince said. "You want to tell me what you're doing?"

I snapped open the cylinder. There were two more cartridges inside. I nodded toward Sheppard. "Sheppard shot Pritchard. So there's got to be gunpowder residue on his hand."

Vince lifted his eyebrows. He seemed impressed.

I wiped the gun on the rag again and pressed it into Sheppard's hand. The tendons in his hand tensed a little.

I fired at the wall at about the same spot Pritchard

had stood. The shot went far right, straight through the jukebox. Glass spilled to the floor.

"Nice shot," Vince said.

I let the revolver slip from Sheppard's hand. "I hated that goddamn thing anyway."

"Not to be a killjoy or anything," Vince said, "but how're we going to explain the two shots so far apart? Timewise, I mean."

"Hell, I don't know. Do I got to think of everything?"

I went around to the back of the bar and scrubbed the residue off my hands and studied Sheppard, watched the slow rise and fall of his breathing. I was surprised Vince didn't notice it. I dried my hands and tossed the rag into the sink, then I surveyed the crime scene. The brains and blood spatter on the floor. Broken table, overturned chairs. Gun shot jukebox. I had no idea what I'd tell the cops. Not yet.

Vince shrugged and walked over to the bar and passed me the bottle of Fireball. I took a long swig.

"Let me worry about this," I said. "For now, you just need to get the hell out of here. Before the cops show up."

Vince looked aggrieved. "Why me?"

"Because, Einstein, you're not supposed to be anywhere near a bar. Remember? Your parole?"

"Fuck that."

"Besides I still owe you one."

He didn't say anything to that. He took another slug of whiskey. He stared at the bodies on the floor. After a moment he said, "Hate to be a downer, but your little plan ain't going to work."

"Why not?"

"Because," he said, "they're smarter than us—the cops."

A TASTE OF SHOTGUN

"Cops ain't smart."

"Well, maybe not the cops, but the detectives. They're professionals. You came up with this plan in what, thirty seconds? They'll have weeks or months to unravel it. And they got blood spatter science and forensics. Medical examiners. Don't you watch TV?"

I knew he was right, but what else were we going to do?

"Dude, we ain't got time for this," I said. "Where's your truck?"

"Out front."

"Oh for god's sake." I went around the bar to the front door. I opened the door and poked my head out. A city salt truck splashed by. Other than that, the coast was clear. "Go on, get out of here."

Vince slipped the bottle of Fireball into his jacket pocket and eased out the front door. He walked across the street and climbed into his truck and gave me a short little wave. I waited till the truck rattled off down the square, then I went over to where Sheppard lay and I rifled through his pockets.

The original was in his suit coat pocket. I strode over to the bar, picked up a book of matches, and lit the bottom corner of the letter. When the flames licked my fingers I dropped the letter into the sink. Then I washed the ashes down the drain.

Over the buzzing in my ear I heard Sheppard let out a low moan. You really had to strain to hear it.

I looked over the room once again. The Fallkniven lay beside the revolver on the table.

I still didn't hear any sirens. How the hell could nobody have heard the gunshots?

Maybe I *had* gone deaf.

Then I heard the sirens.

THIRTY-NINE

A crew-cut cop escorted me back to the interview room. Same room I'd been in before. He took down my statement in all its gory, make-believe detail, then I signed. Then he told me to wait and locked the door behind him. Never a good sign.

I was left to stew in my own juices some forty-five minutes before Stakoff showed up, arms loaded with brown and manila folders.

"Happy Ruination Day, Denis."

I scowled. "I don't know what that is."

"No? April fourteenth?"

"I know what day it is."

Stakoff dumped the folders on the desk and pulled up a chair. "April fourteenth. The assassination of the Great Emancipator, the sinking of the Titanic, the Black Sunday dust storm of 1935, and now this. The Great Brass Lantern Massacre."

I suppose that's what passed for cop humor.

I decided to play it like I was the aggrieved party, the victim. Two drunken idiots wreaked havoc on a small, family-owned business. "An hour I've been sitting here," I grumbled.

Stakoff opened a can of Sprite and glanced at his

wristwatch. "Forty-six minutes." He searched through the folders, then paused and glanced up at me. "Care for a sodie?"

"No, I don't care for a sodie. I gave my statement, signed it and everything. Can I go now? It's been a long day."

He snuffled noisily, opened a folder, and studied my statement. "Sure. Just a few things to straighten out. Shouldn't take too long."

I pointed to the file in his hand. "Everything I got to say is right there."

"Just a couple things to clear up."

I rested my forehead in my hands and rubbed my eyes with the balls of my hands. "Fine. Just get on with it."

He slipped a pair of reading glasses from his shirt pocket and pushed the glasses up the bridge of his nose and pulled a sheet of paper from the file. "Let's see what we got here. Robert Duane Pritchard. Twenty-nine years old. Born Galesburg, Illinois. Arrests for armed robbery. DUI. Public intoxication. Drug possession. Assault and battery. Damage to public property, public urination. Huh. Appears to be a warrant for his arrest. Failed to report to his parole officer." He put the sheet back in the file and looked over his glasses at me. "A real role model, this guy."

I didn't say anything.

He thumbed another paper. "Clark Pennington Sheppard, Esquire." He lowered the sheet and glanced at me knowingly. "Sixty-eight. Retired tax attorney. Business owner." He set down the file. "So your story is these two fellers got into an altercation? A barroom brawl?"

"It's not a story. It's a fact."

"A shitbum ex-con and a tax attorney?"

I drummed on the desk with my fingers. "Just like it says in my statement."

Stakoff tilted his chair back. "So according to your statement Sheppard shot Pritchard—" he paused and glanced down at the paper. "—then Pritchard knifed Sheppard?"

I shook my head.

"No?"

"You got it backwards. Pritchard stuck Sheppard, then Sheppard plugged Pritchard."

"Huh." Stakoff frowned and scrawled something down on the file. "And you saw it?"

"Isn't that what I said?"

"You want to just humor me?"

"Humor you? What is this, improv night at the city jail?" I said. "Look, Butch, I get it. You want to see if I change my story. Maybe if I repeat it enough times I'll screw up some of the details."

Stakoff gave me his best poker face. "I got all day, Denis."

I crossed one foot over the other and folded my arms over my chest. "Like it says in my statement, I saw some of it. After the first gunshot."

"So where were you *before* the first gunshot?"

"In the walk-in cooler. Doing my job."

"So you came out after the first gunshot and what'd you see?"

"I saw two drunken idiots fighting over a gun. Sheppard had the .38 and Pritchard had a knife."

"So it was Sheppard's .38?"

"No idea."

"Was he carrying a .38 when he came in?"

"Couldn't say. He did go out to his vehicle though. That could've been when he got it."

"When did he go out to his vehicle?"

"Right before I went to the cooler. I thought he was leaving."

"Why'd you think that?"

"Like I said, they were arguing. I figured the old fart had had enough and was going home."

Stakoff scowled. "So you came out when you heard the first shot and then what?"

"I ducked behind the bar. I wasn't about to catch a stray bullet, know what I mean?"

Stakoff scowled. "Did Clark Pennington Sheppard, Esquire often carry a weapon?"

"No idea."

He nodded. "All right. What happened then? After you daringly ducked behind the bar?"

"Pritchard plunged the dagger into Sheppard's chest and Sheppard smoked Pritchard." I shrugged. "Then I called the cops."

Stakoff laced his hands behind his head and gazed at me, unblinking. "Where was your brother when all of this was going down?"

"Which brother?"

"The one that just got out of prison."

"How should I know?"

"So he wasn't there at the time of this alleged altercation?"

"That would've been a violation of his parole."

He stared at me blankly, his lips pressed into a fine line. "Of course. How silly of me." He paused a moment, then said, "How do you know Robert Pritchard?"

I took several seconds to search for an answer. He

was fishing, but I wasn't about to lawyer up. Not yet. "What makes you think I knew him?"

"Did you?"

"Barely."

He bit back a smile. "Interesting. How'd you come to know a shitbird like Pritchard?"

"I run a bar. I meet lots of shitbirds. Including cops."

"How'd you come to meet this shitbird in particular?"

"When I picked up Vince from the work camp he offered Pritchard a lift."

"Interesting."

"Not really."

"So Vince knew Pritchard?"

"They'd just met."

"If they just met why'd he offer him a ride?"

"Because Vince's kind-hearted, to a fault."

"A kind-hearted dope dealer," Stakoff said, thinking that over. "Now there's something you don't find every day."

I let that pass. "He's also a war hero. A war hero who suffers PTSD and traumatic brain injury."

"So where's this Pritchard been staying?"

"No idea."

"Maybe with Vince?"

"Like I said, I have no idea."

"I expect that won't be too hard to find out."

I cleared my throat. "We done here?"

Stakoff hawked up something big and gross and swallowed it. "Well now, that all depends." He washed it down with a swig of Sprite and smacked his lips. "Sure you don't want a sodie?"

I slowly shook my head.

Stakoff sat up. "Pritchard ever been in your bar before?"

"Couldn't say. I'm not there every day, you know. I do take a night off every once in a while."

Stakoff popped his knuckles on his right hand. "What I don't get is what Pritchard was still doing here. He was supposed to report to his P.O. in Galesburg two weeks ago."

"Like I said, I didn't know him."

"You said you *barely* knew him."

"I *hardly* knew him."

Stakoff went to work on the knuckles on his left hand. "So you hadn't seen him since you and Vince gave him that ride?"

I folded my arms over my chest and looked at the wall. "I might've seen him once."

"Where was that?"

"I don't remember."

"You remember seeing him, you just don't remember where?"

"Maybe. I can't be sure."

Stakoff scowled. He pulled a cough drop from his shirt pocket and slowly unwrapped it and popped the yellow lozenge into his mouth. He left the wrapper on the table. "Lawyer Sheppard. How long have you known him?"

"I remember seeing him around the bar when I was a kid."

"So you've known him a long time?"

"I've known who he was a long time. Just another bar fly."

"He get into a lot of barroom brawls?"

"I wouldn't say a lot."

"What would you say?"

"One or two."

"When was the last one?"

I pretended to think about that. "Can't recall."

"But you do recall other brawls involving Mr. Sheppard?"

"I think so. Maybe. I can't be positive."

The cough drop clicked on his teeth. Stakoff thumped a stubby index finger on a sheet of paper. "Witness says there was a four-and-a-half-minute elapse between gunshots."

"Seems long, but okay."

"How long would you say?"

"Minute or two."

"Don't suppose the bar had video cameras?"

"Nope."

"Silly of me." Stakoff sucked noisily on the lozenge. "Any idea what they were fighting about?"

"Sports, I think."

"Sports?"

I nodded.

"You're telling me two men are dead over sports?"

"You think that's unusual? People go ape shit over sports. They fought an entire war over soccer in Central America back in the sixties. Ever hear of the Soccer War? Course down there they called it the Football War."

"Never heard of it," Stakoff said.

"All I know is they were arguing about sports when I went to the back room. I got sick of listening to them."

"Sports."

"Uh huh."

"I'm not even going to ask which sport."

"Hockey."

"That's barely even a sport."

I didn't say anything to that. After a moment, I said, "We finished?"

He crunched on the lozenge and chewed till it was gone, then he swallowed. "One more thing I don't get. Sheppard had gunpowder residue on his right hand. But he was a southpaw. I checked with his secretary."

I sat still, brain seizing. It was always the little things—whether someone was right handed or left handed—that trip you up, that turn out to be the difference between going home and going to the chair. I shrugged. "Maybe his left hand was disabled. From fighting. Why ask me?"

"Yeah." Stakoff slowly stood up. He collected the folders and files in his arms but left the can of Sprite on the table.

"Am I free to go?"

"Sure. Free as a mountain goat." He paused at the door and turned back. "Oh, in case you were wondering, we're following some new leads in the Goodwin case. We're not done there. Not by a long shot."

I didn't say anything. I just wanted to get the hell out of there. Only Stakoff wasn't finished.

"And since this is the third homicide at your bar in five years, I'm afraid I'm going to have to ask the city council to shut you down. Nothing personal, you understand. We just can't have this sort of thing in our town." He grinned at me and jerked his head toward the hallway. "You know the way out."

FORTY

Sara wanted to see the three of us.

No doubt, she'd heard about the "incident" at the bar and all the fallout from that.

I got Roy's truck running and drove out to the trailer to pick up Vince, whose pickup had broken down. I rapped on the trailer door and waited. No answer. Not a sound. A minute later the screen door to my grandparents' house creaked open and Vince appeared on the steps, pulling on a Dickies hoodie. "You don't think I'm going to freeze to death in that tin can when this place is sitting here empty?" he said.

I'd finally got the electricity and water turned on in the trailer, but apparently that wasn't good enough for him. I turned and started back to Roy's truck. "It won't be empty for long," I said. "New tenant's moving in next weekend."

"Dude, why don't we rent the trailer and let me stay in the house. Sara will never know."

"I found a tenant for the house, not the trailer. But you're welcome to take over landlord duties. Any time."

We climbed into Roy's truck and I cranked the engine.

"Christ, this truck smells like ass," Vince said. "I don't know how you can stand it."

"It's that or public transportation. And public transportation doesn't come out here." I backed up and pointed the pickup toward town. "You figure out what's wrong with your truck?"

"I've narrowed it down to the carburetor, the starter, the celluloid, or the spark plugs."

"I wouldn't call that narrowing it down."

A light winter rain began to fall. I switched on the wipers. Then I noticed there weren't any wipers.

"Anything on this truck work?" Vince said.

"Engine, brakes and one of the headlights. That's basically all you need, right there."

"I don't know, wipers would be good right about now."

Wipers or no wipers, we made it to Sara's house. I pulled up behind Chad's truck, took out my flask, and popped a couple Ativan.

"Got one for me?" Vince said.

I scowled, shook a pill into his hand, and passed the flask. "Thanks, man, we're going to need this."

Walking through the garage, we could hear Sara hollering over the television. "Another shooting? Is he running a bar or a damn shooting gallery?"

We paused in the hallway. Chad was rooting under cushions and searching under stacks of pizza boxes and newspapers looking for the channel changer.

"Where the hell's the remote?" he yelled.

"There's like six of them," I said. "But good luck finding any of them."

Sara frowned across the room at me. "Your father and your uncle ran that bar for thirty years and nobody ever shot anyone! Not once!"

"Hey Ma," Vince said.

"Hi sweetie," she said, her gaze softening. Then she leveled her eyes at me and snarled. "You better have brung Roy's truck back."

"I did, but I'm going to need it a while longer."

"What?" she yelled.

I went over and unplugged the television. Sara fumed helplessly in her lounger. The room fell silent, the only sounds were Sara's labored breathing, the low hum of the refrigerator, and a neighbor's dog barking idiotically.

Sara turned to Chad. "He stole Roy's truck!"

"You don't have to yell," I said. "I turned off the TV."

Chad said, "Can we get down to business? Some of us have to go to work."

We made room on the sofa and easy chairs and the three of us sat down. Chad cleared his throat. "Ma, the city is going to pull our liquor license and shut down the bar. And once they do, there ain't a thing we can do about it. There's no appeal. There's no other options. I think we need to sell the bar."

"Why am *I* losing my liquor license?" she cried. "I didn't shoot anyone. It's you damn trigger happy kids that ought to lose your license."

"They're going to close the bar, regardless," I said. "We have to put it up for sale. There's no other choice."

Sara folded her flabby arms across her chest and glared at me. "First you ask me to give away my bar, now you're trying to make me sell it. You think I don't know what this is?"

We waited.

"I know exactly what this is," she said.

I wanted to strangle her. I really did. Fortunately

Chad had the patience of a medieval saint.

"Ma, our saloon keeping days are over. Okay?" Chad said. "If we don't sell, it's just going to sit there and depreciate. If we're lucky we can get maybe a hundred grand for it now. Stock and all." Chad glanced at me and Vince. "That is, whatever stock Dumb and Dumber haven't drunk up. If we let it sit empty for years we'll get less. It'll deteriorate. It'll get broken into. We have to sell. End of story."

Sara was silent. I could tell she was calculating her next move. "Fine. But I want half."

"What?" I said.

"I want half of whatever we get."

I exploded. "Jesus Christ! Now my own mother is extorting me!"

Chad turned to me. "Shut up, Denis."

I gave him a look, but kept my mouth shut.

"You boys made this mess, not me, so you ought to pay. I get half or there's no deal."

Chad thought things over a minute, then he said. "Fine. You'll get half the sale price."

I pulled Chad aside and hissed into his ear. "I owe my lawyer like five thousand bucks, and we haven't even started on the divorce," I said. "And in case you're forgetting, I'm not going to have a job anymore."

"Wait," Chad said, "you're getting a divorce?"

Damn it. I forgot I hadn't told him about the separation. "Can we talk about that later?"

Sara's ears pricked up. "Who's getting a divorce?"

"Christ," I said, sagging back into the sofa. "Reva and I are separating, okay?"

"Separating or divorcing?" Sara said.

"I don't know. We're separating first."

The room was silent as the news sunk in.

"Well, I don't blame her," Sara said.

After a while, Chad put his hand on Vince's shoulder. "What do you say? Split our half three ways?"

He shrugged. "What kind of war hero would I be if I didn't take one for the team?"

Chad turned to Sara. "Deal."

Sara started to say something else, but Chad cut her off.

"Don't get greedy, Ma."

She scowled. "Fine. Now plug in my television."

Well, that was easy. Easier than I thought it'd be.

I went over and plugged in the TV. The room filled with inane noise. I gave Chad an awkward pat on the back. "Thanks, man," I said. Then I turned to Vince. "Let's get the hell out of here."

We were halfway out the front door when Sara yelled something.

"What'd she say?" I said.

"She said don't forget to take out the trash."

FORTY-ONE

The next city council meeting was two weeks away. The bar, however, remained a crime scene and closed for business. It was kind of nice having the place to ourselves, drinking up the liquor supply and listening to old country-western songs on the shot-up jukebox.

Toohey called. He said the cops were unable to locate Erica Wainwright; they'd pretty much concluded that she'd run off to avoid questioning. At the same time, Stakoff didn't for one second buy my story about the barroom brawl.

So we waited and popped pills and drank and argued over which decade had the best country music. My view was country music peaked in the seventies with Willie and Waylon and Jerry Jeff Walker. Vince thought the peak was the sixties with George Jones and Merle Haggard and Buck Owens and Johnny Cash.

I countered with Tom T. Hall, Charlie Pride, Kris Kristofferson.

Vince: Roger Miller, Glen Campbell, Tammy Wynette, Patsy Cline.

We agreed to disagree. We killed off a bottle of Fireball and sat in the dark listening to Glen Campbell's heartbreakingly beautiful rendition of "Galveston," the greatest anti-Vietnam War song ever. When the strings faded, I got up to put some more money in the jukebox. More Glen Campbell seemed about right. I punched in "Wichita Lineman" and "Gentle on My Mind," then went back to our table. Vince turned to me and said, "I've had something on my mind too…"

"Yeah?"

"Newspaper said Sheppard died from a knife wound to the chest," he said. "Funny. That ain't how I remember things standing when I left."

I shrugged. "You were kind of shook up. Might've been in a state of shock. Might not be remembering things too clearly."

He cut his eyes at me. "Uh huh."

I closed my eyes and let the ending of "Wichita Lineman" wash over me. "You may be right about the sixties after all," I said. "Damn that's a great song."

"Love how you changed the topic there."

I smiled at that. The front windows lit up momentarily as a patrol car pulled up to the front doors. I went over to the windows, peered out, and watched Stakoff ease out of the cruiser.

"Shit," Vince cried. His eyes darted around the bar. "I told you them cops weren't stupid, with all their forensics and shit!"

"Take it easy, Mr. War Hero. If they were going to arrest us, there'd be more than one cop."

I told him to go back to the office, close the door, and stop worrying. He grabbed a bottle of Southern Comfort, then steadied himself and staggered down the hallway.

A loud rap at the front entrance. It dawned on me that we'd been sitting in the dark, the only light the dying rays that sifted through the smoked window glass. I flipped on the overhead lights and unlocked the door. Stakoff stood heavily behind the yellow police tape.

"Evening Denis. Thought I saw somebody's truck parked out back."

I didn't say anything to that.

He began spooling the crime scene tape around his wrist. "Mustn't waste the taxpayers' money."

I waited for him to bawl me out for trespassing on a crime scene, maybe even cite me, but I guess he had other things on his mind.

"You alone?"

"Uh huh."

"Mind if I come in?"

I stepped aside and he shoved the police tape into his coat pocket and followed me inside.

"Think you missed something?"

"I seldom miss anything, Denis. You know that." He looked the place over. He picked up one of the two glasses from our table, studied it, but didn't remark on it.

"Can I get you something? A whiskey? A beer? A waterboard?"

"No thanks." He walked over to the bar and glanced behind it. "Been a busy month. Winter's usually our slow season."

"Same here."

"There was something I wanted to talk to you about. A recent employee of yours. Erica Wainwright."

I walked behind the bar and opened a jar of olives and popped a couple into my mouth. "Dinner time," I said and offered Stakoff the bottle. He shook his head.

"Heard she's skipped town," I said and spat the pimentos into my palm.

"Who told you that?"

"My attorney."

"A friend of Erica's said she was supposed to visit her in Salt Lake City. Only she never showed up."

"Huh."

"Huh is right. Like she vanished into thin air."

"Maybe things got too hot for her after she murdered her uncle? You ask me, she made up that story about staying with a friend in Utah. Probably to throw you off her scent. My guess is she's probably in Florida right now."

"Florida?"

"Or Texas. That's where rednecks go when they leave southern Illinois. Florida or Texas. Just like being at home, only the weather's warmer."

He scowled at that and zipped up his coat. "Yeah. Thanks." He studied the room again and snuffled loudly. "I wouldn't mind being in Florida right about now."

"What's keeping you?"

He ignored that and turned to leave. "Well, you boys behave yourselves," he said. "And tell Vince hello when you see him."

"Will do, Butch."

After the door closed, Vince strode out of the back room holding one of Chuck's vintage *Playboy* magazines from the seventies.

I said, "Told you it was nothing."

Vince went over to the window and watched Stakoff leave.

"You heard?" I said.

"I heard."

"What do you think?"

"I wouldn't mind being in Florida right now, either." His eyes glanced toward the jukebox.

"Don't even think about playing Jimmy Buffet," I warned him. "I will shoot you."

Vince laughed. A bit uneasily.

FORTY-TWO

I was awakened by the sound of something pounding. It took a while to remember where I was, and even longer to figure out that the noise was coming from the front door and not from inside my skull. I lifted my head from the table. "We're closed!" I yelled.

It felt like the top of my head had fallen off.

The door opened. Toohey strode in, dressed like he was going hiking through a Land's End catalog.

"Oh, it's you," I said, my mouth full of cotton.

"Nice to see you, too."

The bar was dark and the shattered jukebox was still playing old country tunes from the fifties. Vince slept right through it, snoring like a jet engine, a puddle of drool spilling out of his open mouth. Toohey went behind the bar, found a rocks glass, and filled it with ice. He pulled up a chair and unscrewed the cap on a bottle of whiskey and splashed a little over the cubes. He nodded toward Vince. "He all right?"

"Not a care in the world."

Toohey smiled. "What are we listening to?"

"That's old Hank."

"Williams?"

"Thompson."

A TASTE OF SHOTGUN

"Cool."

The hangover was bad. One of those poisonous ones that'd last a whole day if you let it, so you're better off if you start drinking again. After a moment I said, "Stakoff was in earlier. Wanted me to help him find the chick that's trying to frame me for murdering her uncle."

"What'd you tell him?"

"Told him I'm a little busy right now watching my world crumble around my ears."

Toohey took a sip of whiskey. I wondered what it must be like never to have money problems. Or family problems. Any kind of problems. A guy who drinks whiskey for the mere pleasure of it.

I hated the fucker.

"This is good," Toohey said. "What are we drinking?" He examined the label. "Ah. George Dickel. Sour mash. Number 12. Good stuff." He savored a mouthful, then said, "About Goodwin—"

Vince let out a loud sleep fart.

Toohey grinned and continued. "The killer's trail gets colder by the day. Won't be long and it'll be in the cold case file."

"I'll drink to that," I said and slammed back the last of my whiskey. Toohey sipped his drink and frowned at me. "Denis, Dickel is meant to be savored, not slammed."

"Don't tell me how to drink my booze," I said. "What about Sheppard?"

"Right. That's what I came by to tell you. I talked to the prosecutor this morning. For now they're going with your version of events. I think one cold case at a time is enough for them. That could change, but I don't think it will."

Vince stirred and lifted his head. "What could change?"

"Go back to sleep," I said.

Toohey said, "I don't suppose we have to worry about that letter anymore."

"Letter? I don't even know what you're talking about." I refilled my glass. The booze was working. The hangover felt like it was melting away.

One record finished and another began. An old Kitty Wells tune. After a moment Toohey said, "You still need my help with that other issue?"

I nodded toward Vince. "He already knows," I said. "And yes."

"What do I know?" Vince said. He reached for the bottle of Dickel, which I moved just out of his reach.

"About me and Reva."

"Oh yeah. That sucks."

Toohey killed his drink and set the empty glass on the table. "Come by tomorrow at one o'clock. We'll get things rolling."

"I don't know. I'd like to talk to her one more time. Maybe…you know…"

He gave me a pathetic look and stood up and zipped up his thousand-dollar Canada Goose jacket. "Thanks for the drink."

After Toohey left, Vince reached for the bottle and I moved it again. "Who was that asshole?" he said.

"My lawyer," I said.

He thought about that. "Nice jacket," he said.

FORTY-THREE

Chad represented the family at that month's city council meeting. He made a gallant effort on our behalf, noting that neither of the incidents—the first shooting or the second knifing/shooting—were the fault of the bar owners and could have happened any place where liquor flows freely, including Hooters and Buffalo Wild Wings. It was a pathetic argument, which Police Sergeant Stakoff destroyed when he reminded the board about the five pounds of weed found at the bar and Vince's subsequent arrest.

Sara insisted on attending the meeting, and since I was still borrowing Roy's truck, I had to pick her up and drive her there. We sat in the front row and when it came her turn to speak, Sara said it wasn't fair that she should be penalized because of her no-account kids, and that since she was homebound she couldn't be expected to know everything that was going on at the bar, and if the council would let her keep her liquor license she would fire me and get someone competent to run the bar, someone who wasn't so "damn trigger happy."

Mind you, she said all of this with me sitting right beside her.

In his statement to the board, Stakoff noted that the

Carroll family had run The Brass Lantern for generations and it had always been a welcome part of the business community as well as the social life of the town. "Heck, when I was a boy the Lantern sponsored my little league baseball team," he said. "But the current generation—with the possible exception of my friend Chad Carroll—has proven itself unfit to operate such an establishment. In the past five years there have been three violent deaths on the premises, in addition to a drug arrest for which one of the owners served four years in prison. I therefore have no alternative but to ask the board to rescind the Class C license of the Carroll family to service liquor in the city."

In the end, the board went with the recommendation of the police and voted seven to one to revoke "indefinitely" our liquor license. The only no vote came from my alderman and son's basketball coach, Dale "Equal Time" Schuhardt. Funny. I thought the guy hated my guts.

The next morning I began the long, hopeless process of looking for a job. The only skill I had was running a tavern—it was all I'd ever done and all I was good at. And there were damn few taverns anymore that weren't corporate chains. The manager of a place called Hooligans Sports Bar and Grill in St. Louis County called me back and said they couldn't offer me a manager position or even a bartender job, but they could use a dishwasher. Like I was going to drive Roy's truck eighty miles round trip to wash dishes for a lousy seven bucks an hour or whatever the hell minimum wage was in Missouri. That was about as low as I'd ever felt. After a few days I stopped looking for work. I filed for unemployment, which was immediately garnished for child support, and I went back to sitting around The Brass Lan-

A TASTE OF SHOTGUN

tern in the dark drinking up the stock and listening to Conway Twitty and Loretta Lynn on the shot-up jukebox.

Looking back, I suspect if something hadn't happened soon I would've either drank myself to death or sucked on the barrel of my nine-millimeter Smith & Wesson. It seemed like everything had gone sour inside me. I'd taken to fantasizing about Reva driving over to the bar, all set to harangue me over child support, and finding me sprawled on the barroom floor where I'd been rotting a good week or two, the back of my head blown off. I hoped I looked nice and disgusting so she'd have that ghastly image to haunt her dreams the rest of her goddamn life.

Then a couple of things happened. First, we got an offer on the bar—some out-of-state developer who wanted to raze the building and put up a parking garage, contingent on receiving a shit ton of tax abatements and subsidies from the city. He offered us seventy thousand. He acted like he was doing us, the city, and all of mankind a great favor. It wasn't like there was a shortage of parking downtown. That's pretty much all downtown was—an empty parking lot.

That turned out to be the only offer we got. We took it.

Sara got half the sale price and we split the rest. I sent a third of my take to Toohey and mailed the rest to Reva.

The other thing that happened was I ran into Stakoff in the parking lot of a greasy spoon called the Hi-Ho Diner. It was around midnight. He and some buddies had been out drinking, and I had on my usual drunk. He greeted me like an old friend, all back slaps and glad hands. He told me he was truly sorry about having to shut down the bar, but he didn't have a choice. He said he had some news that would cheer me up. Cops had put Clay Goodwin's murder in the cold case files. Off the record, he said, whoever killed Goodwin did St. Clair County a service, maybe even deserved some kind of medal.

Then he shook my hand and wished me luck.

The next afternoon I was moping around The Brass Lantern. We were down to the last of the liqueurs: sweet vermouth, triple sec, crème de menthe. I didn't care, as long as it contained alcohol. I was paging through an old photo album containing ghostly snapshots of Uncle Chuck and Pop and long-dead regulars, thinking how in a month or two the bar would be a goddamn parking garage, when somebody knocked on the door. I yelled that we were closed, but the asshat kept right on knocking. I got up and opened the front door.

"We're closed! Can't you read the goddamn sign?"

It was some tall dude I'd never seen before. A guy with a lantern jaw and prominent gut. "Denis James Carroll?" he said.

"What?"

He shoved an envelope in my hand. "You've been served."

FORTY-FOUR

Thanks to Toohey, the settlement was an even split. I got the twins every other weekend and two months during summer. Reva got to keep the van, while the house went on the market. I got to stay in the house till it was sold, though mostly I slept on the sofa at the bar.

Like father, like son.

The day we closed on the Lantern was frigid and overcast. A late winter storm bore down from the north and threatened a wintry mix of snow and ice. I stopped by the bar to pack up the last of our things. It was my first weekend with the kids since the divorce and I'd promised to take them to a matinee to see some new Disney flick. I didn't care if it would be awful and noisy and crowded as hell, I was going to start being a better father, even if it killed me.

I had most of the stuff boxed up, crap left over from when Uncle Chuck ran the bar: baseball and softball trophies, crumbling photo albums. Old ledgers. A bowling ball and a few autographed pins. Stuff that didn't mean a lot to me, but I couldn't see myself tossing in the dumpster. Better to store it in a garage somewhere, let the mice chew it to pieces. I poured myself a glass of crème de cacao on the rocks. After a solid month of hard drinking we were completely out of liquor and beer. But I didn't care what I drank. As long as it got me where I needed to be.

I carried the last box out to Roy's pickup and squeezed it into the truck bed. I hadn't been gone two minutes, but when I walked back inside I heard the loud crack of pool balls. I glanced across the bar. Randy Goodwin was bent over the pool table, preparing to shoot, his long dark hair in his eyes. "Five ball in the side pocket," he drawled. He drew back and fired at a solid, but the ball ricocheted out of the pocket. When he stood up his hunting jacket fell open and I got a good look at the sidearm shoved into his waistband. My nine-millimeter Smith & Wesson. The one I kept behind the bar over the sink.

The one goddamn thing I hadn't packed.

My mind went into panic mode and I was washed with a wave of adrenaline. I thought about making a run for the back door, but then I remembered Reva and the twins. They'd be coming through the front door any minute now.

Randy cleared his throat, spat on the floor. "Been wondering what I ought to do with you," he said, almost inaudibly. He bent over the table. "Nine ball in the corner." This time he sighted on the nine carefully and knocked in the three.

I swallowed hard. "Dude, I did not kill Clay, if that's what you think." I paused. "Is that what you think? Because I didn't." I tried to sound calm, but my voice kept rising and breaking.

He lifted his gaze at me and stared at me with dead eyes. Then he limped around the table, favoring his good leg, studying his next shot.

A TASTE OF SHOTGUN

I wondered if he'd really shoot me in the back if I ran for it.

He once choked a man to death with his own small intestines. Of course he would.

I glanced furtively around the room. Nothing left in the bar to defend myself with. He had my pistol and I'd taken home the shotgun and the baseball bat. Even the little paring knife I'd used to slice lemons was in a box out in the truck bed.

"Figured I'd let the cops handle you," he said. "Till you went and accused my niece of murder. Now that done pissed me off."

I leaned against the bar, trying to buy some time till I could figure something out, come up with some idiotic plan. "Come on, dude," I said. "Think about it. Why would I kill your brother? Okay, so I got a raw deal. A lousy twenty percent. But is that a reason to kill someone?"

He called the four in the side and took aim and dropped it with a solid crack. He straightened and half smiled at me. "You think I'm stupid? You think Clay didn't tell me what happened? You shot that Sika kid because he was working for the cops. That's what you thought, anyway."

"You're crazy," I said. "It was a robbery!"

"Executed him right in front of my niece. Made sure he suffered too, didn't you? That was some fucking sloppy work, man. If you're going to off someone, you don't leave witnesses." He leaned on the pool cue. "And you let your little brother take the fall." He shook his head. "Guess family doesn't mean shit to you Carrolls."

I held silent.

"Then you go out to Clay's house and shoot him

down like a dirty dog. Afraid he'd tell the law how you executed that Sika kid?"

He picked up a cube of chalk and chalked the tip of his cue.

"One thing I don't get. How you could be so stupid to leave behind the murder weapon?" He shook his head and chuckled. "Amateur. Figured the police wouldn't give a rat's ass, right? Just another dead white trash dealer."

I started to say something when he slammed the pool stick down on the table, snapping it in half. "SHUT UP WHEN I'M TALKING!" he screamed. The top half of the stick shot up, hit the ceiling tiles, then landed a few feet from me and rolled under a table.

I studied the shaft. It wouldn't make much of a weapon.

Randy limped over to the wall rack and selected another stick. He sighted down the line for irregularities and seemed satisfied.

"Tried to frame my niece for Clay's murder, making up some bullshit story about him raping her." He bent down, then stood up again. He leaned into the table and said, "Six ball, corner pocket."

The cue ball kissed the six and went wide.

"Fucking table is lopsided," he said.

I waited till he finished, then I said, "I didn't make that up, about the rape. Your niece told me that. If anyone made it up, she did."

He took up another piece of chalk and chalked the tip. "I'll hand you one thing, though. Pretty slick how you got rid of Sheppard. Can't be leaving any snitches around, can we?"

He set the chalk down on the table. "You know, all

them people you killed—Sika, Pritchard, Sheppard—you're right, nobody gives a rat's ass about them. But you made one mistake." He paused for effect. "You fucked with my family."

My insides iced over and I felt my gut harden. "You're a special kind of crazy," I said. "I didn't kill anyone. Everyone knows Sika was robbing my bar. Everyone knows his death was self-defense." I took a deep breath. "And as for Clay and your niece, that was a family feud. It had nothing to do with me."

He shook his head. "Almost forgot the old woman you left to die in the cemetery. What was her name?"

Wow. He knew about that too. Creepy didn't begin to describe it. It was like he'd been following me around for months.

He snapped his fingers. "Helen. Helen Cole. That's right. Damn if you didn't almost get away with it too. Course you were dealing with the fucking Keystone Kops."

He was enjoying this, taking his good old time. A cat playing with a poor, doomed mouse.

Only I wasn't no fucking mouse.

He straightened and looked at me. "What do you say we make this interesting? You're a sporting fellow, ain't you, Denis? Tell you what, if I miss this shot, I'll just turn and walk out of here. With the .38, of course."

I studied the table. There were at least two shots that a blind monkey could make.

"And if you make it?"

He laughed, showing off all twelve of his rotten teeth.

Outside, tires crunched on snow as a vehicle pulled into the lot. Randy didn't seem to notice. I glanced at the clock above Uncle Chuck's shrine. It was about time for Reva and twins to show up. A cold void opened in my bowels. Any second now they'd walk right into the middle of this hell.

I was out of time. Out of options. This crazy motherfucker, no telling what he'd do to my family.

He was so cocksure he never even saw it coming. He had his back to me, bent over the table, studying his shot. I stooped for the broken pool stick and hurled myself toward him. I waited for the bullets to rip through my body but somehow it never happened. I slammed the stick alongside his head. It splintered into a dozen pieces. I was pretty sure he never knew what hit him.

He rolled off the table and slumped onto the floor. I fumbled the gun out of his belt and shoved it into his rotten mouth. His eyes were dull. He muttered something. Whatever he said, they were going to be his last words.

The van door slammed. Children's' voices rose on the crisp wintry air.

I got up and gave Randy a sharp kick in the groin and seized him by the collar and dragged his scrawny ass across the barroom floor and down the hall to the walk-in cooler. I flung open the door and dragged him inside. I gave him a nice kick in the ribs, for good measure. He let out a muffled groan, so I kicked him again, this time in the mouth. The few teeth he had would have to go anyway and besides, I didn't want any sound out of him, not while Reva and the twins were on the premises.

I closed the door and slipped the lock. Then I went over to the cooler's thermostat and turned it down as low as it would go.

***

I can't begin to describe the relief I felt. Maybe even a little satisfaction. I may not be a war hero like Vince, or a lifesaver like Chad, but sometimes I think I deserve a medal or two my own damn self, the way I've cleaned things up here, made this town a better, safer place to live. Even if nobody knows what I've done. It would be a long time before anyone reported finding a decayed, half-eaten, toothless corpse in a pot field behind Clay Goodwin's compound.

I closed the door to the hallway and walked out to the bar. I dug my hand into my pocket, dropped a dollar's worth of change into the jukebox, and scanned the playlist till I found it. Our song. "I Cross My Heart." The first song Reva and I danced to on our wedding night. George Strait's voice filled the room. Damn if George didn't know how to pull on the old heart strings.

Then I hurried to the front door to greet my family.

ACKNOWLEDGMENTS

For their words of encouragement, assistance, and expertise, as well as a certain generosity of spirit, I would like to thank Jedidiah Ayres, the late Jonathan Ashley, Paul Fairbanks, Dan Kelley, and, as always, Trina. Thanks to Chris Rhatigan and the rest of the crew at All Due Respect/Down & Out Books for their genuine love of independent literature and for putting out great books with apparently little regard for profit margins. Cheers!

Chris Orlet is the author of the crime novel *In the Pines: A Small Town Noir* (New Pulp Press). He lives in St. Louis with his wife Trina and their son and daughter.

On the following pages are a few
more great titles from the
Down & Out Books publishing family.

For a complete list of books and to
sign up for our newsletter,
go to DownAndOutBooks.com.

Flight of the Fox
Gray Basnight

Down & Out Books
July 2018
978-1-946502-61-2

After innocently receiving a mysterious encoded document, mathematics professor Sam Teagarden suddenly begins a terrifying run for his life.

While fleeing hitmen and killer drones through New York, Washington, and Key West—he decodes the document to learn it's a secret diary kept by a former FBI agent. If made public it will reveal dark crimes committed by the FBI in 20th Century.

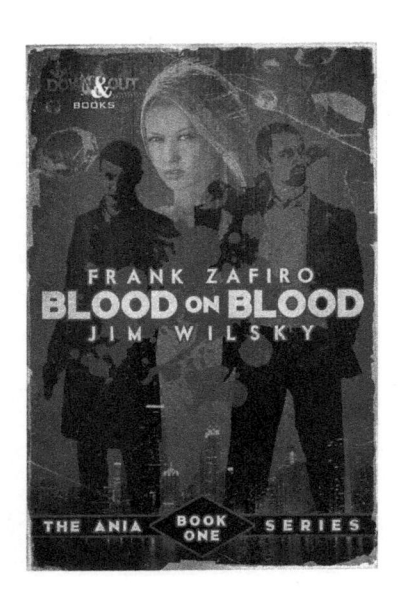

Blood on Blood
The Ania Trilogy Book One
Frank Zafiro and Jim Wilsky

Down & Out Books
978-1-946502-71-1

Estranged half-brothers Mick and Jerzy Sawyer are summoned to their father's prison deathbed. The spiteful old man tells them about missing diamonds, setting them on a path of cooperation and competition to recover them.

Along the way, Jerzy, the quintessential career criminal and Mick, the failed cop and tainted hero, encounter the mysterious, blonde Ania, resulting in a hardboiled Hardy Boys meets Cain and Abel.

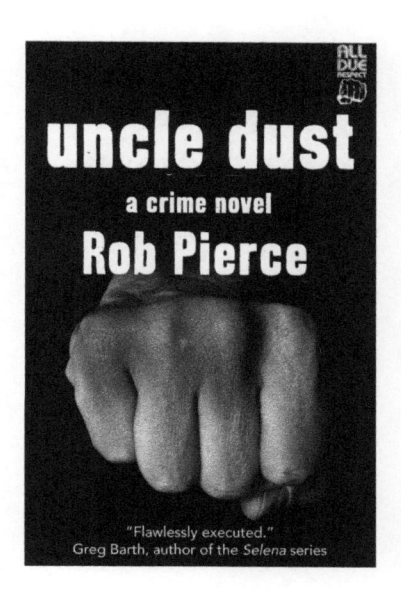

Uncle Dust
Rob Pierce

All Due Respect, an imprint of
Down & Out Books
April 2018
978-1-948235-21-1

Dustin loves to rob banks. Dustin loves to drink. Dustin loves his women. Dustin loves loyalty. He might even love his adopted nephew Jeremy. And, he sometimes gets a little too enthusiastic in his job doing collections for local bookies—so, sometimes, he loves to hurt people.

Told in the first person, *Uncle Dust* is a fascinating noir look inside the mind of a hard, yet very complicated criminal.

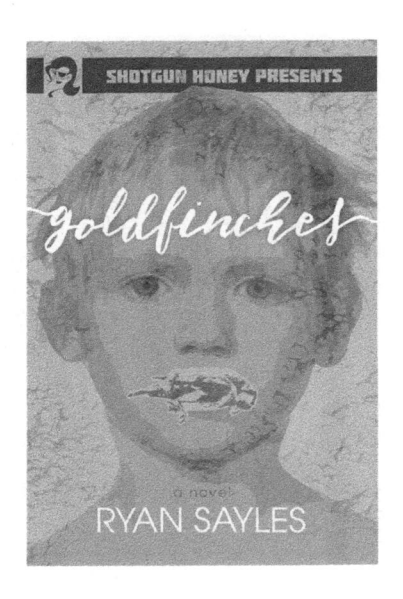

Goldfinches
Ryan Sayles

Shotgun Honey, an imprint of
Down & Out Books
978-1-943402-73-1

Family man Carl, with his wife and daughter, are on their way check on his young son who had been hospitalized for an ear infection complicated by the boy's Type 1 Diabetes. Stopped at a light they are confronted by a gunman who pulls Carl from the vehicle, stealing the vehicle and his family with it.

Desperate, Carl, will do anything to save his family, even commit a carjacking himself. The, when all seems lost, Carl finds a reason to believe, and finds himself amidst a conflict of good and evil.

Lightning Source UK Ltd.
Milton Keynes UK
UKHW01f2132140918
328920UK00001B/138/P